ALISHA NURSE

*To: Jackie
From: Alisha with lots
of love xxx*

The Return of the Key
Copyright © 2014 by Alisha Nurse. All rights reserved.
First Print Edition: 2014

ISBN: 978-0-9931451-0-0

Cover and Formatting: Streetlight Graphics

No part of this book may be reproduced, scanned, or distributed in any printed or electronic form without permission. Please do not participate in or encourage piracy of copyrighted materials in violation of the author's rights. Thank you for respecting the hard work of this author.

This is a work of fiction. Names, characters, places, and incidents either are the product of the author's imagination or are used fictitiously, and any resemblance to locales, events, business establishments, or actual persons—living or dead—is entirely coincidental.

To my Grampie and Ma, whose unfailing love inspired this story.

Prologue

AN AIR OF EERINESS ENVELOPED the atmosphere. It was so peaceful, idyllic, and captivatingly breathtaking but something stirred in the shadows.

I couldn't remember how I had come to the boat I was now sitting in. But I didn't care. I was somehow too distracted by the majesty of the beauty here. The air was fresh and the water in the lake was turquoise, almost transparent in parts. Iridescent fish and what resembled mini dolphins swam around oblivious of my presence. I was suddenly aware of two familiar persons on land, apparently waiting on me. Their faces were blurred, but a strong sense of familiarity assured me it was safe.

'Eliza! Hurry! Take it quickly.'

The voice didn't come from the two people in the distance, but from a girl atop a protruding bit of rock emerging from the headland over the lake. She was standing over a preposterously huge, white calla lily, desperately urging me to pick it. I paddled the boat closer to the mass of rock, trying to get a closer glimpse of the girl's face, but the bright overhead sun made it difficult. She spoke to me as though we were friends.

'Take it fast, Eliza, take it before it's too late, hurry, please!' she pleaded with great urgency.

Confused, I reached up to examine the source of her anguish. The twenty-five-inch flower was growing peculiarly down the rock towards the lake. It could have been a typical calla lily, except I'd never seen one this enormous that its weight made it hang clumsily along the lime-scaled rock. Still, it was strangely beautiful with its velvety texture, brilliant white colour, and curvaceous body.

It beckoned me to it. I suddenly wanted it, needed it. I knew it should be mine. Somewhat unsure, I stood up persuading myself to pick it; after all, it was growing wild off a rock and could not have belonged to anyone. But the boat rumbled violently, startling me, and I quickly gripped a bit of rock so as not to fall into the lake.

As I listened to my heavy, uneven breathing breaking the perfect calm, my eyes scanned the waters around the boat in panic. A dark shadow moved in the water, blanketing the lake with blackness. The fish and dolphins hastily swam away as the shadow moved slowly towards me.

ENGLAND

THE EARLY SUNDAY MORNING BREEZE was cool and a kind of serenity rested on the small community at the very foot of the majestic mountains of the Northern Range. In this community, in a humble and quite nondescript house, Eliza Aurelio stirred in her sleep. Her vision was becoming blurrier by the second. She squinted, hoping to see her surroundings more clearly, but it didn't work. She was in the strange but familiar mystical place again desperately gripping onto some slimy protruding rocks so she wouldn't fall into the rough waters that harboured evil.

Soon, the unexpected happened. Eliza's subconscious state became obvious when, in the distance, she could hear her grandmother complaining over her absence at the breakfast table.

"Where's that child? She's not waking up?" her grandmother grumbled.

Eliza was now struggling to wake herself, but the dream lingered. The boat she was in continued rumbling violently beneath her and she was terrified, despite knowing it was a dream. It was one of those where everything felt real as most of her dreams played out. She felt herself edging closer to consciousness when a deep, sinister hiss bellowed loudly in to her ear.

"Ahhhhhhhhhhgggghhhhhh," she screamed, rolling off the bed all tangled in her grandmother's floral sheets.

Braps! The sound rang in her ears as she hit the wooden floor.

"Owwww."

"Child! What you doing there? Dreaming again? Hmm... Hurry we can't be late for the flight" said her grandmother, Indira, while hastily pulling the sheets on the bed.

"Ok, Ma," Eliza muttered in slow response.

Eliza tried shaking off the chills as she stumbled towards the breakfast table. The wooden floorboards were warm against her bare feet, and they creaked in protest as she stepped on them. The entire house smelled of roasted aubergine. On the table next to it, Eliza's grandmother had laid a plate of freshly made Sada roti—her favourite meal of local flat breads and fried pumpkin. Her grandfather had already devoured his share and was digging in for second or probably third takings.

"Hurry before I eat yours," he muttered through a full mouth.

She laughed and picked up a piece of flat bread. She was barely halfway through it, into her meal when a loud crashing sound came through a nearby window. She dropped herself to the floor in a panic, covering her head with her hands. A large stone broke through a different window at the front of the house, barely missing her before it fell to the ground and rolled next to the table. Wrapped around it was a crumbled piece of white paper with a big X scribbled on it.

"These damn bloody children, if I only catch them..." Eliza's shaking grandfather grumbled aloud with his thick grey eyebrows turned downwards.

She could hear him breathing heavily. Her own heart was thumping.

It had happened again.

Still on her knees, it took her a while before realising she should say something to comfort her grandfather and now her grandmother, staring wide eyed from the corridor.

She got up and walked over to his chair and rubbed his back in a circular motion.

"Don't worry, Grampie," Eliza tried to assure him. "Don't worry, you just stay inside until it's over," she whispered, feeling tension in her forehead from the frown.

Elections.

It was a bad time to be mixed race in Trinidad. Not that her grandparents were, but she was, and they took care of her.

The stone through their window might seem harmless, but in truth the times were perilous.

National elections were coming up and racial tensions were spiralling. The leading political parties were playing the race card in a desperate bid to win votes. They were using race and the people played along. A dangerous game, it was. You see, on an island largely polarised by race, you were either one thing or the other. Afro Trinidadian or Indo Trinidadian. There was no room for an in-between, like Eliza. No. That jeopardised things, so, Afro Trinidadians aligned themselves with the United Political Party, which promised them a better life, while Indo Trinidadians typically voted for the National Peoples' Party which was offering the same results for the other half of the population. Of course, there were the minority ethnic groups like the Syrians, Chinese, Portuguese, and other White Trinis, but Eliza wasn't sure where they placed the X on Election Day. She wasn't even sure if they voted. No one ever asked those questions, or seemed to care about marriages between them, or their little mixed children. After all, they weren't feuding. She only knew about herself—a by-product of the two feuding races. The small pool of young mixed race people like herself was torn. Ostracised with nowhere to fit in, they had no party to join because they belonged to neither side. Better said, they were somewhere in the middle of nowhere.

"Child, I told you not to write that thing in your school paper. Look at what you've caused now!" Eliza's grandmother shouted in her lilting accent, pointing to the worn copy of The El Dorado Times folded on the mantelpiece.

Eliza sighed heavily and considered a fitting response. Her grandfather ignored his wife's grumblings and reached for the television remote while letting out a loud, winding belch.

Police are investigating the murders of five people early this morning in what is believed to be the country's second wave of racially-motivated attacks since the start of election campaigning. Investigators have not yet released the identities of the victims who were shot at their homes in East Chaguanas, but say they have evidence the attacks were linked to several key political figures.

"Stupid, stupid people! Letting themselves be brainwashed by these selfish sycophants calling themselves politicians!" Eliza protested to the television while her grandfather nodded.

"Child, watch that mouth of yours!" her grandmother warned from the kitchen.

"Sorry, Ma," she answered.

Eliza's grandmother had warned her to take no sides in the upcoming elections. Yes, because times were dangerous enough with all the politically and racially motivated attacks. But also because she was more at risk than most. She, a little mixed race girl in a society feigning togetherness above deep-seated bigotry and suspicions of 'the other race.' She was the token anomaly that both sides seemed to think they could do without.

Eliza felt that technically she wasn't taking sides by writing about the contradictions and absurdities of racial politics on an island where there was bound to be a growing mixed population some day. The article had been placed on page five of her school's otherwise unpopular newspaper, but garnered such critical reviews that soon Eliza Aurelio went from being virtually unknown to becoming a common subject of gossip whispered across classrooms and staffrooms in her little town. Moreover, as most gossip tends to be, it wasn't all good. That same week she had been slammed against a wall by rivalling school bullies. They didn't need a good reason. Who she was was reason enough. Suspicious enough. They each accused her of belonging on the 'other side.'

Now, there was the stone that ruined her grandmother's traditional windows, which had been there long before any of Eliza's aunts or uncles had been conceived.

Her grandmother was furious.

"Ma, you know Mr Ching has windows just like ours in his shop. I bet he'd trade us one if I climb his mango tree for him again." Eliza tried to sound carefree. Indira said nothing, and Eliza's stomach churned in response.

Secretly, Eliza was worried, but she remained stoic for her grandparents, her lifeline and backbone for as long as she'd lived. They were all that mattered in her small existence, and any sadness of theirs pained her. Her mother was dead and her father just another absconding man who turned away from the shame of fathering an impure child.

Her grandfather, Jose Aurelio, was the only father she knew, and he would not risk their safety. He was sending her and her ma to the southwest of England to stay with her great aunt Rosie until elections were over and the violence quelled. Jose was to join them later after he'd harvested their season's crops.

Eliza didn't like leaving him behind—she and her grandparents had barely spent any time apart since her mother died.

"Child, hurry up! And comb that hair!" Indira was calling out again an hour later.

Eliza sulked. Freshly showered and powdered, she now sat on the swing in their back garden, in the high-collared flare dress ma had laid out for her. She was gazing at the cardinal red ixoras as she forced a comb through the endless tangles in her voluminous curls. A little green hummingbird zipped past her towards the flowers, and she gasped in delight at the chance to observe such a creature. She crept in closer on her toes to get a better look, but when her comb hit a knot, she sighed aloud and the hummingbird zipped away in a buzz.

Hmmph!

She looked at the comb and flung it behind her.

"Oops!" she said merrily as it landed in their little pond with a soft splash.

"Aye girl, watch where you throwing things!" the young male voice startled her.

It was her long-time neighbourhood friend, Ricky, who she greeted fittingly.

"Go away," she growled, all semblance of cheer vanishing.

"Eliza, I'm sorry, I never should have...." he started saying, but she cut him off.

"Never should have what?" She spun around at him. "Admitted what you really think about your friend who is unfortunate enough to be mixed? Mmm? Mmm?"

"No, no, it's just that...I was under a lot of pressure, you know at school and everything...."

"Please! You're lucky enough to not have anyone calling you a watered-down bastard... Just go away."

Her rant was met with unexpected silence. Ricky's face went blank, completely void of anything like a canvas waiting to be painted on.

"You know," he charged, "don't blame me because society doesn't accept you, Eliza! It's not my fault you don't have an identity," he blurted out before storming out of the garden.

She gasped, but before she could feel the warmth of tears on her cheeks, her grandfather was calling her inside. It was time to leave.

Eliza's Aunt Rosie met them at the airport, dolled up in a washed-out blue sari with her hair rolled up in pins, just like Indira's. Her spectacles sat on the tip of her nose and amazingly stayed there even while she leaned forward to plant a wet kiss on Eliza's forehead.

For as long as Eliza could recall, her childless Aunt Rosie had doted on her, sending gifts religiously every birthday and Christmas holiday.

The drive to Aunt Rosie's house was utterly long and drawn out. Eliza had been out cold for some time, dribbling helplessly on herself while her grandmother and great aunt chattered away endlessly in the front seat as Rosie steered them home.

When she opened her eyes, Eliza was astonished. The little town of Abbeydale was even more picturesque in real life than in photographs she'd seen. Driving along the undulating, narrow roads, Eliza pressed her hands against the car window and marvelled at the strange intimacy behind the small red-bricked houses and green hilly landscapes.

Tiny cottages fitted into spacious green yards short of no beautiful flowers and trees, home to sweet, singing birds. Besides their melodious tweeting, there was little else to hear. Aunt Rosie's street was so quiet, and Eliza couldn't see a single soul on it.

"You're awake, child?" Aunt Rosie asked lovingly in a Trini-British accent. "Here we are, Currysome Avenue."

"Really?" Eliza asked sarcastically, only to realise Aunt Rosie wasn't joking.

"Curry some what?" Eliza added in jest.

Aunt Rosie smiled, and along the side of her face, Eliza could see the wrinkles forming three curved lines.

On the way into the house, Eliza couldn't help but notice the unmistakably tall hill standing in the distance with a tower at its very peak. It looked like it was emerging from the red rooftops in the community.

"What's that?" she asked.

"An ancient monument full of history and magic, much like the rest of Abbeydale, as you may come to learn," she said, before walking off into the house. Eliza smiled, shook her head and followed after her aunt.

Aunt Rosie's house smelled a tad musty despite its clean appearance. On the walls hung old black-and-white family portraits, with mostly familiar faces to Eliza. In one corner of the room, a humungous white-and-black beaked red macaw sat on some artificial tree.

"Arrrrkkk, mawnin Rosie, arrkkkkk," it said.

"Ohhh," Eliza heard herself mutter in marvel.

Eliza didn't know Aunt Rosie had a bird, for she neglected to mention it in all her correspondence.

"Eliiiii?" Aunt Rosie called out from another room.

Eliza was lagging behind, lugging the suitcases clumsily around the living room, eyes fixed on the macaw, who stared back.

"Yes, Aunty Rose?" she replied without enthusiasm.

"I've already signed you up for school, so you can start tomorrow. Isn't that great?" she smiled.

"Oh, Ma!" Eliza sulked. "You promised I'd get the week off!"

"Hush child, just go and see nah. It will be different from home," Indira buttered her up.

She sighed heavily. She already didn't want to be there without her grandfather, and she was certainly not looking forward to school. In fact, only one word came to mind. Dull.

However, Eliza Aurelio couldn't have known that her trip was going to be anything but that.

Eliza didn't sleep that night. The recurring nightmare about the flower and the dark shadow haunted her again. She woke up cranky as ever, missing her grandfather and wanting to go home.

She had slept in a small but cosy room while Aunt Rosie and her grandmother slept in separate rooms down the corridor. The house had a very homely aura to it, but it was no doubt very old and in need of some repair.

Eliza stumbled down the creaking staircase and, as usual, was the last to sit at the breakfast table. She suddenly remembered it was far cooler in England when she felt her pores standing on her arms and wished she'd grabbed a sweater.

Her grandmother and Aunt Rosie were already in their element, freshly powdered and enjoying what Eliza assumed to be an English breakfast. The extremely large white plates were overflowing with eggs, toast, bacon, and mushrooms.

"Mornin,'" she said to her ma and Aunt Rosie.

They nodded, both inspecting her from head to toe. Indira's forehead was creased.

"Child, you're still having those dreams?" she asked. "You were screaming again in your sleep again last night."

The women in Eliza's family had what was presumed to be a 'gift' of premonition through dreams. Usually someone would dream an event clear as day and would know the spot-on interpretation for it. It was quite an art when Eliza thought of it, for dreams were not always as straightforward as they seemed. For instance, her ma would tell you if you dreamt a funeral, you had nothing to worry over, because dreaming a funeral meant there would be a wedding and vice versa. It was complicated business. Eliza couldn't interpret dreams, but dreamt so vividly that sometimes she couldn't tell when she had actually dreamt something from when it really happened. That in itself was scary because there were some in her family who believed that you could cross realms while dreaming.

Eliza couldn't figure out what to make of her recurring nightmare, though, and it was so farfetched that Indira told her it just sounded like she'd been watching too much late-night TV.

"Ma, it's the same dream from the last four weeks. Me on the boat, trying to pick some stupid flower in a really nice place that turns out to be all spooky. I just wish I knew what the message was," she grumbled while walking towards the parrot.

"Well don't worry, you'll figure it out in time, when you need to," said Indira with her mouth full of toast.

The parrot was nibbling on sunflower seeds but dropped them and advanced towards Eliza when she drew near. Fascinated, Eliza beckoned him with an index finger and surprisingly, the bird bent his head over to be scratched.

Eliza smiled in awe while hesitantly scratching the bird's yellow-topped head.

"Amazing. So Patrick likes you. Funny bird, that. He's not usually social with strangers. You've always had a spirit that animals love, Eli," Rosie beamed.

Patrick's orange irises widened and his feathers became lightly ruffled like he was happy. Eliza stopped scratching his head to admire his plumage, and he looked up at her as if wanting to play.

"Child, breakfast is getting cold, come and eat. You could play with Patrick all evening when you come home," Indira instructed.

Eliza felt like sixteen going on five and reluctantly sat at the table and gobbled down a mouthful of breakfast before trying to excuse herself.

"Eliza, your grandmother told me you'd been having trouble at school again. You mustn't worry about those ignorant people. Just let them talk," Aunty Rosie said with conviction.

Nobody understands, Eliza thought.

"What, child? What?"

"Aunt Rosie, you don't understand. The Afro Trini kids call me 'Coolie' and the Indo Trini kids call me 'nigger.' And if that's not bad enough, I don't fit in anywhere! Nobody accepts me," she ranted, having no choice but to stop when out of breath.

"Child, what do you want them to call you?" Aunt Rosie asked while stroking her face.

"Eliza. I just want them to call me Eliza. That's who I am. I don't want to be the anomaly anymore. I'm proud of who I am and who my ancestors are, but under all that I'm just the granddaughter of Jose and Indira Aurelio. Why do people have to be so stupid?" Aunt Rosie sat up on her chair and paused for a second to think, before leaning back towards Eliza.

"I understand, but, child, if you truly accept who you are, then you won't need other people's approval. You can't rely on that, because they'll always let you down. Be proud of who you are regardless," said Aunt Rosie.

Eliza sighed heavily before giving one of her classic fake smiles and heading upstairs to shower.

Chapter 2

UNUSUAL WEATHER

Walking uphill to Linkage's Secondary School, the wind blowing against her face and caressing her bare skin through her purple blouse pacified Eliza. That is, until she got to the school gates and encountered a rowdy group of boys congregating on their bicycles, peals of their laughter cutting through the morning silence.

Instinctively, she hung her head low, letting her heavy, swirly curls cover the side of her face.

"Oye!" one of the boys called out.

"Oye, curly hair," he said in an accent quite amusing to Eliza.

"The entrance to classes is past this way, yeah," said the boy with the low-lying fringe almost covering his left eye.

Eliza shyly thanked him and quickly walked past the group, into the main office. The school was relatively small and must have housed about three hundred students at most. The rooms were all tiny, holding a maximum of eighteen students each, and from the outside, if not for the fading sign with its name, the school could have been mistaken for any old arbitrary building. Still, it had character to it, with little ugly-faced gargoyles manning the rooftops and outer walls.

Eliza was directed down a narrow corridor to a classroom where other young people were streaming in. She headed for the first row of desks. Soon, a pallid, lanky blue-eyed girl with a white-blonde bob followed and dropped herself on the seat next to Eliza's. She had a well-defined jawbone that accentuated her well-proportioned features—high cheek bones on an oval face with small eyes, thin lips, and a turned-up nose.

"So where you from, mate?" the girl asked in the same bemusing accent as the boy from outside.

"Um, Trinidad. I'm Eliza," replied Eliza nervously, extending her hand.

"Gwen Callaghan, nice to meet you. Love yur hair," she grinned, intrusively tugging at a ringlet of Eliza's curls.

Eliza smiled back, and before they could say anything else, a frail middle-aged man opened the door and gesticulated for the remaining teens in the corridor to take their seats inside.

"G'mornin,'" he beamed. "For our newcomer, the name's John White. You can call me John; I'm your Spanish teacher."

John made the entire class do introductions, and this kindness made her uncomfortable. Eliza was no doubt the only foreigner and odd one out. In her mind, she rolled her eyes. Deep down, she also hated the awkwardness of having the brownest face in the room.

In this session, they were to learn about how to deal with certain scenarios in Spanish, which would be a breeze for Eliza, having done this at her own school a year earlier. She would have noticed if she were paying attention.

Thankfully, someone knocked on the door. Eliza was happy for a break of any kind, and she rummaged through her bag for munchies.

A fat, red-haired woman beckoned John outside, and

as he closed the door behind him, a piece of crumbled paper hit Gwen on the head.

"Oye! Weasel brain, what you do that for?" Gwen shouted as she spun around.

The pretty boy with the overgrown fringe was grinning helplessly with his friends.

"Find yuh witch mother yet, Gwen?"

Gwen's face was turning red with rage.

"You little plonker! I'm gonna beat you good, Aaron!" Gwen said as she rushed off her chair, pouncing towards the boy before throwing a fist towards his face.

All around chairs were collapsing as the other girls and boys scampered to safety while cheering them on.

Gwen and Aaron were rolling on the floor now, no one making a move to part them.

Eliza forgot that she was foraging for a snack and looked on with her mouth hanging open.

"Don' pay dem no mind, tomorrow they'll be talking like it never happened," said a pimpled boy with deep black hair and round, piercing eyes, two rows from Eliza.

"I'm Ronald, and they over there are mi best mates, Eric, Olly, Pete, and mi sis Katie," he said.

Eric, a handsome red-haired boy, waved at Eliza while Olly, Pete, and Katie managed half smiles.

Eliza hesitated. "Um, nice to meet you Ronald, and your friends too. Err, shouldn't someone call a teacher or something?"

"Nahh, they'll work it out," he assured her.

Okay!! As long as they keep it over there, I'm cool, Eliza thought to herself.

"Oye! What is going on in here? Break it up before I have all your heads!" screamed the fat red-haired woman amid the sound of shuffling chairs as people rushed to their seats.

Aaron and Gwen froze where they were.

"Mr White has to go sort out some things in the office.

Pete, go to the office, yuh mum's waiting for you," she added.

"This is to do with mi pa? Innit?" Pete said shakily. "Innit, Miss Foster?"

His eyes looked tired, and for the first time Eliza noticed how unkempt he was.

Pete rushed out the room, fumbling past the overturned chairs with tears welling in his eyes. Everyone looked on in silence. Olly, the shaggy-haired friend, ran out after him. Eliza wondered what Olly's excuse was for his overgrown hair and shabby appearance.

She soon learnt from the fat red-haired lady, Ms Foster, that Pete's dad was one of four fishermen who'd gone missing off the coast of Watchet fishing village, some twenty miles away from Abbeydale. It had been three days and police now reported that their boat had washed ashore that morning empty, with no sight of the four men or their fishing gear: the worst had been feared. But the boat wasn't empty.

Only one knew there had been a little wooden box shut tightly in the boat. In this sealed box lay a queer-looking round clock-like device with strange inscriptions where numbers might have been on an ordinary clock. The device had ended up in the hands of an unsuspecting wanderer who had alerted the police to the bare boat rattling with every incoming wave on the shore. Somehow, this clock-like device had become entangled with Eliza's fate, though she was yet to know it.

For most of the day, Eliza gazed off into space. Though she hardly knew Pete or the community, she felt upset by their misfortunes. In her gut, she felt sick, but Gwen sensed this and offered a distraction by doodling on Eliza's clean, crisp notebook page.

"What's that?" Eliza's screwed her lips.

"It's a dog, you can't tell?"

Eliza looked at Gwen in a most pathetic way, and the

two burst into quiet giggles. This was how a friendship between an unlikely pair began. Gwen, an over-confident tomboy of sorts loved wearing oversized sweatshirts with her patched jeans; her beauty radiated, and everywhere she went she drew attention with her lithe walk and strange charisma. The only jewellery she wore was a plain silver necklace adorned with the rare peridot gem at the centre of a leaf. Eliza was the exact opposite of Gwen—unassuming, self-doubting, and considered herself average and thus not needing distinguishing clothing to make her stand out unnecessarily. She rarely drew attention and always preferred to keep it that way, but together the two girls had a chemistry that was unexplainable and almost immediate.

That evening Gwen walked home with Eliza, having found out they actually lived on the same street; and they talked about everything from which boy band was their favourite to what flavour crisps was the best to gobble in successive packs.

"So since we're being all personal, I hope you don't mind me asking, but what happened to your mom?" Eliza asked fearing she might be scaring her new friend away.

"Well... She went missing... when I was eight."

"Oh that's really sad, so sorry to hear, Gwen," Eliza uttered hoping to ask some more follow-up questions.

"It's ok. I've gotten used to it."

"Um, Gwen? Why did Pete call yuh mum a witch?" Eliza asked.

"She wasn't," Gwen sputtered out defensively. "Peep... people here are very superstitious and my ma had very different beliefs, yuh know? She believed in nature and spirits and foresight, yuh know what I mean?"

"Well nothing's wrong with that," assured Eliza. "My family and I kinda believe in foresight; we dream things before they happen," she added, inspecting Gwen's face for reactions.

Gwen genuinely seemed impressed. "Wow that's so cool! You definitely have to tell me more tomorrow," she said as they stopped in front Aunt Rosie's house.

Rosie and Indira were sitting in the veranda beckoning Eliza to come inside.

"Um, I'll see you tomorrow, Gwen," Eliza said embarrassingly before they parted ways.

During dinner, Indira and Rosie told Eliza of how Abbeydale Road was turned upside down that day when a young child of the Wethertonnes had gone missing.

Four-year-old Emily was used to playing in the front yard every day, but mysteriously disappeared after her mother turned away for a mere minute to answer a ringing phone.

Eliza's forehead furrowed as she remembered the missing fishermen and the upset feeling set down upon her once more.

"You must try and come home early child," Indira urged her.

"Ok, Ma. Aunt Rosie, do you know anything about these missing fishermen?"

"Child, people saying all kinds of things, I don't know what's going on. Twenty years I've been living right here and never even heard so much as a robbery on this street. Something isn't right at all. You better listen to your ma and come home as early as possible," Rosie warned with concern on the edge of her every word.

In the coming days, it became easier to forget the misfortunes that had befallen the community. All was quiet and life went on as usual in the simple town—Eliza was settling into her classes, making new friends here and there while becoming closer to Gwen, who she now spent considerable time with. Then one afternoon, sudden torrential rains and gusty winds broke the calm.

Class was in session and no one noticed the dark

grey clouds drifting to cover the bright blue sky. It began drizzling, and before Gwen could say, "Holy crisps!" the skies unleashed a heavy downpour.

"How unusual, the weatherman said it would be sunny today," John White said, distracted by the sudden darkness.

"It's Gwen's ma working up some magic, John," said a voice from the back of the classroom.

"Oye!" Gwen shouted, spinning around to give Aaron Spindler a piercing look again.

"Ok, settle down you two," John said in a less-than-authoritative tone.

Gwen turned back to face the teacher, but Eliza noticed that she never unclenched her shaking fist. It was some forty-five minutes later when a drenched Ms Foster stumbled into the room to announce that classes would end early due a sudden Storm Watch that had come across on breaking news.

Without wasting time, the kids scampered out the classroom, some to waiting vehicles, others gleefully in the downpour towards their bicycles. Eliza was at the main entrance staring into the rains and the thick developing haze when Ms Foster approached her with Gwen.

"Eliza, I'm heading in your direction, so I will take you and Gwen home now."

"Oh? Um, thanks a lot, Miss Foster, that's really nice of you," Eliza said in the flattest, most unenthusiastic tone.

"Mmm," she heard Ms Foster grumble.

They ran through the cold rains to the car park and jumped into Ms Foster's red mini Volkswagen.

"Can't remember the last time we had such heavy downpours," said Ms Foster, twitching her mouth while looking through the rear view mirror as she reversed out of the car park.

Eliza couldn't remember the last time she was in a vehicle that drove so slowly it might have been crawling;

neither could Gwen, who was now propping her chin against the car door and sighing audibly every few minutes.

"You kids buckle up," said Ms Foster.

"But we'll be home soon, Miss," Gwen complained.

"I said buckle up, Miss Callaghan, the two of you. You see this rain? No telling how slippery the roads are," Ms Foster said.

No sooner had Gwen and Eliza's seat belt buckles clicked in, than in a sudden flash of black, what appeared to be a huge animal leapt in front of the car before disappearing into the fog.

Ms Foster mashed the brakes immediately, and the impact jerked all their bodies forward. The car skidded down the street and the frantic girls screamed as Ms Foster hysterically tried to regain control of the vehicle. When the car halted horizontally across the street, all three said nothing while panting and looking around at each other. Gwen seemed to be shocked and was staring off wide-eyed while Eliza pursed her lips as she squeezed Gwen's hand.

"You girls ok? Everyone ok?" Ms Foster rambled with a shaky voice. "Did you all see that? What was that? Did you see it?" she asked confusingly.

"Hardly," Eliza whimpered while staring at Gwen. "What was that? A horse? A... a bull?"

"No, it couldn't have been," Gwen muttered.

All three looked around the car, across the nearby fields, up and down the empty street. There were no signs of any animal running wild, as far as they could see past the fog anyway.

"Better get you girls home now," said Ms Foster still peering around through the car's windows.

When they got home and bade Ms Foster farewell, Indira asked Gwen to stay over for some tea until her father returned from work.

Indira and Rosie listened attentively as Eliza recalled every second of the earlier mishap.

"So what do you think it was?" Rosie inquired, forehead all creased.

"Don't know, Aunt Rosie, but it was big and black and so fast none of us could see it well," Eliza responded.

Gwen soon motioned for Eliza to make an exit so they could head upstairs to her room.

"Thanks for the tea, Gwen and I are going upstairs to get some warm clothes and talk for a while," said Eliza.

"Yeah, thanks, Ma'am," Gwen echoed.

"Aunty Rosie and Aunty Indira to you, child," Rosie smiled at Gwen.

"Ok, Aunty Rosie," Gwen smiled back fondly, as she followed Eliza upstairs.

Eliza sunk into her bed verbally reasoning through what animal it could have possibly been. Gwen sat cross-legged making funny shapes with her mouth.

"C'mon, you're not helping me here," Eliza complained while munching on some butter cookies.

"It wasn't an animal, Eliza," Gwen said flatly.

"Well. What do you mean? Do you know what it was?" Gwen furrowed her brows.

"Gwen, you know what that was?" Eliza asked with a look of shock, then concern when she realised Gwen went mum with a heavy sigh while looking away.

Eliza moved over and embraced her.

"It's just me, what's wrong? Come on, we're friends," Eliza tried assuring Gwen.

Gwen looked up at Eliza.

"What..." she hesitated, "what if I told you that thing that ran across Miss Foster's car wasn't one from this world?"

"Well, what...what do you mean?" Eliza stuttered in bemusement.

"Eliza, what I'm about to tell you might seem reaaally, really farfetched and very much made up, but you have to believe me, promise you'll believe me," Gwen pleaded as she breathed in heavily. "And you can't tell anyone."

"Ok, Gwen. I promise," Eliza said, bending her head to meet Gwen's eyes. "Go ahead."

The room became silent, and all that could be heard was the torrential rains and roaring thunder.

At first, Gwen opened her mouth but nothing came out. She vacillated for about forty-five seconds, then shakily blurted out, "I'm not supposed to tell anyone, but I think we may all be in danger." She sighed heavily. "I think the creature that ran across Miss Foster's car might be the same one that took my mum, possibly Emily Wethertonne, and the missing fishermen." Gwen paused again to breathe. "Phookas. That's what they're called. They're violent, prank-playing shape-shifters that usually take the form of great black animals. They can turn into many animals—you know, cats, goats, horses, dogs, birds even—but they're always black and shaggy...."

"Pokas? Pookas? What are they called?" asked Eliza, who was now more befuddled. "And where did they come from, Gwen? And how do you know so much about them?"

"Poo-kazz," Gwen over-exaggerated her pronunciation. "They come from a realm that exists on the same plane as yours, Eliza. A realm where creatures of all sorts reside. We call it Annwn[1]."

"Okay, um, who is *we*, Gwen?" Eliza interrupted with a raised left brow.

"I'm getting to that Eli... We call it Annwn1, but to the humans who know of it, it's The Otherworld. To cross realms, there are certain doorways, hidden in various places. But for a very long time, these doorways have been closed barring races from both sides crossing over," Gwen explained.

"Ooookay," Eliza said, nodding her head slowly while processing the information.

1   Annwn is pronounced Anoon

"*We* means my kind. Well sort of. Annwn is known especially for one race, the fair folk or what humans call faeries. My ma was a faery, so that makes me a...emmm... a rhwoski. It's *very* hard to translate, but I suppose in the human tongue it might mean the same as half-blood."

"Ohhhh?" Eliza muttered.

"Kinda like how you're mixed race, Eliza," said Gwen.

"So you're saying you're a faery? Wow, um, Gwen, this is all a lot to digest. I'm still trying to connect the dots here with the poka and stuff. You don't look like a faery. Does this mean you can do magic? I mean you're telling me all this mythology with faeries is true? I trust you, but this doesn't sound very logical. Do you know what I mean? If the doorways you speak of are supposed to be closed, how did the poka-thing...get through? And what's it doing here anyway?" she spluttered in one go.

Eliza had many more questions. Before she could ask one, three more popped into her head. It was definitely a lot to process, especially when Eliza had thought she lived in the real world where the only magical things happened in the movies.

She had seen and visited the many alluring shops at the small town square that had colourful showcases packed with dangling winged-faery chimes and figurines, peculiar jewellery that promised luck, and books on a so-called goddess that resided in the mysterious monument on the hill. However, to Eliza, these myths were anything but true, only a clever tourism tool to lure curious travellers to the otherwise quiet town.

She was downright confused. She trusted Gwen as a friend and usually dared to believe her despite any lack of logic and air of madness; but this time she remained as sceptical as you might be now.

Gwen had expected this scepticism, and she quickly whisked her slender right index finger in the air as though it were a wand. Before Eliza could ask what she was doing, opposite them on the cream bedroom walls, thick rope-like lianas were springing forth, growing here and there in accordance with Gwen's finger.

"Huhhhhhhhh," Eliza gasped with an opened mouth. "Gwen! How did you do that?!"

"Shhh you silly cow, that's what I'm trying to explain," Gwen chuckled at Eliza, whose mouth remained agape in awe.

"Ok, firstly," Gwen said, putting her hand down, "fair folk look very much like me, they're not always the tiny buzzing-around cuties you see on Peter Pan. I did take some of mi pa's human attributes, so I'm not full common fair folk, but I possess some of the traits. I can sorta glide on air, and I possess some but limited powers over plants and animals of the other realm. I didn't grow up in The Otherworld with fair folk training, so my grasp of spells and potions is limited to what mi ma taught me before she was taken.

"Secondly, I suspected for weeks now that something wasn't right, when the fishermen went missing and then little Emily, and, well, I think I know why the doorway is opened. The fishermen found a...a thing at the bottom of the sea. The Key. I don't know what it was doing there to begin with, but it controls the few known doorways, including the one beneath the tower on the hill."

Eliza was dumbstruck. She eventually managed to mutter, "How do you know someone found this key, Gwen? And where is it?"

"I don't know where it is, but I saw it. My ma showed it to me in a dream. I'm afraid something terrible is going to happen, Eliza. The phookas are among the most feared by fair folk. They're tricky and vicious kidnappers who like to play pranks. If they're here, it can't be that they're up to any good."

"Well, what can we do, Gwen? I...I dunno what we can

do. This is just crazy! I mean, there's no one here you can ask for help?" Eliza said.

"Noo! You must tell no one, Eli! No one! Not even your ma, understand? Who will believe us anyway? My pa knows, but I've already put myself in deep poo by breaking a sacred rule and telling you of Annwn and the existence of my kind. There is nothing that can be done from this realm. If anything can stop whatever madness is about to happen, it will have to be done from the other side."

This was how unassuming Eliza came to know of the mystical Annwn. A realm so beautifully enchanting that in past centuries humans who had stumbled into it were reluctant to leave. It was filled with exotic flowers and plants, breathtaking, landscapes, and delightful creatures who tickled the fancy of humans. Yes, Annwn had a mesmerising grandeur about it, but belying its magnificent splendour was a steep darkness, which came to enter the realm in a time past when the doorways between realms stayed opened and beings from both sides stumbled over either unknowingly, in case of humans, or intentionally, in case of many of Annwn's creatures. Many of the myths you know of today might have probably come about from older generations having seen faeries or elves or other unusual creatures who were too lax in remaining unseen from the human eye. Then, there were those creatures that saw our human kind and fell in love, like Gwen's mother who, after seeing a young David Callaghan, fell eternally in love, but more of that story another time....

"Gwen?" Eliza whispered after lying in bed listening to Gwen's many tales of this faraway place. "Why did you risk telling me about Annwn? How did you know I'd believe you?"

"Hmm," Gwen smiled confidently. "Because you already know it, Eliza, you just haven't realised it yet."

"Ehh?" Eliza asked.

"I saw you coming here in a vision. I, as most fair folk,

can see bit of the future as far as it involves myself. I didn't know why I was dreaming of you, but I saw us as great friends in the fair Annwn. I don't know why, but you seem to have some business there. It will come to you, don't worry," Gwen foretold.

Business? In Annwn? Eliza thought, long and hard she did, but just couldn't figure out why she would have anything to do with some place she'd never even heard of.

By late evening, the rains had eased and it drizzled lightly with an occasional rumble of thunder. When it was almost 7 p.m., Eliza walked Gwen to the front door as she headed home.

"Here," Gwen said, putting a small object in Eliza's hand at the front door.

Eliza looked at the little brown nut with a string pierced through it. She held it to her nose, and then looked up at Gwen curiously.

"Gwen, why have you given me a nutmeg on a piece of string?"

Her friend smiled. "It will keep the phookas away from you. Keep it on you, and try to get some around your house. It repels them."

Gwen started to walk away, but turned back to Eliza who was staring at the nut in her hand.

"May you and your family stay safe from the clutches of evil, my dear friend," Gwen said to Eliza in a tone that sounded foreign to her usual carefree demeanour.

"We have to fix this" Eliza fumbled long after Gwen had walked out into the dark, wet night.

Chapter 3

ENCOUNTERS

"Eliii? Come downstairs. Someone is here to see you."

"Aunt Rosie, I'm soo sleepy. I need a few more minutes," Eliza stuttered drearily as she sank deeper into sleep.

Faintly, she could hear a familiar voice in the living room.

Grampy? She thought. She became excited at once and was happy in her sleepy state.

What she heard next triggered something in her subconscious. He was sobbing profusely.

Her aunt was comforting him. "Shhh, it's been more than a month now, Jose. I don't know if we'll ever find Indira. She's gone," the words lingered in Eliza's mind.

She awoke in a flurry of panic. The night was young and her room was dark. Outside, the thunders bellowed. She ran down the corridor to her grandmother's room and flung the door open.

"Ma?" she whispered while standing at the doorway.

The howling wind hurled the opened windows back and forth violently, and the white curtains blew freely in the air. The bed was empty and Eliza's heart sank: her grandmother was gone.

The Return of the Key

A roar of thunder jerked Eliza out of her deep and disturbed slumber, and she woke up panting. It was as she had dreamt—the deluge continued, interrupted only by a chorus of thunder. She sat up and wiped the beads of sweat off her forehead. She could see little in her dark room, lit up only by quick flashes of lightning. Reluctantly she inched off the bed, fearful of reliving her nightmare, but knowing she could not rest until she was assured that all was well in the house. Step by step, her feet drew her closer to her grandmother's room down the dimly lit corridor. Her heart thumped profusely and her breathing grew heavier and heavier. She paused in front of the door and slowly, the tip of her fingers pushed it in. The creaks in the door's hinges wound on endlessly, adding an edge of eeriness that Eliza didn't like. She closed her eyes for a brief moment as she stepped forward, and then reopened them to see Indira sleeping soundly in the dark.

She could hear herself breathe a heavy sigh of relief, and she placed her hand over her heart as she did so. But just as the load lifted off her shoulders, she was startled by the sound of something falling to the floor downstairs. Instantly, she spun around and tiptoed out of Indira's room, her heart throbbing again. Eliza was frightened once more, but she walked as quietly as she could down the creaking old staircase.

"Patrick, is that you?" she whispered on reaching the living room.

The sound of flapping wings across the room could have given poor Eliza a heart attack. She gasped, bending over so her hands held tightly to her knees.

Phewww! She took one last breathe and reached for the light switch.

"Gees, Patrick, you gave me a good fright! What are you doing there, little buddy? You should be sleeping on your branches," Eliza tried talking to the shaking bird now walking farther under the dining table.

"Hmm...what's frightened you, Patrick? It's okay, little fella," Eliza whispered, furrowing her forehead as she reached her hand out to Patrick. When he climbed onto her hand, she placed him atop his perch and stroked his head before heading to the kitchen for a glass of water.

After she gulped down half a glass of cold water, standing in front of the fridge with the door wide opened, Eliza burped and thought that nothing had ever tasted more refreshing. She fancied a bit more, and reached into the fridge to pour another glassful. When she pushed the door shut, she had a niggling feeling that she was not alone in the kitchen. Slowly, she turned around, still swallowing her mouthful, and saw only the abnormally monstrous, black hairy feet when she dropped her glass. She wanted to scream, but before any sound could escape her lips, she was clobbered with a blunt object.

Later that morning, when the sun rose and the heavy showers had ceased, wailing could be heard from Rosie's cottage on Abbeydale Road. Had it not been for the boisterous thunder, they would have heard the glass fall to the floor, shattering into pieces. In addition, they might have heard the commotion as Eliza's limp body was dragged through the back door. The unfortunate tragedy that had befallen other families in the community in the days gone past had now unexpectedly hit home to Rosie's own. The grief was sudden and the pain ran deep. The police were already there investigating what was now the third disappearance in Abbeydale. Despite the telltale signs of all not being well on the street, Gwen walked over to Eliza's house and rang the front doorbell, as she had every morning from the time they'd become friends. She didn't know that she wouldn't find Eliza there, for she had not seen her friend's disappearance in her sleep. The moment teary-eyed Rosie opened the front door, Gwen's shoulders sagged as they bore the sudden burden of a missing friend.

Standing in the living room with her friend's stricken family, it didn't take her too long to conjure up a first guess as to where Eliza might now be, but this was nothing she could say to the police. They might have laughed or even reprimanded her for making a joke of a tragedy. She'd found that the nutmeg necklace she'd given Eliza was on her friend's bedroom nightstand. Eliza, it seemed, forgot to put it on before leaving her room. Gwen gave her best wishes and ran all the way home; she had to journey to a place where no police would go searching for her friend. A place where she had been only once as a child before her mother was taken. Gwen would have to cross realms into The Otherworld.

Through the damp, dismal, and meandering subterranean passages, Gwen's feet hastened. In the mouldy, cavernous tunnels deep beneath the tower on the hill, the darkness was set as though her own eyes were closed. Yet her legs carried her instinctively, showing no caution for the darkness.

This darkness seemed to swallow the bright beams of light shining from her torch, and she was hesitant to venture down certain pathways for fear of what lurked in the shadows.

These passageways might have led to another realm of things glorious and worth gazing upon, but fabled stories known to Gwen spoke of the most dreaded, unsightly creatures trapped between realms in this under-earth labyrinth.

This doorway was infamously the most dangerous of doorways linking both worlds, because it was said that trapped beings were always seeking a way out, either way, so if your footsteps were heard or your presence felt, you were likely to be followed to the entryway of the tunnels.

That is, of course, if you managed to find your way out without getting trapped in a dead end.

Luckily for Gwen, her mother had told her of the secret to the safe way through the labyrinth.

She eventually came to the last Y in the path and looked down to the left, where she could see the light emerging from the end—the obvious corridor to the other side. She took a few short steps towards it and stopped abruptly.

No.

It was the other way. The dark passage to the right was not welcoming. There was no light emerging from it, suggesting an end to the blackness, but alas, in these places logic wasn't always one's friend.

A memory quickly set down upon her of the time her mother was plaiting her hair, for the very last time, in fact, when she told of how many unlucky farers were joyous at believing they had come to the end of those dastardly tunnels, only to find that they had been tricked by the magic living there.

Gwen tightened her jaw, gripped her torch, and marched on to the right passage.

She walked on and on for a while before she came upon a huge wall in the way.

A dead end.

"Orriaes surrir," she whispered to the mossy wall, but nothing happened.

Perplexed, she whispered the words again and again.

Then, from somewhere beyond her, a fierce roar echoed through the passages.

Gwen gasped and spun around in horror.

It seemed that she was not as careful as she might have been and her presence in those parts of the tunnels was no secret, for one creature at least had become enraged by her choice of the right passage over the deceiving left. No mystical being likes being outwitted. Let alone by a human, or so it thought Gwen to be.

She turned back to the wall and desperately whispered the enchantment again, for fear of alerting the coming creature to her precise whereabouts.

In frustration and anger, she boldly spoke the words in a demanding tone with much authority, which was what she had lacked initially. In these parts, enchanting words bore no fruit to those who uttered them with no confidence.

A great rumble did sound when part of the wall slowly began to move out of place.

Relief came over Gwen, but lasted little time as the creature's heavy footsteps moved in closer.

"Come on, open faster! Come on!" she urged on the wall futilely.

At the end of the long corridor before her, a beast was now standing.

Gwen hesitantly pointed her light towards it, and in the distance, all she could see were its red, glowing eyes and great horns that stood upon an upright, muscular frame vastly bigger and taller than hers.

The creature roared again and the sound echoed through the tunnel.

Trembling, Gwen began squeezing herself through the small opening in the wall as the creature began charging towards her. Just in the nick of time, she eventually got her grazed body through the small opening and landed on all fours, before spinning around to shout another strange and foreign phrase.

She scrambled to the door and rested both hands on it, pushing while shouting the phrase again.

Through the shrinking gap, she could hear the creature quickly drawing closer as the wall slowly closed in.

Nevertheless, her words were of great effect and the door

quickly jammed in, causing the ground to shake. Behind, the creature's loud roars faded into nothingness, and the vanishing doorway was soon veiled by fast-growing weeds and vines springing from the hill Gwen had emerged from.

"Phewww," she sighed heavily, before taking a quick glimpse around her.

She was exhausted but still smitten by the grandeur of Annwn. It was strangely full of life.

In this place, a kind of bewildering charm flowed in the very air Gwen breathed in. A charm that made even the bare ground feel alive, as living as the fields of thriving flowers—Snowdonia Hawks to be precise, their orange blossoms bending in the whistling winds before her.

In truth, Annwn was indeed full of life, and much of it was to be revered.

Any unwitting being that dared misuse or disregard certain elements of this place faced punishment by the Dryads who guarded certain of the trees, plants, and animals. Take the said fields of Snowdonia Hawks for instance; they were many in numbers—as far as the eye could see, they sprung forth from the ground and created a seabed of swaying orange.

However, anyone who dared pick more than a single petal from one of these rare flowers, hoping to take advantage of its powers to bestow great strength and speed, was likely to be swivelled into a vast whirlwind and thrown down the nearby slope into the deep, gushing waters of the Black Lake.

It was a precarious place to be, and few new to it could survive without counsel.

Gwen contemplated this as she stared into the fields of flowers.

She made a full circle on spot, peering carefully around at her surroundings. Ahead of her, the fields seemed never-ending, stretching in the distance and almost touching the neon pink skies. To her right, a stony path led to the wooded forest, and to her left the lands became hilly and mountainous. Behind her, the flat green lands ended abruptly, sloping down to the noisy lake, the sound of which she didn't like.

She turned and approached the beginning of the flowerbeds and stooped. Carefully and with honest intention, she pulled a single petal from a flower and dropped it in a wide-rimmed bottle she carried in her knapsack. To it, she added some liquid from a fine tube, and lastly, some strands of Eliza's hair that she had taken from a hairbrush. She shook it violently and then threw it out on the bare ground, gesticulating with her hands.

"Umrriae ashmai elusi dosti Eliza Aurelio. Show me, oh bright Snowdonia."

Her forehead furrowed as she studied the emerging patterns on the ground.

"I hope you're safe, Eli. I'm coming to find you," she muttered to herself, before getting up and setting forth towards the wooded forest.

Gwen didn't know what she would find when she set foot in the wooded forest, home to common fair folk.

She trekked on quietly amid the colossal Red Woods towering over the green forest at over five-hundred-fifty-feet high. These grand giants had reddish-brown trunks as big as six feet wide and sometimes had snaking, gnarled roots spreading across the forest floor. High above, they formed a grand canopy that sheltered the enchanting forest.

Her inherent faery senses were coming alive again in her other natural habitat.

Up in the trees, she could hear the wind rustling leaves, the movements of animals shuffling through the bushes, and in the near distance the streaming waters of the lake. All was quiet, except somewhere ahead there was the sound of heated debate in a strange tongue.

She made her way closer to an encircled clearing in the

forest where there was a large gathering of common fair folk.

"I need to get in closer," she mumbled to herself, hiding behind a huge trunk.

She took a quick scan of her surroundings and eventually spotted an oak whose thick, leafy branches spread over the clearing.

"Bingo!" she said to herself.

Gwen climbed the tree with ease and, on looking down, saw a meeting of dozens of fair folk having a fiery debate. They were tall in stature and fair faced; most had distinctive markings about their pale skin.

"She is a liability," affirmed an elder female faery, draped in a long violet robe and poised with a glittering metallic rod. Her glass-jewelled diadem sat atop a crown of plaited silver locks, which fell behind her short, pointed ears.

"This isn't right, Mother. This is *not* the way of our folk," argued a fae male standing opposite her.

"Bring the human," ordered the elder faery, ignoring the arguments of her son.

Eliza staggered into the clearing, led by two armed fair folk, a cloth bag over her head. She fell to her knees and sighed in exhaustion. Though her face was concealed, she appeared haggard in her torn nightgown and bare feet.

Great sadness swept over Gwen upon seeing Eliza, and she clutched onto the tree and wept, but her sadness soon turned to anger.

"What shall we do with her then, my fair lady?" one of the armed fair folk eventually asked.

Gwen swiftly pulled a light wooden bow with arrows from her knapsack, and, despite the clamour, what was heard next was the sound of her running and fearlessly leaping off the oak branch, strung and suspended midair over the gathering by lianas she'd sprouted from the tree.

Ready to shoot, she announced, "Do *anything* to her

and this arrow will fly through your fair head." She kept her arrow trained on the armed faery.

"Gwen!" Eliza said with some relief as the gathering gasped in awe and murmured.

Everywhere arrows were now pointing at Gwen herself.

"The human has brought a friend. A fae friend, albeit. How many more of you are there?" the elder faery asked.

"It's just me," Gwen uttered. "Just let us leave in peace, we want no trouble."

"It's not that simple. *You* should know. You *are* one of us, no?" asked the elder fae.

"I'm not from around here. "I'm from the human realm. I'm only part faery," said Gwen reluctantly.

"Ahhhh... a rhwoski! Haven't seen one of you in moons! Unless of course... no it can't be. Child of Niada?"

"Yes. She was... is my mother," Gwen stuttered again.

The elder fae, Lady Drwyrwen, twiddled her fingers on the metallic rod, and lifted her chin while she pondered deeply.

"Lower your bows," she instructed her own with a nod, before she looked to Gwen expecting same.

Reluctantly, Gwen obliged.

"Why have you come here with this girl, Child of Niada? This is no place for a human," said Lady Drwyrwen, her eyes locked on Eliza.

Gwen explained how The Key had been fished out of deep waters by the missing fishermen, and how the phookas had been kidnapping people from the human realm. The crowd gasped at the mention of the fearsome beings.

"Have you humans not caused enough trouble here? You've stolen The Key, opened the doorways, and now you complain as you reel from the consequences?" asserted Lady Drwyrwen.

"No! Listen, no human stole The Key," assured Gwen.

"It was planted in the human realm. I don't know why, but someone's trying to stir up trouble for us."

Lady Drwyrwen looked upon Gwen's face with great curiosity.

"You speak truth. Extraordinary indeed. Though extraordinary has been the order of affairs in our realm of recent."

"I empathise with you, Child of Niada, but we cannot offer you safe shelter and neither can we come to your aid. New rules here outlaw humans. Anyone found harbouring one will face the ultimate punishment," warned Drwyrwen.

"You must set out on your own before anyone sees you here and reports it back to the Council."

"Mother!" clamoured Drwyrwen's son. "You send these fair beings to their deaths! You know they'll never make it back home without help!" her son argued.

He was angry, but the timbre of his voice was like music. His pale skin was flawless and smooth, his pink lips welcoming and his grey eyes captivating.

"You will have us risk our own to save these foreigners, Arden?" questioned the unyielding Drwyrwen.

"Yes."

"Your courage is worth praise, my son, but you know the days of helping humans have passed."

Arden marched past his mother and pulled the cloth bag from Eliza's head. His intention was to continue with his argument, but instead he did a double take and he gazed upon Eliza's face with much awe.

He sighed heavily before turning to his mother, visibly void of any emotion.

"I respect your decision as our leader, but as my mother, I say to you I will not depart the side of this human until she and her friend have gone safely past these lands. So if you must send them to their untimely deaths, then you shall do the same for your son, as well!" said Arden, the last of his words trailing off into a whisper.

Lady Drwyrwen was shocked, and a silence had befallen her.

"Your compassion is folly, brother," asserted a young fae sitting cross-legged above the gathering on a tree branch.

She jumped off the branch with ease and clutched the elder fae's arm. "Come, mother, leave brother to his madness."

"Know your place, Fialka!" Arden shouted at his now scoffing sister.

Lady Drwyrwen slowly walked off before turning to Arden. "The foreigners can sleep in the lower end. I expect you to set off by sunrise," she muttered with sadness.

"Thank you," Arden responded.

Gwen and Eliza offered their thanks.

He looked to them with kindness, but to Eliza especially he maintained a visible admiration.

"This way," he beckoned Eliza and Gwen. "You must be exhausted and hungry."

"Aquila, come!" he instructed with authority, and a magnificent mammoth of an eagle swooped down from nowhere to fly low over them.

"Weeaaaaaaaaa," shrieked Aquila as the young Arden spoke to her in a strange tongue. Before long, his winged friend was off again.

As the crowd dispersed, Arden led the girls out of the clearing and back into a forested area that eventually led up a slight incline. Gwen supported Eliza by the arm and they walked in silence. Eliza's eyes roamed unceasingly as she tried to take in her surroundings, which were constantly changing. She noted the odd thistle-coloured tree trunk scattered sparingly amid the reddish-brown bark of the Red Woods until they were walking only among thistle-coloured trunks. It was strangely beautiful to her human eyes.

As they walked, Arden asked their names.

"Eliza, and Gwen," Eliza answered nervously.

"Fair names for fair beings," he smiled.

The trees grew sparser than before, and soon further past that point, she could see a magnificent thistle tree—The Great Tree—a gigantic fortress fitted with many carved holes about its enormous branches. It was into one of these holes in a lower branch that Arden guided Eliza and Gwen. Two large beige pods fitted with thick cotton lay on opposite ends of the room on the other side of the doorway, which was lit by dozens of fist-sized glowing stones sitting on the ledges of the small, circular windows.

"I'll bring food. If you wish the lights out, touch the stones once, and again if you wish them on," Arden whispered.

"Arden!" Eliza called out before Arden passed through the carved doorway. "What *is* the ultimate punishment for helping us?"

"Death," he whispered before stepping out the door.

Chapter 4

UBIQUITOUS DANGER

THE NEXT MORNING, PEALS OF laughter that rung like a symphony in the wind woke Eliza from her slumber. She had not slept very well that night. Her dream, the same one as always, became more haunting, and she could hear strange whisperings of her name as she sailed into the faraway magical land. When she opened her eyes, she noticed first the curious fae children peeping at her through the room's circular windows. Their faces were round and fair and held a glowing radiance to them. They ran away shrieking with delight on seeing Eliza wake. Gwen was fast asleep in the pod across the room, and on the back of the door, someone had placed two simple but fine hooded cloaks for them. Eliza took one off the rack and slipped it over her shoulders before going outside.

She had never seen a sight so beautiful, she thought, as she examined the blossoming and verdant lands around her. The air smelt pleasantly sweet and below the bright neon pink morning sky, a cornucopia of shades bloomed in lavenders, amaranths, fandangos, carnation pinks, and many, many more than you could imagine—they were in the plants, flowers, trees, animals, and even the bare earth. There was no part of this place that wasn't a beauty to behold.

Eliza walked slightly down the incline and sat on a nearby rock bordering an odd flower-shaped fountain spewing shimmering water up into the air.

She was watching the droplets splash back into the bowl when she heard a musical voice call out, "Hello, Eliza," from behind her.

She spun around to see Arden, freshly bathed with his pale blonde hair neatly combed back in a single plait. He wore an earthy yellow belted vest with archer's sleeves and loose-fitted trousers neatly tucked into his leather boots.

It was the first time she had had a proper look at him, and she stared at his beautiful face and became embarrassed, as she was lost for words. He blushed with delight, appeased that his feelings were shared.

"Hello, Arden. Thanks again, for everything," she muttered as he approached and knelt before her, a pair of petite leather boots in hand.

"I brought these for you," he said. "May I?" She nodded. She bore a ladylike smile, but on the inside, her heart was throbbing uncontrollably.

Arden slipped the bole brown boots onto Eliza's small feet, and slowly, his gaze travelled up to her blushing face. He wished to stay kneeling before her, but it would have been lacking in propriety. So instead, he sat beside her and explained how his skilful cousins had rescued her while she was unconscious from a fearsome phooka during their patrol.

"I don't understand. Why did the phooka bring me here?" Eliza asked.

"I wish I knew the answer," said Arden. "But there is... something about you, Eliza. You must have the favour of Annwn, of this land. We usually avoid the phookas. Well, my kind are petrified by those horrendous monsters, but my cousins Rohan and Arrae decided they could not leave your fate in the hands of such a beast. They were brave only for your sake and barely escaped to tell us the tale."

Eliza expressed gratitude once more, shivering at the thought of her possible end had she not been rescued. She figured that she'd been clumsy in forgetting to put on the nutmeg necklace Gwen had given her for protection.

At the same time, she was becoming distracted by the oddly familiar shape of the flower fountain. Arden could not help but notice her curiosity.

"I've seen this before. In my dreams... I've seen this flower before, Arden. What is it?" she asked.

"It's not possible," said a voice before Arden could answer. It was his mother, Lady Drwyrwen. "*This* is a sculpture of a rare flower that blooms once every century. It is a sign of prosperity and good fortune, but more importantly, it offers to one worthy and noble fae, an extraordinary gift—a gift from the very heart of Annwn. A gift that can only be claimed by the chosen fae," she asserted.

Eliza's forehead was now furrowed. "I'm certain I've seen it before—it's white, and the tube is about twenty inches long, and it grows off a rock in the middle of a lake."

Lady Drwyrwen gasped. She deemed it impossible that Eliza, or any human for that matter, could have foreseen the Gift of Annwn whose blossoming was greatly anticipated every century by faeries all over the land. Understanding of this was esoteric. You see, every hundred years, Annwn offered up a rare flower, which bestowed an extraordinary gift to its beneficiary. No one knew which rare flower would blossom, which noble fae it would choose, or what gift would be bestowed. As Drwyrwen's minute sympathy for Eliza and Gwen quickly ebbed, she glowered at Eliza.

Infuriated, she grabbed Eliza by the shoulders, looked deep into her eyes and whispered an ancient mantra in song:

Ethmaro assinct roush dro pi,
kayee chay yan firokti,
eswar quiori vustnaha,
zaronhuut dejzut sionnth itz ma

In the human tongue, the closest translation might have been:

Noble the being, pure and whole
Who shall reap the gift of Annwn untold,
Uncorrupted and fair they shall be
Who be blessed of this land eternally

Eliza didn't know this, of course, and was horrified as she gazed into Lady Drwyrwen's colour-shifting eyes. "What does this mean?" she whispered shakily.

"It means that *only* an exceptional, *pure-blooded* fae can be chosen by Annwn for this bounty! Once, I was chosen! Certain of my forefathers were chosen, and someday perhaps one of my offspring shall be chosen. How dare you! *You* are not fae! You are not even a human of pure blood! This is blasphemy! Beg forgiveness, lest I smite you!" shouted Drwyrwen, whose voice was starting to rumble like a thunder.

"Mother! Stop!" cried Arden before he removed Eliza from his mother's grip.

Eliza felt numb from the vitriol in Drwyrwen's remarks. She cared little for the flower, but on the inside, she felt herself imploding from the contemptuous accusation of not being whole enough. She lacked the wholeness in her human realm and there, in a distant land, things were hardly different. This made her rebellious, and suddenly she felt like taking the flower just to prove her worthiness. Just to prove that someone of mixed race like her could be still be worthy and pure and noble.

"Mother," Arden began innocently, "who are we to question the mysteries of Annwn? She chooses a noble heart, and if a human girl is chosen and she has foreseen the gift, then she must take what is hers, but if she speaks untruths, we know she cannot take the Great Lily. She will be struck down by the same forces that put the flower there."

Arden's sister, Fialka, and his cousin, Arrae, had appeared quietly beside them. Arrae had come to aid Arden in returning the girls home and Fialka for no good or decent purpose.

Fialka, being her surly self, was not pleased. She cared not for aiding the brother who she loved but considered inept and imprudent at times. More than that, she shared the growing sentiments across the land that humans were untrustworthy and to blame for Annwn's beleaguered state.

She stared at Gwen, who was now running to Eliza after hearing the strange thunder in Lady Drwyrwen's voice.

"Here comes the half-fae," scoffed Drwyrwen.

"Eliza!" screamed Gwen in a panic. "Eli, you alright?" she panted, halting suddenly before the group.

Eliza was about to answer when Fialka butted in.

"Rhwoski! What's that in your pocket?" pointing to Gwen's left pocket, which was slightly bulging.

"I have a name, you insolent git. It's Gwen, not rhwoski," Gwen chided.

"Empty your pockets, Child of Niada! See where rebellion ended your mother. Don't make the same mistake here! Empty your pocket!

"It's no business of yours," Gwen replied.

"Gwen?" Eliza tried to politely butt in.

Fialka gestured with her hand and uttered a simple spell, lifted the bulging contents of Gwen's pocket.

Everyone, including Arden, gasped as Fialka pulled The Key from Gwen's pocket.

"Liar and thief!" exclaimed Drwyrwen, who was now certain that her initial suspicions were true—that Gwen and Eliza stole The Key from their realm and were out to cause further havoc just as other humans had reportedly done in recent times.

Eliza looked at her friend in confusion. "Gwen? What's going on?"

"No, this isn't what it looks like, I found it in my realm and I intended to return it," Gwen stated defensively.

Eliza sighed heavily. Had her best friend lied to her? "Gwen?"

Gwen turned to Eliza. "Eliza, I swear, I found it in the fishermen's boat that washed ashore. I was the one who discovered the boat and called the police. I couldn't let them take The Key away, they don't know its importance."

"What about me, Gwen?" asked Eliza. "You, you lied to me."

"Eliza... I... I did it to protect you, please. I didn't want you to have this burden...." Gwen pleaded, but she was interrupted.

"Arden, bring those traitors to me! The Council will deal with them!" ordered Drwyrwen.

Without fair reason to the witnessing eyes, Arden slowly shook his head in defiance, and most on that day believed him to be bewitched by the human Eliza and so followed her lead, but he did have good cause for standing by Eliza, as you will find out later.

"Arden, I said bring them to me," commanded his mother once more.

"I am sorry, Mother," he whispered. "Aquila! Come hither," he called to his bird as he gestured for Eliza, Gwen, and Arrae to follow him quickly. Out of nowhere, Aquila swooped down, squealing continuously.

Lady Drwyrwen stood still in shock for a minute before she closed her eyes, raised her face, and lifted her metallic staff to conjure a wind spell that would bring them back forcibly.

"Sorry, Mother," Arden heard himself muttering as Aquila struck Lady Drwyrwen down with a single swerve of her heavy body.

Arden, Arrae, Gwen, and Eliza ran east and down some narrow steps towards the Black Lake at the bottom of the incline.

"Arden, what are we doing? Your eagle just knocked your mother over unconscious!" said cousin Arrae, whose cheekbones were tattooed by double streaks on either side. His frame was superiorly muscular to Arden's, but this had only to do with his faery trait as a primary shape-shifter. On the other hand, what Arden lacked in stature, he made up for with his advanced archery skills and his special relationship with certain winged creatures.

"Trust me, cousin, they need our help. The Council's spies hide in waiting at the South doorway—we must take the river up North," Arden answered.

"Who else is after us?" asked Eliza naively.

Her three companions turned to her simultaneously, and Arrae broke the bad news.

"You're a human. Humans are outlawed here. *Everyone* is after you," he said, before calling them on.

They came to the end of the stairs leading to the Blake Lake, one of the largest and deepest masses of water in Annwn. Arden pushed one of the nearby boats into the water and ordered Eliza and Gwen into it, while he and Arrae got into another.

Eliza hesitated—not thirty feet away was the Calla Lily of her dreams, flourishing off a headland rock amid the setting with which she had become so familiar in her sleep.

"No, we can't go there, no, no, no...." she trailed off, but Arden didn't listen.

"Eliza, we have no time," he urged, looking behind him frequently, knowing very well that if his mother didn't bring them back herself, she would inform the Council of their whereabouts, and that was hardly a desirable outcome. Informing the Council meant that its eleven rulers, each belonging to differing races across the lands, would unleash guards to capture Gwen and Eliza and then their fate would no doubt be sealed.

Humans were now regarded enemies of the realm, and any found within its borders were to be imprisoned or banished, and appropriately punished for any crimes committed.

Arden rushed to Eliza, physically lifted her, and placed her in the boat with Gwen.

"No, no, no It's coming true, Gwen, my dream is coming true," she muttered in a frightful daze. Eliza then thought that the only way to avoid the darkness in the water was to do the opposite of what she'd done in her dreams. She would not pick the lily off the rock and all should be well, or so she reasoned, but every decision she made hoping to lead her away from her fate actually brought her closer to it.

"Grassor eere!" Arden commanded, and the boats started moving through the waters.

Eliza never stopped scanning all around her as they gradually increased their speed through the tranquil waters of the Black Lake. As they approached the emerging headland, heavy panic took hold of Eliza, and she became inert.

Suddenly, a heaviness weighed down on the atmosphere, and all four occupants began to feel quite glum. Simultaneously a great blackness, just as Eliza had dreamt, appeared in the water, blanketing sections of the lake and moving quickly towards their boats.

"Gwen, Eliza! Quick! Get onto the headland and stay there no matter what!" Arden shouted with urgency. He and Arrae stood up in their boat and began looking around them at the water. Arden readied an arrow in his incredibly powerful bow while Arrae took out a handful of magical silver star-shaped shuriken—sharp, star-shaped blades that, when thrown, could fly for long distances, causing great damage to whatever they struck.

The darkness in the water moved with swiftness now and was closing in on them.

Gwen motioned her right hand and lianas rapidly grew off the headland and into her hands. She pulled the boat towards the rock and then scaled up its mossy side, almost slipping a couple times until she was at the top. She reached her hands to Eliza.

"Eli, come on, quick!" she said, but Eliza didn't move.

Incapacitated by her fear, she sat still, gripping the edges of the boat and nervously looking around her.

"Eli! Take my hand!" Gwen appealed again. Finally, Eliza looked up at her, but the rays of overhead sun filled her vision.

She was about to stretch her hand to meet Gwen's, but then she glimpsed the Calla Lily, so beautiful, so pure, and so delicate growing marvellously mere inches from her. Eliza became spellbound, losing her senses, and for that short moment was enamoured by the flower. Her hand was outstretched and ready to pick it, when her boat started rocking uncontrollably. The darkness in the water was now surfacing nearby them.

"Elizaaaa," Arden shouted still standing in his boat.

She didn't hear him. She was barely gripping onto the rock for dear life, but still bewitched by the flower. She finally got hold of it and picked it! At that very moment, several things happened.

The Gift of Annwn (the great Calla Lily) released a shower of glimmering particles which fell onto Eliza, disappearing into her skin. She gasped liked something had possessed her, but as quickly as it began, she was released from the flower's hold, left only with the wilting flower in her hand.

Then a mighty rumbling sounded as the darkness rose to the surface of the lake. A massive snake-like reptile emerged from the waters, bellowing and creating violent waves that overturned the boats. It towered over them, iridescent scales along its hooded head glistening in the moonlight, and gave a fierce hiss—its ugly forked tongue darting out of its mouth. The hiss echoed hauntingly in Eliza's ears, just it did in her nightmare, as she fell screaming into the icy, rough waters.

Gwen acted quickly and ensnared her friend with two vines of lianas, pulling Eliza from the water and onto solid ground. That was of little use though, because with the behemoth towering over them, standing on the headland offered little protection and in fact only brought them to the creature's attention faster.

When the monster sighted them, the two girls gripped each other and cowered in trepidation. There was nowhere to run or hide. The heavily forested land on the other side of the lake was still a good swim away and appeared dark and uninviting. Just as the creature's head was moving in on them, it writhed and shrieked in pain before retreating. Arden had fired two arrows into its neck, as did Arrae with his throwing-stars, but they appeared to do insufficient damage beyond giving it two new targets. The monster was now turning on Arden and Arrae, who had climbed up and crouched on their capsized boat.

The reptile began eerily crawling across the surface of the waters towards Arden and his cousin. Just as it drew near enough to strike, Aquila appeared with a flock of golden eagles that swooped down on the reptile launching a fierce attack, aiming for its eyes and head. Few creatures were as magnificent and strong as the great eagles, but the odds were against them. They attacked the reptile with all their might, piercing its scaly skin with their sharp talons, but the creature was enormous and with every mighty move, it lashed the squealing eagles left, right, and about. It was a despairing thing to see. All hope seemed lost when the creature suddenly appeared stunned for a moment. Arden and Arrae took advantage of this and quickly equipped their weapons once more, aiming for the creature's eyes.

The weapons hit their marks, causing the monster to squeal in pain. It retreated to the depths of the lake, and the waters calmed down.

"What was that? Since when have such horrendous monsters dwelled in our lake?" Arrae asked Arden, both still out of breath.

"Since the plague, cousin."

"We were lucky to escape, though it was rather close," Arrae added.

"No. It wasn't luck," Arden answered, looking to the land behind them. He saw no one in the distance, but Arden suspected someone had come to their aid.

Arden and Arrae quickly got out of the water, deciding that it was probably best to stay out of the Black Lake lest other dark surprises be hiding in its murky depths.

Arden sent thanks to the golden eagles with Aquila and set off at a run with the group.

The four made their way stealthily past the faery community and into the thick of the Wooded Annwn Forest. Arden scouted the path ahead of Eliza and Gwen, and Arrae guarded the rear. The gnarled tree roots on the forest floor made running more hazardous than it should have been, but really, the only one made clumsy by it was Eliza. Gwen's half-fae heritage made her naturally lighter on her feet, and she sashayed easily over the obstacles. She thrived in this environment, and Gwen let the air carry her body as she pushed it upwards and forward, pausing on occasion to let Eliza catch up. As they manoeuvred their way through the forest, Arrae spotted a haunting shadow shifting in the skies above the forest.

"Spies! Look for cover!" Arrae alerted the group.

The Sluagh, as they were called, are a kind of evil spirit that took the form of angry birds and often appeared as black shifting shapes in the sky. Though typically used as spies by evildoers, the Council had started using The Sluagh for their own business due to the spirits' effectiveness in tracking those the Council wanted. Being used for good could not ever change the nature of The Sluagh, however. They were, by their very essence, an iniquitous force that drew evil with it, attracting darkness to those they spy on. So Arden and Arrae, knowing the truth of this force, had reason to shudder in fear.

The fact that The Sluagh were onto them meant that other powerful evil forces would now be aware of their presence, alone and vulnerable in the forest without the safety of numbers. As they ran seeking a hiding place, Eliza collapsed very abruptly and started hyperventilating. The others initially thought she'd stumbled on one of the many gnarled tree roots, but when Arrae picked her up, foaming white froth poured from her mouth. Arrae alerted the others and panic moved through the trio, now more unsure than ever how to proceed.

"What is it? Is she breathing?" Arden questioned.

"Yes, but her heartbeat is faint and she has a high fever," replied Arrae.

"I don't understand," Gwen spoke, barely a whisper.

"Something must be causing this reaction, but we've all been together since leaving the lake," said Arden.

It was then, it dawned on Gwen that Arrae and Arden might not have seen Eliza picking the Great Calla Lily off the rocky headland. Indeed, they hadn't. Once they sounded the warning to the girls, Arden and Arrae had been busy scanning the waters for the creature in the Black Lake.

After Gwen made this known, the group fell silent. A few moments passed, and Arden spoke first. "I should have kept an eye on her."

"What? Are you blaming me?"

"No...."

"Well, what are you trying to say?"

A nonsensical row escalated, and an irritated Arrae had to silence them with a beastly grumble that sounded more animalistic than fae. Gwen and Arden stared wide-eyed at Arrae who was still grumbling under his breath.

"You're allowing yourselves to be influenced by all that is around us. Fill your inner space with goodness, and keep that negativity out," Arrae instructed.

It was now obvious that Eliza needed some kind of help, but they couldn't return to the fae community and Lady Drwrywen; and with The Sluagh foraging the great forest for them, they needed to get going sooner rather than later.

"I know somewhere we could go," Arrae said.

"Good," Arden answered. "Let me take her, you lead the way."

Keeping a close watch out for The Sluagh, Gwen and Arden, with Eliza in his arms, followed Arrae gingerly through a bushy course off the forest's stony pathway. They ran for about fifteen minutes before Arrae stopped them in the middle of the forest.

"The less you say, the better. My friend is of a peaceful nature, but he bears no liking for human or fae. In fact, better keep a still tongue. Both of you."

"What nature of being is this *friend* of yours?" asked Gwen.

"What nature? He has the eyesight of a golden eagle, is seven times stronger than most of us fae, and can move the world with his wrath. To say the least, it is best to not test his patience or anger him. So say nothing," Arrae replied.

Arden stared in disbelief and Gwen shifted nervously from foot to foot.

They followed Arrae a short distance farther until a

massive tree came into view. They stopped to rest, and Arden lay Eliza against a thin tree trunk. Arrae told them to wait in the shadows while he approached the Great Holm Oak. It was majestic; laden with acorns amongst an abundance of greenish-blackish leaves that crowned a huge, dark trunk imprinted with square fissures. Arrae knocked on the tree's trunk, and a doorway that reached the height of his shoulders opened on one side of the tree.

"Come on," Arrae beckoned toward the shadows where his friends stood. Arden scoop Eliza back up and made his way briskly to his cousin with Gwen close on his heels. They lowered their heads and stepped into the Great Holm Oak.

Chapter 5

A PLOT

SOMEWHERE IN A DARK FOREST...

In the dark, cold shades of the Strangler Figs, four slender figures hashed out the details of a plan. Not just any old plan. A big plan. A big, sinister plan. It took place on the other side of the Black Lake. The 'other side' was known to all fae as the place they must never, ever, ever, under any circumstances, cross over to. It was the side of the river that marked the start of the *Dark Forest*—a forest so evil that those who entered it rarely came back out. It was so filled with doom that many an unsightly creature thrived there, feeding off the darkness and all that was evil, and even the fae with the strongest arcane magic dared not think, even once, about setting foot in it. However, this forest hadn't always been dark, once, it had formed part of the Annwn Forest where common fae like Arden and Arrae grew up and played and sung and lived with their community in harmony with nature.

The cataclysmic events of The Unknown Plague decades ago had changed everything, and new evil had emerged and corrupted the soil with the seeds of the evil Strangler Figs. These monstrosities began their lives as epiphytes on the branches of the lofty oaks and redwoods and elms and all other good trees, before off shooting a network of deadly roots that encircled and snaked down their hosts, eventually suffocating them and all the beautiful things that grew out of the land. Their thick leaves eventually covered the once-pristine forest in darkness—a darkness used to harness more darkness. And so, the forest was lost to evil.

It was in this forest that Eliza's plotted end began.

"It is as our Lady said it would be," said the elf whose yellow irises glowed against his skin, which was darker than the night itself. "They possess The Key and intend to return it to its home, the human and the half-fae, but they have unexpected company and help," he said in a staccato voice.

The elf directly opposite him smiled slyly. "This is no problem. Their escape from the clutches of our Lady's magic is by mere chance, or luck, as the humans name it. Soon, we shall hold their puny lives in the palm of our hands."

The other two elves, one female with bright scarlet hair, laughed heartily in agreement.

On setting foot inside the Great Holm Oak, Gwen gasped in awe.

"It's bigger on the inside. Eli, it's bigger on the inside!" Gwen stuttered in disbelief to Eliza, though her friend remained unconscious in Arden's arms.

Eliza might have been unconscious, but in her subconscious, she was well aware of the sickening feeling on her insides of something powerful, bubbling away and travelling fast to every edge of her body. Her body felt the energies rumbling inside her wanting to explode, but there was no way out.

"Watch your step now," said Arrae, walking ahead.

They followed him down a set of wide steps in a dimly lit corridor and through a large, circular, well-lit room with a table and short seats, decorated by many, many colourful and shiny ornaments.

"Arrae, I'm in the workroom, mi friend," shouted a throaty voice from beyond.

Arrae led the group through another doorway into an even larger rounded room with two huge cotton bedseats and intriguing gadgets of every kind crowding nearly every surface.

The ceiling was low in some places, but for the most part, the tallest among them could stand without bumping their heads.

Gwen and Arden were apprehensive as a tall, eerie shadow came out of a nearby doorway, approaching the room where they stood, but for all their fears, as the shadow approached, it quickly reduced to less than half its initial height. Soon, the diminutive gnome Skoran was revealed.

He was hardly as scary as Arrae had made him out to be! He had tan skin and was clad in a blue tunic with matching trousers and a heavy toolkit attached to his belt. His face was round, his cheeks rosy, and his mahogany hair curly and thick.

"Who are these strangers?" he asked Arrae with concern.

"We need your help."

When Arrae looked to Eliza, Skoran hustled Arden to get her onto one of the long cotton seaters. After Skoran inquired about Eliza's state and was shown the slowly withering Calla Lily, he said he knew just the thing that could help her. He rushed to his kitchen and the sound of pots and pans clattering and tumbling resounded through the room. After about five minutes, the most malodorous smell permeated the house. Arrae, Arden, and Gwen blocked their noses to no avail. Soon, Skoran was back, handing a cup of the smelly mixture to Gwen to feed Eliza, and a bowl and cloth with some more for her forehead.

"This should help her recover, but it could take several hours before she regains full strength," said Skoran.

"What caused it?" asked Arrae.

Skoran glimpsed at the Calla Lily in Gwen's hand.

"The Gifts of Annwn penetrate the skin once picked from their roots, and their components tend to be very, very powerful. I am not well-learned in these matters, but I cannot recall any other race than the fae being destined to pick one of the Gifts of Annwn. It could be that your friend's human body isn't as strong as the body of a fae and her immune system it seems, took the substance as though it were a poison, but she should be well, as I said. Nothing that a fresh cup of popidops and Perilous Python leaves can't fix!" said Skoran.

"Perilous Python? Eckkk," Gwen burst out.

"Yupsidoo! Only the sweetest smelling, but most deviously deadly plants in the Kingdom!" answered Skoran.

"Sweet-smelling you say?" asked Gwen still covering her nose.

"Ahh... sweet until it dies or its leaves are picked! They immediately give off quite a stench! Stinky! But a medical wonder!" The dwarf let loose a hearty chuckle.

"Mind you," Skoran added in a whisper, "if your friend hadn't been treated quickly, there's no telling what The Gift might have done to her."

"Thank you," muttered Gwen in unison with Arden. She tilted her head and furrowed her brows. "Why's it called a gift anyway, if this is what happens to you when you pick it?" she asked.

"Well, this was a very rare case—the only one I know of. Your friend has been given a great gift, whatever it is. Have you not noticed what it is yet?"

"No, not really."

"Ahh... Well in due time she will figure out what it is, but be sure it will be nothing short of extraordinary."

After Arrae properly introduced Skoran to each member of the group, he explained the situation and the danger in the lake that they had earlier escaped.

"So let me get this straight. Gwen, you possess The Key, which you found in the human realm. Creatures from our realm have been causing havoc in yours and you wish to return The Key to its rightful place to end this, but of course you need help, as your ailing friend is forbidden from our lands?"

"Yes," Gwen said. "I was initially hoping to just hand The Key over to someone else to return, but I had no idea of what was happening here."

At this moment, Eliza stirred, opening her eyes, and tried to sit up.

Skoran said to her, "You will be weak for several hours yet, lie and take rest." She leaned back her tired body but her eyes stayed open, fixated on the small man with the large voice.

"We have to do it, Gwen," Eliza said.

"No, not *we,* Eliza. This is not your burden," Gwen interjected.

"But it is, don't you see? The people we love will never be safe until that doorway is closed, Gwen. This is our burden, and I am not leaving until it is done."

Skoran stood up. "My friends, if you wished my advice, I would say to you, go home. This journey is perilous, and you will have more enemies than friends here. The very nature of this realm makes it perilous, and the events of The Unknown Plague magnify the danger awaiting you along the way. I know you do not want this advice, so I will tell you plainly: you need a miracle. Hope that whatever gift was bestowed on your friend will help you. I must say, it is rather unusual that a human was chosen for this—a human who has never been to our realm, for that matter. She must be special. On another note, the sighting of the lake creature that attacked you is worrisome. Our lake has never been home to such monstrosities. It sounds the likely product of dark magic," said Skoran.

Skoran didn't look his years, but he had many centuries of experience and had lived through the fateful events of The Unknown Plague. He, for one, knew the evil that had descended their lands making lone journeys precarious for any who dared wander. Anyone could face an attack, but humans were more at risk given the new law that demonised them. Any attack on humans could be excused now, no matter who was on the offensive.

Skoran told them that their possession of The Key only added to their risk. Its finding would make realm creatures suspicious of Gwen and Eliza's motives, and The Sluagh spies being aware of their presence made almost everywhere unsafe.

"What... What is The Unknown Plague?" whispered Eliza as she writhed in pain.

Arrae looked to Skoran, horrified that the question might anger his gnome friend, but it didn't. Arden, Skoran, and Arrae's faces all wore looks of discomfort at Eliza's words.

Skoran nodded in silence and took a half a second before he began speaking again.

"Many years ago our vast kingdom was called The Underworld and was inhabited by many varying races of beings that lived in harmony and at peace with one another and nature.

"The kingdom was ruled by Drezairlar Ruythorin, a fairy king of great stature. He was respected in all the lands by all beings, the grand and the diminutive.

Among his many duties, he was charged with maintaining the balance of good and evil. This he did fearsomely, and his rule was never questioned or scorned, but something happened to change all this.

"A great darkness, never seen before, swept over our lands, corrupting many of the pure of creatures, and forever making volatile the balance of our kingdom. It spread fast, like a virus, covering the farthest reaches of the kingdom that many of us were yet to even set foot upon.

"No one knew how this evil crept upon us like a thief in the night, and Drezairlar was overcome by so much grief that he was incapacitated. For a long time he remained in denial, and he failed to confront this evil. Many beseeched him, but he harkened not unto our cries. Many lives were lost.

"The races of our lands were left with no other choice but to fend for ourselves. Most created impenetrable veils that hid and sealed the entryways to their territories, making it impossible for any evil to pass through. Even if a veil was discovered, not even the strongest magic could cross it. This was how our peoples became divided by fear and anguish. Even now, the races mistrust each other.

"To this day, no one knows how that evil came to us. Many blame the humans who crossed over to our realm. In the past, most of us had embraced your kind, but some feared your people, and the spread of human diseases like malice and greed, and a human plot to overtake and corrupt our peaceful realm.

"From then on, this has been no place for humans. The newly established Council forbade the return of your kind here. All humans already resident in our realm were banished to distant lands to live in isolation. It is a life I wouldn't wish even on an enemy, if I had one. Anyone in league with a human risks the ultimate punishment.

"As for Drezairlar, no one knows what became of him. Some say his grief consumed him, others say he was corrupted by the very evil he failed to confront. No one knows, but these lands have dwelled in fear ever since. And, there are those who even hunger for the human longing you call vengeance."

Gwen and Eliza looked at Skoran in shock as his tale drew to an end.

"This Council," said Eliza, "where do they sit? And is there no chance at all that they would hear us?"

Skoran looked down, feeling a sense of despair for Eliza in particular.

"My child, I wish it were so simple for you. Hear my words—in the aftermath of The Unknown Plague, we were without a leader. The evil became widespread and we knew not how to fight it or who to trust. This is no longer the realm we called home. Everything has changed. Now, always, we live with evil on our doorsteps," Skoran paused and clasped his hands together.

"Members of most of the races came together and formed a confederation, headed by a Council of eleven elder representatives. They are charged with ruling us and restoring order and peace, yet among them there is discord. Rumours rage of evil penetrating the Council."

"What do you speak of?" questioned Arden, who was shocked to hear this.

"Young fae, all is not as it seems. Word has spread of an infiltrator who sits on the Council, influencing the votes and the rule of law. We don't know who to go to. Those who have spoken out have disappeared, and the brave-hearted are no longer brave. Spies are among our friends and neighbours," Skoran forewarned.

This greatly troubled Arden.

"You don't seem surprised, Arrae," said Arden in an accusing voice.

Arrae maintained a straight face with his silence.

"You knew of this and said nothing to me! We have to warn mother and our elders!" asserted Arden.

"Stop! You WILL tell no one! This is precisely why I made Arrae swear his silence," shouted Skoran.

"Arden, as I have said, be wise and hear my words. Spies are among us. Let what I have said today stay among you, or else we are already dead."

Arden nodded, understanding the error in his hastiness. For a while, no one said anything.

"Back to business!" Arrae announced, breaking the silence. "Do you know where exactly in the North The Key must be returned, dear friend? And is there a safe doorway nearby, so Gwen and Eliza can get home afterwards?" questioned Arrae.

"Hmmmm..." muttered Skoran before he turned his head and called out a name.

"Rage, mi gnomie gnome, bring mi looking glass," called out Skoran.

Some seconds later, a small individual clumsily walked into the room, carrying a hefty, rectangular, double-sided mirror on a tall, lean stand. It covered much of the poor child's face, but the little hands that firmly gripped the mirror's stand made it apparent this was a child. He rested it on a little table among Skoran and his guests. When he stood up, Eliza, and all company besides Arrae, gasped—Gwen and Eliza for different reasons than the rest. Little Rage had radiant skin, but his eyes were yellow and piercing. Eliza and Gwen had never seen such a thing, but for Arden, he immediately knew the race from which Rage came. He was an Aradath Elf.

"You hold an aberration in your dwelling, gnome!" Arden shouted, jumping to his feet.

Skoran looked on in shock. He never thought of alerting them to the fact that he kept the company of a young Aradath Elf, but as a typical gnome, he expected his friend's guests to respect his home and act within good reason.

"Arden! Sit down," shouted Arrae.

"No! What friend is this to have, Arrae? One who keeps our enemy on our doorsteps?"

Eliza covered her mouth in fright, not knowing what was happening or where this would lead.

"Arden, calm down, I'm sure there is a reasonable explanation for this," butted in Gwen.

"No! We cannot trust him!" Arden rebutted.

No one noticed, in the background, Skoran was desperately trying to comfort, or defuse rather, little Rage.

Arrae's anger was just mounting to its peak, but before he could let out a furious roar, Rage unleashed an unfettered, deafening shriek that painfully rang through their ears, causing unimaginable distress and breaking anything made of glass within close proximity. It was a wonder the double-sided mirror didn't break. They cupped their hands over their ears, but it was of no use. The deleterious shriek travelled through their bodies as fast as lightning, bringing a crippling pain to every joint and muscle. Gwen, Arden, and Arrae had fallen to their knees in agony. Eliza was curled up in a ball on the bed, shaking.

The shriek stopped abruptly and they all gasped in unison, their bodies sagging frailly from the onslaught of Rage's scream.

He was sobbing, his face pressed into Skoran's chest, who had his arms wrapped tightly around the small creature. When Rage lifted his face, his eyes had gone from yellow to a fiery red.

"Dear, dear, gnomie, t'was a silly mistake by the fae, silly fae, mi sure," said Skoran looking angrily at Arden.

Arden clenched his teeth.

"Um, yea silly mistake, uh please, Rage, forgive this fae, I beg your forgiveness."

Skoran patted Rage on the back and sent him off into another room.

"Skoran, my sincerest apologies. My cousin has shamed me," said Arrae.

Arden pursed his lips, folding his arms over his chest defiantly.

"It is forgiven. Arrae, you are a loyal friend, but if there be a next time, I cannot promise to remain in peace. I have held Rage since he was a baby and nurtured him as my own. He may be Aradath Elf, but he has the heart of a gnome! And any offence to him is an offence to me," said Skoran.

Arrae nodded in agreement with his friend.

"Now, let me show you whereabouts you must head. Gather 'round," cheered Skoran as if nothing had ever happened.

He positioned the mirror so he stood to one side and everyone else could look on through the other side.

His index finger traced invisible patterns on his side of the mirror, and very soon the group could see emerging colour and lines demarcating territories, before it unfolded into a proper map. It was the first proper map Arden and Arrae had ever seen of Annwn Forest and beyond.

Skoran pointed on the map firstly, their current position in The Oaks of Annwn Forest. He traced his finger again on the glass's map, this time showing what he considered the safest route to their destination—The Sacred Valley— all the way past the Great Mountains of the Never-Ending East. Skoran jotted down the key points on piece of parchment once he pointed it out on the looking glass.

Head Northwest through forest and past Mermaid's Lair (beware of the screamers).

Continue to Mirror Lake and keep Northwest

Cross the Canyons

Cross Misty Bridge (Note: bridgekeeper must be paid to pass)

Leads into Mountains of the Never-Ending East. Pass through quietly

Head into The Sacred Valley

Note: the nearest doorway lies just beyond The Sacred Valley

"What payment are we to give the bridgekeeper?" asked Arrae.

"Ahhh, yes... I do not know! A rumour abounds that the payment rolls only on the ground of 'the living waters.' I've never heard anyone talk of what that could be! If you don't find out, you will have to answer a riddle, I hear, but you must be wary. The bridgekeeper is fabled to belong to a race of sacred guardians, some of whom can be deadly to touch, friendly and willing to come to your aid, or neutral, caring for nothing but its duty as keeper of the bridge.

"Have you been there before?" asked Arrae.

"No, never in mi gnome years."

"Won't The Sacred Valley be under guard?" asked Gwen in a panic.

"It is not what awaits you in The Sacred Valley that worries me. I fear for what you might meet on the way," said Skoran, handing worn out copies of the map to Arrae, and Arden. They had water stains on them and the edges were ripping.

The group spent the night at Skoran's, since Eliza had not fully recovered. Skoran in particular persuaded them, having thought it best that they set out at dawn. The Sluagh, he said, were more active at night, and they needed to plan where they would rest at the fall of light.

In the early morning, when the dew was still fresh on the Holm Oak's leaves, Skoran woke the group and gave them each brown satchels filled with freshly baked bread and biscuits, fruit, and water."

"Eat carefully, Eliza. This food is safe for you, but some foods of our realm will endow you with abilities too powerful for you to return home, back to a normal life. So eat only this, unless Arden or Arrae can confidently point out a safe food source for you," said Skoran walking them to the door.

"Oh! I have a rather strange feeling that you best give The Key to Eliza for safekeeping," Skoran added, looking to Gwen.

Gnomes do not typically have the gift of foresight. Instead, just like dwarves, they were gifted with crafting ingenious inventions and jewellery out of the gems they loved to cut.

For this reason, it was strange that Skoran had this, well, 'strange' feeling. Nevertheless, Gwen obliged and passed The Key to Eliza.

"I don't... I mean, Gwen is fine carrying The Key, aren't you, Gwen?"

"Oh it don' matter, Eli, long as it gets to where it belongs," said Gwen, handing the object over to Eliza, who handled it clumsily.

On the way out of The Holm Oak, Skoran said to Gwen, while staring at the jewel hanging on her chest, "Dear, Gwen, do you know the gem you wear?"

"The peridot. Lovely innit? Twinkles in the light," Gwen said, looking at it.

"Very rare gem and so is the fashion of its chain, both from...."

"From this world yeah, I know—really special—only one of its kind here," said Gwen smugly.

"No. Not the only one, and it doesn't only twinkle in the night."

"What? What do you mean?"

"These old hands dug the raw stones from the earth of a realm of ours. I made your necklace and its sister, which both twinkle when near each other."

Gwen looked to him with suspicion.

"Gwen, the only other one belongs to Niada, your mother. And the peridot twinkles when in close proximity to its own kind."

Gwen stared at Skoran intensely for a moment, let out

a deep breath, and then briskly walked up the steps and into the forest without a word.

Eliza pulled the hood of her cloak over her head and approached Skoran to thank him for saving her life.

The fae cousins looked on, waiting.

As she stopped in front Skoran, blocking the view of him from the outside, he appeared grim and whispered to her so softly it was like it wasn't being spoken at all.

"Do not get caught. The Council is draconian and will not spare you." He gripped her hand tightly in his. "Trust no one. Not even your own shadow."

Chapter 6

DEADLY DIVERSION

*A*T A MEETING OF THE *Council far, far away in the mountains*
Around a large round table made of gold, the eleven elders of The Otherworld's Council deliberated. They sat in a regal hall fitted with antique gilded walls. The gold highlights stood out against the white walls and spiralled upwards onto the ceiling, curling back and forth in the most intricate patterns. Complex coloured reflections fell across the room through the ancient faery-stained glass fitted into the tall gothic windows around the room.

Hiatar, a yellow-skinned centaur seated at the table, grunted.

"Yes, the human has stolen The Key, according to reports. But, an itch down to my mane tells me we know not half of this story's truth," said Hiatar.

"I feel this too, Hiatar," agreed Emyrees, the glowing white-clad ice faery of the Riashore Water Valley. He lifted a brow in consideration.

The Council was deliberating the latest threat facing the realm—a human, her half-fae counterpart, and two defecting forest faeries. A grim report had been made by the faery leader, Lady Drwrywen.

The Council had beefed up its security and ordered

its guards and The Sluagh to find the suspects. Rumours were spreading fast across the realm, and an upheaval was brewing.

"Is the truth of significance, my brothers?" interrupted a pale female elf, tossing her hands in the air to garner their attention. "Does the truth bare importance when the human has stolen our only key to the most accessible doorway, opening our realm to unimaginable threats? She and her friends roam our lands freely when they are prohibited by our very laws!" argued Eolande, whose long crimson tresses flowed over her shoulders and spilled onto the glimmering stone floor.

She leaned over the table and whispered, "They have stolen something precious, and it must be for a reason. And I cannot foresee good behind this reason."

"Eolande...." interjected Emryees in a whisper, his head tilted down.

She ignored him and continued her rant.

"We passed the anti-human laws with just reason. The anti-human groups were right. This species must possess far greater intelligence than we have given them credit for. The greatest threat is we know not what is planned against us. Against our realm. Another great plague? Imagine!" Eolande added in an ominous voice, looking around the table to the faces staring at her intently.

"Eolande," Emryees tried reasoning, staring at her with his green eyes, "we cannot seek war with those we know *not* for certain to be our enemies."

"You gave your vote on the anti-human laws willingly, brother," Eolande answered.

"Yes, but voting to bar humans from our lands is moons from what this Council now prescribes! We might as well be asking for a war with the humans. We have no proof against them in this instance, yet you wish to condemn the human girl and her friends to death," said Emryees.

"The proof we carry, Emyrees," interjected the heavy

male voice of Vonroth, the wizard gatekeeper sitting at the head of the table, "are the nascent evils dwelling in our once-peaceful realm. The proof, which we live daily, is the pain left in the wake of The Unknown Plague. The disappearance of our formerly adored King Drezairlar. The corruption of innocents and the taking of many lives!" snarled Vonroth, gripping his chest.

Eolande nodded in consent, while the gnome beside him patted his back in support.

Vonroth pointed out what every council member already knew. Among the perpetrators in question, was the half-fae Gwen, daughter of a faery banished for cohabiting with a human. As one of the realm's first half-faeries, anti-human sentiments were directed towards Gwen as well. Vonroth reasoned that surely she couldn't be a happy trooper. Moreover, a human who had mysteriously been chosen by their motherland for The Gift of Annwn? Something was amiss.

"We must extract the threats against us! For the sake of our peoples and the existence of our realm!" Vonroth shouted lifting his fist in the air.

"They infiltrate our realm, conspire against us, and seek to murder ours again. Before any war can come to us, we will bring them down, torture them till they cry out the details of the human conspiracy and then terminate their evil lives." His fist bounced up in the air again.

"Aye!" shouted numerous voices around the table, throwing their fists into the air in consent.

Emryees looked around the table at his co-council. His indifferent expression betrayed the deep suspicions rife within him.

"This is anything but right, Hiatar," he muttered incoherently to the centaur sitting next to him.

Eolande noticed his quiet upset, and raised a suspicious brow at him.

They might have sat on the same council, these eleven

rulers coming from a total of nine different races of the realm, but their differences were many, and rumours of discord among them were far from untrue. In fact, 'discord' was putting it mildly. Among the small group, Emryees could see indifferent faces like his.

There was his friend Urhouri, the yellow-skinned salamander, crowned by a full head of fiery red hair, and with the most unusual shade of amber-ringed eyes. Then, there was the hairy and sometimes frightening faun. Seated two places from him was the reticent Sylph. Her huge hawk-like eyes and distinctively sharp, angular face were distractions from the imposing, yet almost invisible, wings folded on her back. These three seemed like him and his friend Hiatar, who annoyingly bore a pleasant look no matter the occasion. Still, he couldn't be sure what secret feelings their indifferent expressions shielded. The majority of them had voted in favour of the anti-human laws, at the time believing it a harsh necessity in the wake of The Unknown Plague that left their lands ravaged and without a ruler. All, except another Sylph, who had abstained from the vote. Why, none of them were entirely sure, as she downright refused to say. All the other members of the Council—his ice faery counterpart, a stocky gnome with a curly white nest of a beard, a common forest fae, and a woodland elf, seemed to share similar sentiments about humans as did Eolande and Vonroth.

However, around this table, one could never be sure of who was who. When he had been asked to sit on the Council, Emryees obliged, seeing it as an important call of duty at a time when his realm needed him the most. His people at the Riashore Water Valley bore concerns and emotions following The Unknown Plague, much like any other community. Suspicion and fear were rife, and while many races removed themselves rather than joining the confederation, his people would not do that. For if another plague was to come, the confederation would not protect those outside of their umbrella. Remarkably, two entire races took the risk. Namely the dwarves and the isolated, social outcasts, the Gwragedd Annwn. No one asked them why. In those days, a staunch arrogance was levelled at anyone putting up such resistance to the confederation and its ruling council. Emryees wondered if the decision to remain independent of the confederation exhibited a degree of wisdom or if it was foolishness, as some council members called it.

These days he found himself wondering many things like this. Since news of this strange human had come to the Council, they convened daily. A human so powerful and destructive, yet their motherland had gifted it above the fae of the realm. Still, it was only a human. A mere human. What danger could one human bring? Many questions led only to more questions, all left unanswered.

How could a human steal The Key from what was considered to be one of the 'safest' places in their realm? The Key was guarded at The Sacred Valley. No ordinary Nixy Fae or Rratchrog Gnome could just fairydust in and take it. Few, if any, could bypass the lone guard. Yet a human managed to steal it, to potentially open the doorways, to let its own infiltrate the realm, but why? What was the motive? Before The Unknown Plague, humans had been friends of the realm, to those who befriended the humans anyway. Those unfortunate ones who had stumbled over accidentally, through unknown doorways and holes between the realms, were encouraged to stay, for few humans could return to their world with the knowledge they would have acquired in Annwn and the wider realms of The Otherworld. Those who stayed had become friends of the realm. They seemed harmless enough, unlike some of their kin who had caused bloodshed in the human world, over shiny jewels and ludicrous ideals. It seemed, from his little interaction with the human species, the vast majority were good, as the humans called it. Emryees knew better than anyone else that these arguments couldn't withstand the impassioned rebuttals of those anti-humanists always eager to point out a realm-accepted axiom—before the humans, order was intact, and whatever evil they combated was incomparable to The Unknown Plague. Never in the history of their realm had they known a devastating tragedy like that scourge. It wiped out entire communities, infected many more, and sprouted more evil, as a darkness ravaged the lands and any communities that couldn't veil themselves in time. It happened so fast. Without warning. No one knew what this plague was, or what had caused it. The accepted truth was that everything went downhill after the arrival of humans. That he couldn't defend.

Back in the Wooded Forest....

Eliza trekked on quietly through the forest, which was slowly coming alive as the morning wore on. Intriguing winged creatures fluttered in the air amid awakening flowers, which were spreading their delicate petals open. Despite the teeming beauty all around them, Eliza's thoughts were far away from Annwn Forest. They were in the tiny cottage on Abbeydale Road, with her beloved grandmother and Aunt Rosie, and all the way back in Trinidad with her grandfather. In her heart, she was worried sick over her family's safety, over the possibility of her loved ones being abducted like her but facing less fortunate ends.

She so longed to be in the arms of her grandmother where it was always safe, where she was always shielded from the harsh realities of her world. Somehow, in some way, her grandparents had been able to protect her from cruel things that seemed bigger than them all, and Indira and Jose never showed fear in the face of danger. They were always strong, and they had always protected her, whatever the cost and now, *she* had to protect *them*. She and her family had gotten entangled in this mess somehow, and her friend Gwen had lied about not knowing where The Key was. She wanted to be mad—fist-clenching, teeth-grinding mad, but she didn't have time for that.

She had to finish the journey that would put things right, back to the order they should be in. She needed to free her world from the dreadful creatures that could take havoc to her home and to her grandparents. She understood her grandmother and great aunt's vulnerability in particular, being so close to a main doorway of the other realm, and she wondered who else had gone missing after her. She thought about the distress that her abduction was causing Ma, Aunt Rosie and Grampie. She wished she could let them know she was alive and would be home soon. She wanted to tell them that she missed them and that they meant everything to her, more than life itself. Being in Annwn made her realise that she couldn't live in a world without her grandparents. She would be empty without them. She closed her eyes and imagined their faces. Then she cursed the gift of dreamed foresight bestowed on the female members of her family. She wished she had never dreamt this place of haunted beauty, this place that took her away from love. These things weighed on her mind and made her heart heavy. Noticing her quietness and detecting something was wrong, Arden fell back to walk alongside Eliza.

"Eliza," said Arden, taking her hand. "Look." He pointed at a group of huge bubbles floating in the air ahead of them.

She stared at them in wonder but kept her silence, though infatuated by the feeling of his hand in hers. As they approached the abundance of bubbles, they could hear enchanting music faintly playing somewhere nearby.

Of the bubbles, Arden said, "See how insubstantial, fragile and temporary they are. Yet, each has its own purpose. Some carry the songs of the mermaids near and far. Others carry the memories, stories, premonitions and dreams of the mermaids."

Arden held up his hand to touch one of the bubbles. It rested on his hand before eventually popping, releasing the beautiful notes of a mer-song.

"You, too, have a purpose, Eliza, a great purpose, and you are so much stronger than these bubbles. I wish you could see. Fret not, your troubled heart," he said looking into her eyes as the back of his hand gently moved down her cheek to her chin.

"Arden," called out Arrae from ahead, "Do you think the mermaids will know the price we have to pay at Misty Bridge? They are after all creatures of the waters."

"Yes, yes, Skoran said, 'that which rolls on the grounds of living waters,'" Arden replied. "Good thought, cousin. Let us ask, though my stomach churns queerly at the thought of these watery creatures."

They headed left towards the steady stream of bubbles coming from the green waters of the Mangrove known as Mermaid's Lair. No one noticed that the music had stopped, and in the quietness one could almost hear a bubble burst. All around the Mangrove was stillness, and Arrae walked around intending to peer over the rocks and beckon the mermaids. He walked past two towering Perilous Pythons with huge heads that bent over their thick green stalks. They were isolated from the others of their kind in beds at the other corners of Mermaids Lair. As he passed by, he breathed in the sweetest scent he had ever smelt and stopped abruptly to inhale deeply again. Then, Gwen noticed something no one else had—the extremely subtle but quick movements of the flowers when their prickly thorns started emerging from the back of their heads.

"Arrae!" she screamed as she ran towards him.

He spun around to Gwen as the flower above him twisted

over to reveal sharp, deadly thorns and a monstrous mouth that reached down to swallow his head.

In the blink of an eye, without thinking, Gwen lassoed two thick ropes of lianas that wrapped around the neck of the deadly Perilous Python. It was fast, but not fast enough. It had gotten Arrae by the neck and was now flinging his body back and forth trying to escape Gwen's nooses. As poor Arrae's body dangled in the air like a lifeless doll, the other Python tried to grip onto him. Arden lithely ran up Gwen's strings of lianas, jumped into the air and slashed the heads of the Perilous Pythons cleanly off of their stems with a sharp magical dagger that he wore strapped onto his left foot. Arrae fell with a thud, the flower's head still clenching onto his neck. Arden kicked the Python's head off his cousin's neck. He supported Arrae's neck and back as he gasped for air. Warm blood trickled down from Arrae's neck to his back, staining Arden's tunic. Arden ripped off one of his archer's sleeves and wrapped it around the wound.

"You'll be fine, Arrae! Don't worry we have you now," assured Arden to his semi conscious cousin.

The stench of the dead Perilous Python spread across the Mangrove. As the group gathered round Arrae, the sound of stifled giggles in the distance grew into brazen laughter. All around the Lair, mermaids rose up from the green waters and from behind rocks laughing heartily and splashing their tails up and down.

"I'll show you, you...," grunted Gwen already spurting lianas forward to lasso a mermaid's neck when Arden shouted.

"No! They're screamers, somewhat like Rage. They outnumber us and can cause us much harm," Arden interrupted a disappointed Gwen, who was hoping to show one of the devious devils who the joke was really on.

Gwen and Eliza looked around the waters at the half-fish creatures with long, slender, grey-scaled tails and strikingly gorgeous human-like bodies.

"What brings the fae to our Lair?" sung the amused mermaid with the plum-coloured hair. She came up against the rock closest to them.

Arden looked angrily at her. "We came seeking your counsel."

The mermaid nodded while glancing over to Gwen, who had broken the leaves off the stinking Perilous Python and was handing them to Arden to wrap them behind Arrae's neck.

"What counsel could be needed by those who know the remedy to the poisonous bite of the lovely Python?" She smiled.

"We wish to know what rolls on the bottom of the living waters."

"Ahhh..." she mused.

"We too have heard of this glorious mystery found only at the very bottom of so-called living waters, but we have neither seen it nor know its name."

"If you are wise, you will take care in how you ask for it. Tellers of the legend say it evades those who speak its name."

"Then what must we do to find it?" pressed Arden.

"Come closer and I shall whisper it in your ear," beckoned the mermaid.

Arden was frequently accused of being foolhardy in his youth, but even he knew that he should decline such requests by half-fish water-dwellers.

"Tell me now, and I will return to you later, my lovely," he smiled charmingly.

"Say nothing, Loshthrie. He deceives you!" shouted a black-haired mermaid far behind in the waters.

Loshthrie smiled back at Arden.

"You must first find the living waters, and then ask for that which rolls on its floors. It is very precious and will only be given to he who really needs it. The greedy heart that yearns for it will have it too, but only in death, lying in the living waters," whispered Loshthrie.

Grateful for an answer, though feeling no more the wiser, Arden thanked Loshthrie in sincerity and promised to show his gratitude.

Arden arose, carrying Arrae, and called the girls to follow him. They had barely put much distance between themselves and the Lair when Arrae writhed in pain. The poison had been slowly travelling down his neck and infecting his spine. The leaves from the Perilous Python pressed against the open wound on his neck were healing him from the outside, but on the inside, the poison was taking hold faster than the medicine could work.

"Argggggggghhhhhh!" he screamed in agony. On his neck, red, bumpy veins were surfacing and slowly spreading all over his body like the growing branches of a tree.

"We should have given him the leaves orally," said Eliza, her voice soaked in concern.

In fact, the Python leaves, though the remedy to the flower's own poison, were too tough to chew, let alone to swallow.

"He must drink it, then. Like the potion Skoran made for you, Eliza," said Arden.

Gwen nodded and ran back to the dead plants, picking as many of the leaves as she could carry. On her way back to the group, a bubble floated down on her and popped on her nose. In a flash, she beheld a premonition of the mermaid from which the bubble came.

In her mind, Gwen was taken from where she was standing, fast ahead and much farther down the path on which they were walking. Somewhere there, four tall, hooded shadows congregated and plotted in whispers. One turned around and looked into her eyes with his glowing yellow ones. In a split-second, her wits came back about her, but not without a great degree of vertigo. The group saw her sway and bend over as she shouted slurred sentences at them.

"What is it, Gwen? What happened? Tell us!" pleaded Arden, as Eliza ran to meet her.

"I saw something."

"What? Gwen?" asked Arden.

"I think Aradath Elves wait on us in the path ahead. They know where we are and where we intend to go. They're powerful, Arden—vastly beyond our competencies. We'll *never* make it past them. Somehow...I don't know how it's possible, but one of them saw me while I looked through the mermaid's premonition," she stuttered.

"How do we know they're there now? Suppose...." Eliza trailed off.

Fear gripped Eliza. Gwen's worried face gave her no assurance. Panic permeated the group as they considered the odds against them while they were carrying an injured Arrae and supporting a still fairly weak Eliza. Still, all looked to Arden for guidance.

"We won't take any chances. If they are there now they expect us, and we won't disappoint them," he said after thinking for a moment.

Eliza, Arrae, and Gwen looked to him, confused.

"Gwen, I need you to power up. We must create an illusion. One that will keep the Aradath Elves expecting us along this route...."

Gwen hesitated. "Uh...we? Arden, my mastery of illusions won't suffice to give one powerful enough to create a diversion."

"You won't be doing it alone, and I'll tell you exactly what to do," Arden said. "We must try."

Gwen looked at Arrae and Eliza and then nodded reluctantly back at Arden, who filled them in on his plan.

Once he and Gwen created the illusion, their next priority would be finding a secure setting to mix a medicinal potion of the Python's leaves to administer to Arrae. After they overcame this obstacle, they would regroup and figure out how to get back on track with their mission. They were at an obvious disadvantage. Without support from the faery elders, Arden and his friends had been sent to their deaths. He secretly wondered why no elder among his kind had backed him.

They returned to hide in the shades of the Mangroves and stayed low as Arden and Gwen conjured magic to create the distraction they desperately needed. Arden instructed Gwen accordingly. Eyes closed and hands outstretched, they whispered strange utterances and conjured a bright ball of light between them, which rolled away through the air, splattering in millions of tiny particles. It made a voosh kind of sound, and in the distance, the light created an illusion of the group walking down the path.

"Oh my guu...." Eliza muttered. Her head was tilted and her mouth left open as she looked ahead at the likeness of herself.

"Quickly, friends, we must change route and head the other way before we are found out. I don't know how long our diversion shall last, but it may give us just the time we need to save our friend's life and get a head start," said Arden, looking to Arrae lying among the shrubs. His cousin's eyes were now sagging and his body was growing cold and slightly tremoring. They all looked to him with great sadness—the fair fae who had given much to aid the human and her half-fae friend was dying a slow, untimely death.

Arden lifted Arrae in his arms, straining but strengthened by his love for his cousin, and began walking northeast through the forest to its edges.

When it became obvious they were continuing that way, Gwen stopped.

"Wait, Arden, why do we head to this edge of the forest? You know it leads back to the Black Lake," she said.

"I know."

"Well, why? Why...."

Arden stopped and turned around to face Gwen and Eliza.

"The only chance we have is to venture where no one expects us to go. We must head through the Dark Forest," he said turning back and walking on.

Eliza made to follow him, but stopped as Gwen freaked out.

"What? This is madness! I beg you, please, we cannot do this."

Arden took no further notice of her.

Eliza wanted to ask the obvious question: Why was Gwen so disinclined to going that way? However, she refrained out of fear of what the answer might be, and waited for her friend.

Gwen looked around her at every tree, plant, and rock and imagined danger peering from behind each one. She then looked at Arden, with Arrae shivering in his arms, and her dear friend Eliza, and sighed before running on to catch up with them.

They eventually came to the edge of Annwn Forest, through the last rows of trees, which ended suddenly before the land met water. Arden summoned Aquila, who shortly turned up with three other great eagles, and with much caution, they were lifted and flown over the Black Lake to the other side of land with the forbidden forest. The distance was just about short enough for the eagles to fly with the friends.

The other side, as you might imagine, was uninviting. Huddled together, the group walked gingerly through the Dark Forest. Its floor was damp and had thick piles of dead leaves stacked on it. In the air, there was a chill and everything was heavily shaded by the overhead canopy of leaves. Little beams of light from beyond the treetops peeked in through tiny gaps. Gloom was present in everything—the trees, the ambience, the dearth of light, and the arbitrary noises of movements, shuffling, and rustling from creatures that they could hear but did not see. The sight of the evil Strangler Figs, wrapped around the dead trees they suffocated, was overwhelming.

They eventually came to a low drop in the land behind a great tree that hadn't yet been consumed by a Strangler Fig, and stopped there to help Arrae. Arden laid him down gently and took the leaves from Gwen. She and Eliza comforted Arrae while propping him up while Arden grinded the Python leaves to make the elixir.

"Do you hear that?" whispered Gwen.

"Hear what?" asked Eliza and Arden in unison looking around.

"The voices."

"What?"

"I think... the trees are talking. I can hear them," said Gwen peering around frantically.

"Are we in danger?" quipped Arden.

"I don't know. I don't think so, but I'm not sure. There're so many voices talking at the same time. They seem to know that we're here, but they're mostly talking about other things. They're so evil!" Gwen muttered shaking her head. "How can trees be so evil? All they desire is to suck the life out of every living thing that gets close to them," said Gwen in disbelief.

Arden nodded. "We must take care not to get too close then. It's a unique gift you have Gwen, conversing with plants. There's a lot you can learn to do to harness your gifts so you can get the most of them. Like with hearing the trees, you can learn how to focus on one specific tree at a time," said Arden still grinding the plant leaves.

"Wow. How?" asked Gwen eagerly.

Eliza spoke up before Arden could answer. "How did you do that back there? With...with the illusions of us?" she asked.

Arden took pride in explicating to the girls how faeries are each gifted with unique, innate talents that they can develop. Some fae, he explained, also shared similar talents, like for instance, photo kinesis—the common but complicated ability to project and control light and magical energy in small degrees, which allowed them to do things like create illusions. The stronger a fae's ability grows, he said, the more powerful things they could do with that gift. The gift of photo kinesis had, throughout time, been mastered by only a small number of fae, typically the most powerful or elder ones.

"My mother can create much stronger, more convincing illusions because she's more powerful. Her manipulation of that energy can inflict great damage too," added Arden proudly.

He stopped grinding the leaves and added some water, stirring it rapidly. He then slowly fed it to Arrae.

"So what other abilities do you all have?" queried Eliza.

Arden explained how he was able to speak with Aquila, who had been his best friend since childhood. He also had an affinity for archery that helped him hone his skills to the point where he could hit a target over exceedingly long distances without fault. This was the talent he'd chosen to spend time developing and practising over his other innate abilities.

Arrae was primarily a shape-shifter, but this was something Arden said would be better seen than explained.

"I wonder what gift Eli's been given...from the Mother, I mean," she said with excitement, looking to Eliza, who smiled back shyly.

"I'm sure it will be the envy of all, whatever it is. It usually is the case with those gifted by our realm," said Arden.

"What gifts did your mother possess, Gwen?" asked Arden.

Gwen's face went blank, and she said she wasn't completely sure.

"Hmmm...I heard she was gifted at what she did," said Arden.

Gwen's eyebrow went up and her mood sour.

"'*IS* gifted,'" Gwen corrected Arden.

"Yes. *Is*. I'm sorry, I just...."

"Just what? Everyone speaks of her in the past tense! Like she's... Like she's dead," Gwen spat, unaware of the welling tears in her eyes and her shaking hands.

She had been irritable since returning to that realm, increasingly thinking of her mother, questioning the things Niada had told her and those things she hadn't. Gwen now had many questions about who her mother was and wondered if she had been told the whole truth about why she had been banished in the first place.

For years, she had buried the hurt of losing her mother, but now it had resurfaced in the place where her mother was probably suffering from desolation. She was in the same realm as Niada, but she would never get to see her face. It was as if her mother wasn't even there. So, you see, the slightest trigger set her fuming with anger that was slowly bubbling like a volcanic eruption waiting to happen inside her.

The group sat together monitoring Arrae's slow recovery from the deadly poison. His body temperature was returning to normal and the veins that had been visible under the surface of his skin were slowly disappearing. Nightfall was eventually upon them, and with it came fear in the Dark Forest. The forest was black and they could see very little. Arden produced a faint ball of light that floated in their little circle giving them just enough light to see each other's shadows. Arden feared attracting unwanted attention of nocturnal creatures in the stillness of the night. After they had eaten some of the food that Skoran had stored for them, they decided that they should rest while Arrae recuperated. Arden offered to stay awake and keep watch while the others closed their eyes, but Eliza didn't wish to sleep. She feared the encompassing darkness and what dwelled within it, but she had little choice, because her exhausted body eventually began shutting down and her mind soon followed. She nodded off with her head in Gwen's lap. Gwen fell asleep sitting next Arrae.

Arden stared at Eliza's face as she slept soundly, dozing off into what he imagined a much more peaceful and carefree place.

In her mind's eye, she was a child again, as her brain dug up an old, incomplete memory that haunted her dreams.

She was back on her sunny island, a little girl skipping three houses away from her own to the tiny shop converted from the front of a neighbour's house. She bounced through the door gleefully, about to pick out her favourite sweetie, when the drunken shopkeeper emerged, wielding a bottle of rum clumsily like a weapon. His words stung her like poisonous venom; just like the one that was consuming her in Annwn.

'Get out of here, you little blithe!' he shouted at her with a heavy tongue and slurred speech,

but little Eliza didn't understand. 'What's blithe?' she asked innocently tilting her head of curls.

He chuckled. 'Blithe? That's you and your dirty blood. Your dirty, diluted, contaminated blood, you bastard,' he sputtered out, before continuing in a foreign dialect, saliva spilling out at the corners of his mouth.

The words were like a knife, ripping her insides out. She'd heard them before. *Dirty blood. Mixed blood. Bastard....* She dropped her four quarters, and they hit the shop floor with heavy clinks. She backed out the shop clumsily, almost falling over the edge.

'And you tell those reckless grandparents of yours to

keep their shameful racial transgressions from infecting the community!' he pointed a rough finger at her before she staggered off in tears.

Her dream always ended there. This time, it morphed into a new dream. Not a memory, but a fear.

Eliza pictured her grandparents.

She looked a little like both—taking the eyes and brown complexion of her East-Indian grandmother, and the nose and eyebrows of her dark Portuguese grandfather. She had a mixture of their hair. A full, thick body that was curly in some places, wavy in others and straight in other places. A complex head of hair, like the complex person she was. Yet her grandparents loved her and were proud of who she was, even if she didn't fit her society's purist mould. As she considered this in her dream, her grandparents vanished from around her, and suddenly their lingering screams surrounded her, ringing through her body like painful pangs.

She covered her ears with her palms and looked all around her, but couldn't see them. Unable to bear the pain, she shut her eyes and fell to the ground moving back and forth in a rocking motion. When her eyes opened, it mattered not that it had gone completely quiet, because staring at her was the hideous face of a great black phooka taking the form of an ape-like humanoid. Eliza looked into its eyes. She could see a coldness. An emptiness. Bitterness, and there was malevolence. It terrified her, but there was something behind it even more terrifying.

Another phooka appeared suddenly, skipping in the opposite direction, in its arms the limp bodies of her grandparents. A shrill scream escaped her mouth. She began running away. Running, running, running. She pushed so hard, yet her feet carried her at a snail's pace, the phooka always right on her tail, though never reaching her. Images of Lady Drwrywren's disapproving face, suspended midair, began moving in towards her with an accusing voice.

'You shall never realise the true power in you...human of *impure* blood,' the voice echoed.

Eliza spun around and around looking as the faces swooped down on her.

In the end of her haunting dream, Skoran's ominous voice echoed, "Trust no one! Not even your own shadow."

Chapter 7

A CLOSE CALL

A RUSTLING SOUND, BARELY LOUDER THAN an insect, fluttered amid the wild foliage and trees as the group slept in the dead of the night. Still the forest hadn't gone to sleep. In the Dark Forest, many creatures that hid in the daylight came alive in the darkness—though, even in the daylight, much of the forest remained shaded from any sunlight anyway. The forest was hardly quiet, so it's no surprise that no one heard the faint sound of movement from somewhere nearby. Arden's ball of light had blown out some time ago. He had stayed awake long after he should have passed the shift on to another in the group. He had ignored all the telltale signs of his own exhaustion—the occasional yawning, droopy eyelids, and bobbing head until he eventually fell asleep.

He had earlier woken Eliza, who had been mumbling and rolling around in her troubled sleep, but she soon returned to her dreamy state.

When she did wake a few moments later, it was because somehow, strangely, in the forest's distant orchestra of nonstop chirping, tweeting, throat clucking, and flapping wings, her ears had noticed something unlike the other noises that was rather close to the group. No more than a stone's throw from where the group had set up camp. She opened her eyes, now fully awake, and cautiously lifted her head from Gwen's lap to try and locate the source; but in the stark darkness, Eliza couldn't even see her hands when she held them up.

"Gwen," she whispered into her friend's ears.

"Gwen, wake up," she tried again.

She swallowed as her heart's pace picked up gradually and her eyes scanned left and right despite their inability to see anything.

"Gwen," her voice cracked into a soft tearful moan as she gripped her friend's arm with both her hands in fright.

She could hear her teeth starting to clatter and a tear had just rolled down her right cheek, when just above them on the earthy incline, a fearsome roar came echoing into the night. Eliza's horrific scream reverberated through the trees while the group awoke in frantic terror. They had all, without thinking, instinctively scampered a short distance from their camp, away from the loud roar, and huddled together in a tight group.

For a while they heard nothing and stood shaking next to each other—Arden was concerned that creating a ball of light would draw too much attention to them, and so they stayed in the dark, clinging to one another for fear of getting lost in the pitch black of the night around them. After the silence went on for about ten seconds, Arden decided it was safe enough to conjure a ball of light, brighter than the last so they could see their immediate surroundings. As the ball rose from his hands illuminating the air, they heard another fierce roar and screamed in sheer horror as a magnificent beast leapt from the incline towards them.

In a flash, Arden pulled his bow and equipped it, but never let the arrow fly. Instead, he passed his arms over the huddled group, pressing down for them to bend as low as they could. The massive creature didn't land on them, but the fur of its belly grazed their skin as it leapt overhead. When its feet hit the ground, the earth around them trembled from the impact. They could see the golden fur of the sabre-toothed beast shimmer in the light as it darted past them and stealthily crept towards some bushes and trees ahead, growling under its breath. Its sharp sabre canines protruded nearly a foot from its mouth. The creature froze, staring toward the bushes, waiting. And soon, out of the dark shadows ahead, came a yellow-eyed werewolf with brick red fur, saliva dripping from the corners of its mouth.

As it crept closer towards the golden sabre-toothed beast, two webbed wings emerged from the wolf's muscular torso, and it howled. Gwen and Eliza gasped loudly in trepidation.

The sabre-toothed animal snarled back at the wolf aggressively, but from the shadows on the group's left, another demonic winged wolf appeared.

"Arden," whispered Gwen, and he quickly drew his bow and aimed the arrow at the wolf on their left.

The huddled group slowly inched to their right, away from the latest threat.

"Where's Arrae?" Eliza panicked as she noticed his absence for the first time.

Gwen gasped, looking all around them for any signs of him.

"That's him right there," whispered Arden pointing his head at the fierce sabre-toothed beast.

Arrae had shape-shifted to defend them from a threat they hadn't even known about. Gwen and Eliza were interrupted from their reverie of Arrae in his animalistic form by a sinister growl approaching from their right. A third winged wolf emerged from behind a tree on the right.

Come meet your fate.

Eliza gasped as this growling voice penetrated her thoughts.

What was that? Eliza thought to herself.

RRRrrrrip apart your flesh, filthy human. The voice

seemed to come from the wolf whose yellow eyes were trained on her own. They flashed in the darkness as if to confirm her theory.

"Ohh..." Eliza muttered, unsure whether hearing the wolf's thoughts, or what it was thinking, frightened her more. Her trembling knees collapsed beneath her, and Gwen quickly grabbed her under the arms and tried pulling her up but to no avail.

"Eli, get up," encouraged Gwen unconvincingly, for her knees were threatening to give way too.

As if the situation could get no grimmer, from atop the incline behind them, another winged wolf, this one with black fur, strutted back and forth, watching the scene play out. It flexed its wings in preparation to pounce on the group.

Nowhere to run now, Eliza heard one of the wolves think.

Whom shall I gnaw on first? she heard another ponder.

'Spare none, creature!' a female's voice in the thoughts of one of the wolves.

Trickedy trickedy tricks.

'No forget tricks, just kill them!'

Kill prey mmhmm but trick first!

'Aggrediora Inimicusos! Creature! I command you by the sound of my voice! Hesitate no more in your task!' the female voice commanded.

Someone was out to get them. To kill them. The realisation hit Eliza hard, and she gripped her ears to block off the overwhelming thoughts of the wolves coming at her from all angles. Gwen remained hovering over Eliza, unable to pull her to her feet, while Arrae and Arden protectively moved around them and waited for the first move.

The pack leader launched an ominous howl, summoning his pack to attack and from all angles. They pounced on Eliza and her friends.

Arrae, in his animal form, jumped to meet the pouncing wolf. The two clashed against each other and rolled on the ground, locked together as they viciously attacked one another. Arrae used his sharp claws to scratch the wolf, which whimpered in pain as he drew blood. In this fight, Arrae had the advantage—he was much bigger than the wolf and his deadly teeth and claws were sharper and stronger. The only problem was Arrae could only fight off one wolf at a time.

Behind him, three more wolves pounced on the group.

Arden's bowstring twanged repeatedly as he fired arrows at the oncoming wolf on their left. It was frighteningly swift as it flew through the air, dodging the onslaught of arrows. Arden flicked the dagger from his waist pocket and ran towards the wolf. He leapt with a fierce cry, thrusting his blade into the wolf's nearest wing. Behind him, Gwen uttered the first spell that came to mind.

"Ventuso vis vires!" she screamed while violently swinging her two hands forward towards the wolves that were charging her and Eliza on the ground. The force was insufficient and only served to slow the wolves momentarily. As they resumed their charge, Gwen instinctively swung both hands aggressively at nearest wolf and shouted with more conviction, "Ventuso vis vires!"

This time, a violent wind pelted the wolf, sending it back in the direction from which it came. It howled in pain when its body hit the ground.

"Ventuso...." she heard herself start saying, but she knew the time was so short, she'd never complete the spell, and she didn't.

The wolf was about to land on them, and a terrified Gwen had fallen to her knees, her arms wrapped around her best friend.

Eliza never thought that this was how her end would come. In a black, malevolent forest, far, far away from her grandparents and the world she knew. In that split second, her grandparents' loving faces flashed into her mind. She smiled at the image, but the wolf's growl quickly brought her back to her dreaded reality. She defensively braced her arms to protect her face, knocking Gwen back, and the wolf's right paw scratched her forehead. Before she could take another breath, powerful energy rapidly built up inside her filling her chest. A blinding light exploded from her palms and chest, throwing the squealing wolf back against a tree. She lay on the ground whimpering, her eyes tightly shut, when a bewildered Gwen, still holding onto her, said, "Holy crisps! Eli, look! Eli!"

Eliza timidly opened her eyes and sought out the wolf her light had hit, but there was no wolf. Just Eliza and Gwen on the ground, staring ahead. A limp elf with dark blue skin lay in a pool of its blood against a tree some three metres away.

Arden raced over to protect the girls but found that all the wolves had been defeated. It dawned on the group that they hadn't been fighting wolves but shape-shifting elves.

"How...?" Arden's voice trailed off as he realized there had been an explosion of light behind him just moments before.

"Eli killed it with that light," Gwen whispered, her arms still around Eliza's neck and her tear splattering onto Eliza's face.

A faint smiled crossed Arden's lips, but he spoke no words. He was in awe of Eliza's newfound ability, and was about to offer praise when he remembered his cousin.

He looked behind him to find Arrae finishing his attack, sinking his teeth into the neck of the last wolf. When the wolf breathed its last, its wings shrunk down and it transformed into a blue elf, as the others all had.

"One's missing," he said.

"Are you sure?" asked Arden.

"Yes. An elf got away."

"What are these things, anyway?" Gwen asked, arms

still locked around Eliza. In all her time in the realm, she'd never encountered such beasts.

"Aradath elves," Arrae muttered.

"I heard the thoughts of the wolves," Eliza spoke up. "I heard a female voice speaking to them, too, in the head of the one of the wolves. She... She spoke in a foreign tongue, like she was using a spell, and...she wants us dead." Eliza swallowed. "Oh my...," Gwen muttered. A look of shock fixed on her face.

"This wolf, the one being controlled by the female voice, it was different from the others. The others were thinking more like animals. But this one called me a filthy human," Eliza said.

"But they weren't animals, they were shape-shifting Aradath Elves," answered a concerned Arrae.

"Yes, but this wolf... It, it didn't think like the others. All he wanted to do was play tricks on us. The others just wanted to attack us," Eliza said. She felt sick thinking about it.

"It wanted to play tricks?" queried Arden in disbelief.

"Yes."

Arrae blurted out, "I don't know how wolves think, but that sounds more like a phooka." Arrae shivered and the hairs on his arms stood.

"Yes," concurred Arden. "Phookas only ever want to play tricks. Nasty, evil, violent tricks, but they're not necessarily evil creatures. They're driven solely by their desire, unlike these Aradath Elves who are capable of at least some reason. This has always made phookas perfect vessels for control by dark magic," reasoned Arden.

"Oh," Gwen said aloud. "You mean the phookas in our realm, I mean the human realm, could have been kidnapping humans on someone's else's command?" asked Gwen.

"It's very possible," answered Arden.

"But who's been controlling the phookas?" asked Arrae in a pressed tone.

"The Council maybe draconian, but it would not have us killed before an enquiry. Neither would it resort to using dark magic to get at us. Well, at least I think not. Of late, this fae seems to know little about his own realm," said Arden sceptically. "So who else wants us dead, then?" he asked.

The concern over the phookas was greater than confronting any incensed Aradath Elves with death warrants. Though due to no purposeful intention, phookas had become a key enemy of most fae. Few fae were unafraid of them and rightly so. Phookas were vicious pranksters by their very nature, rendering them useful tools for workers of the dark arts. They possessed little limitations in their shape-shifting and could take the form of almost any living creature, including humans, but most often took the form of mostly black creatures with unkempt fur.

Arden eventually turned to Eliza and stared upon the bloodied scratch on her forehead with much sympathy. He lifted his hand and delicately touched the deep scratches.

"Let's clean this up before it gets infected. Eliza, I am sorry I failed to protect you, but I promised to help you and Gwen return The Key and get you home safely, and this I will do. I swear I will protect you with my life," he vowed. "I am just thankful that our realm has gifted you enough so you were able to protect yourself and Gwen when I couldn't."

Eliza looked into his eyes and saw sincerity, but that was not all she detected in his gaze. In Arden's eyes, she saw love, which surprised her given the short time they had known each other. What was even more perplexing was the realisation that she felt it too. She smiled at him shyly, barely able to contain the fluttering of her heart. They stared deeply into each other's eyes, unaware of their friends or their dreaded location.

Eventually Arrae broke the silence. "Come. We must make haste. We know not who else may be on our tracks." He gesticulated for Gwen and Eliza to walk ahead of him.

"Yes," concurred Arden, exhausted from the fight and lack of sleep, and they walked into the blackness of the forest.

It was approaching dawn, and little streaks of light snuck through the odd holes in the forest's heavy canopy. The earth was damp and the forest smelt old and mildewed. The four had stayed on the move since the attack, guided only by Arden's faint balls of light. Eliza walked with Gwen, holding her best friend's hand. Arrae lead the group, and Arden lagged behind keeping a watchful eye on their surroundings.

Eliza was exhausted but still thinking obsessively about what had happened to her during the wolf attack.

"What'd it feel like?" whispered Gwen eagerly.

Eliza felt a broad smile stretch across her face. "Like I was erupting on the inside, in a good way, instinctively, and when it came out I felt so relieved but also drained."

Gwen marvelled at Eliza's new gifts.

"I knew you had a purpose for coming," Gwen smiled. "We'll put things right, Eli, and everything will be ok. We'll be able to go home. You'll see," said Gwen.

Eliza smiled at her friend's words and squeezed her hand.

As the light of day fell upon the realm, the darkness in the forest lifted off like a thick blanket, and gradually they could see around them, though it was still dim.

"Thank Annwn we've made it through the night," commented Arrae while cracking his back muscles. He was still sore from the wolf fight, but relieved to see the trees beginning to thin and the sun shine through more easily.

Past him, Eliza could see brilliant lights shining and sparkling in the distance.

"Wow," she murmured.

"That's Mirror Lake." Arrae smiled at her.

Chapter 8

MIRROR LAKE

AFTER THAT FATEFUL SHOP INCIDENT when Eliza became aware of race and so called racial transgressions on her island, there'd been many more occurrences that had shaped her into the person she was now. Many more events and backward people her grandparents had tried to shield her from. They tried to protect her like she was an egg and the slightest fall could crack her shell. Moreover, they feared without someone to watch over her, she might end up in the greedy mouths of lurking predators.

Eliza didn't want to be an egg, but until now, as strong as she thought her shell to be, her grandparents had always been there, ready to prevent her from even stubbing her toe. They'd not just been protecting her from the cruelty of strangers, really, they'd been protecting her from herself. She was fighting for others to accept her, but she'd struggled to fully accept herself too. That was the bigger problem. Until now, in her grandparents' absence, she hadn't realised it.

A sinking feeling beset Eliza as she gazed over the glistening waters of Mirror Lake and ruminated on these things. The thought was prompted by another dream of her grandparents being abducted after she had nodded off in the boat. Public boats were stationed at many of the larger bays around Annwn so the group didn't have the worry about how they would cross over this large lake.

"Eli...Eli," Gwen called her for the third time.

Eliza hadn't heard her, though Gwen was sitting mere inches away.

"Sorry, Gwen. I didn't hear you. I was thinking about them," she said, feeling uneasy and refusing to make eye contact with her friend.

Gwen sighed heavily as her eyebrows furrowed. She felt the pain that her best friend bore. She knew much about the gaping holes left by a loved one's untimely absence.

Arden stared on at Eliza with great concern etched across his face. He shifted slightly from his position on the far end of the boat to take Eliza's hands between both of his. He rubbed them and gave her an assuring look. The four of them sat quietly and said nothing as their canoe manoeuvred its way through Mirror Lake. They headed northwest towards the magnificent Great Mountains of the Never-Ending East. Far in the distance, the grand peaks seemed to merge with the white billowing clouds.

The pink skies were bright, and the morning light shone down causing the lake's waters to shimmer enticingly. It smelled pleasant, like the petals of sweet peas after a light drizzle. These waters were among the most pristine in all the land, beckoning anyone who came close. Out of its deep waters, the great branches of the Annwn Waterbeard trees sprang up high towards the skies, but silvery strands of Spanish moss hung low from these branches in thin curtains that grazed the water's surface. The abundance of these trees in Mirror Lake made their journey cumbersome, as their canoe navigated carefully through the waters.

Eliza stared at the water curiously, wondering why she could see nothing beyond the surface of its shimmery sparkles. It wasn't just the light reflections on the water's surface—Arden explained that Mirror Lake rarely showed itself to anyone.

"Do not look too deeply into the waters, Eliza," advised Arden, still rubbing her hand. "They are misleading."

"Misleading?" Eliza repeated.

"Yes. Please ask no more of this. It is better to not dwell on these things while we are here."

"Ohh," Gwen moaned in annoyance. "You make a big deal out of everything. Legend has it that the waters can foretell the future."

Arden's thin lips trembled as he ground his teeth and glowered at Gwen.

She scoffed.

"Why don't you have a look then?" Arden taunted Gwen.

Eliza sighed at the two of them.

"Ok," whispered Arden in an assertive tone, clenching his jaw. He leaned over to Eliza. "These waters may tell you your future, but they tell many lies. Mostly lies."

Many fae stories spoke of the lake's capability to foretell one's future, even answering a question for those daring enough to ask, but it was never entirely truthful, sometimes showing only possible outcomes and not definitive ones. It was infamous for its tendency to reveal unfortunate tragedy to those seeking their future. In fact, Mirror Lake was often the demise of those who sought its answers, and reasonable creatures of the realm had grown to respect it in a profound way.

Still, there was something even more special about this expansive mass of water. Mirror Lake was idyllic and serene and its opaque facade was intentional. It betrayed the enormity of the underwater cities of the Gwragedd Annwn[2] —water faeries of the realm and beyond who resided in lakes, ponds, and other freshwater pools. Mirror Lake was reputedly home to one of the biggest cities of the Gwragedd Annwn.

2   Gwragedd Annwn is pronounced 'goo raag eth anoon.'

Like most young fae, Arden had heard endless stories of the cryptic Gwragedd Annwn, but was never lucky enough to have come by one. Tales spoke of drab, peculiar faeries so lonely at the bottom of their watery dwellings that they'd beckon unwary fae or humans deep into the waters to keep them company. Such fae or humans were never to be seen again, according to the popular lore of the land. Whether the stories were true or made up, Arden wouldn't take any chances with Eliza.

Eliza nodded and lifted her head to the direction they headed, determined not to be tempted by the ubiquitous waters.

After they'd been rowing for about an hour, Gwen nodded off, leaving the others sitting in silence as the canoe moved steadily through the waters, the sound of which was mostly all they could hear.

Eliza was busy fiddling with her wildly curly hair, trying to tame it as strands went flying about in the light wind. The glistening waters twinkled even more than Eliza could have imagined. They came to a section of the lake where scores of flowers with oversized petals and hard bristles at their core floated on the surface of the shimmery waters. Arden reached out to the water, his finger gently gliding along it, before he picked a Morning Dune from its watery bed. Eliza was surprised when he handed her the dripping flower.

"Uh, um, thank you, Arden," she eventually managed to mutter, blushing, and smiling all at once as she reached her hand out.

He chucked lightly, ignoring her outstretched hand.

"Look," he said, holding the Morning Dune with its bristles against her hair, and gently brushing downwards through to the ends of her thick, black strands.

She blushed shyly, feeling slightly embarrassed.

"Morning Dunes grow only in fresh waters like these," Arden smiled at her. "And their uses are many."

She looked into his eyes and smiled back, forgetting for the second time that day where they were and why they were there.

Arden's upturned lips soon evened out in a fine line, though he continued brushing Eliza's wild hair.

"This place... things used to be so different before The Unknown Plague. So different," he said, his voice trailed off as he focused on brushing her hair.

"How?" enquired Eliza in a hushed voice no louder than a whisper.

"We were happy. We could go about our business freely, without worry, fear, or suspicion of other races. Before the doorways in our region were closed, our kind could even occasionally visit the human realm. It was so magical," he said dreamily.

"Magical?" uttered Eliza in disbelief, her thick brows rising. "You found the human realm magical?"

"One time, I went to see a dear cousin who lived in your realm and I beheld the most beautiful thing. A human man gave the strangest gift to a little girl. She had golden hair, and the thing in her hand was a peculiar swirl of magic, the colour of our skies, atop a wooden cone. Her laugh reminded me of the mermaid's songs in the spring. And then, she did the most unexpected thing! She ate it!" said Arden.

Eliza's widening smile burst and she giggled jovially. She marvelled at Arden's beautiful face.

He looked at her curiously.

"Why do you laugh?" he asked perplexed.

"I... I'm sorry I don't mean to. You appreciate the beauty in things humans take for granted," she smiled, and looked away to the shining waters. "It's called ice cream."

"What?"

"The swirl of magic you saw the girl eating, it's called ice cream. And it tastes amazing," said a smiling Eliza.

"Ice cream," he uttered dreamily while staring off in

the distance. "Peculiar. Should I be most lucky to see him again, my cousin Indrior would love to know its name."

"Wait...." Eliza said as she paused to ponder. "You said you went to see your cousin. In *my* world?"

"Yes, he lives in a forest near a human settlement," said Arden.

"Oh my...." Eliza said in surprise to Arden's response. "So your kind lives in my realm too?"

"Yes, of course. We are everywhere, just like you humans. Except in your world, we take great effort to keep out of human sight. None of this matters now. Not since The Plague and our king's disappearance." A trace of deep regret edged around Arden's words.

"Arden!"

Arden spun around to see what had alarmed his cousin. Behind them, black shifting shapes darkened the bright southern skies. The thick black shapes swirled menacingly, eventually fashioning themselves into an enormous macabre face. The face travelled quickly and steadily towards them. Arden looked ahead of them in panic. Land was in sight but at least another five miles ahead of them. That was enough time for the sinister Sluagh to give their location away to the Council and draw the attention of other evils. In those seconds that his attention went to The Sluagh, Eliza's was drawn elsewhere. To the side of their canoe, on the water's mirror-like surface, movement had caught her eye. The sparkles in the water had disappeared, leaving only a smooth reflective surface. She bent closer to the canoe's edges, searching for the tiny flicker of movement she swore she saw. As she stared into the water, the sunlight fragmented across the surface and a scene unfolded before Eliza's eyes. She beheld an image of herself on a vast summit, about to venture after a hooded figure into widespread darkness.

In the vision, she hesitated, looking to Gwen and Arden at the wayside of the peak.

'Come,' she said to them with her hand outstretched, but they didn't budge.

'We can't go with you, Eli,' Arden answered.

The hooded figure in the vision whispered, 'You must choose.'

Confused, Eliza's gaze followed the figure's outstretched arm pointing beyond the darkness to a glowing likeness of her grandmother. As she moved towards Indira's warm face, the hooded figure waved its other arm, and Arden and Gwen were thrust down into the unending depths besides the summit. In the vision, Eliza swung back and reached for their falling hands.

Gwen and Arden's hands reached out to hers in desperation, their haunting cries piercing her lungs as they vanished from the image.

The lines between the vision and reality became blurred, and Eliza became enveloped by what she saw. She reached her hands out to the water to touch theirs, but they were falling too fast. Desperate to save them and unable to discern fiction from reality, she plunged into the water.

The moment her body hit the water, the image of her friends vanished, and she quickly realized she was being pulled by a great force down toward the bottom of the lake. Water began filling her lungs, and as her consciousness faded, she felt another, stronger force tugging her back towards the surface.

Violent coughs rattling her small frame jerked Eliza from her unconsciousness. She felt an arm wrapped around her torso and a hand pounding into her back. Water erupted from her chest and dripped down the sides of her mouth.

Two hands cupped her face and lifted it. Arden's eyes searched Eliza's face desperately, and he muttered over and over, "You're ok, you're ok, you're ok."

Gwen released her arms from around Eliza and sat back

panting, her soaking wet hair splayed over her shoulder. Eliza sought her friend's gaze, but was not met.

What was Gwen staring at so intently? Eliza's eyes followed Gwen's, somewhere past Arden, to The Sluagh in the skies above them. Their thick shadowy shapes contorted this way and that, making Eliza's stomach churn with sickness and dread.

"Shoot them," Gwen eventually pleaded with Arden.

"Can't," Arden said sadly. "My arrows will fly straight through them."

No sooner had he said that, he sprung up and quickly drew his bow. Gwen and Eliza both spun around to see what Arden was aiming at.

An imposing female faery with blood-red hair and draped in a flowing black cloak appeared on shore they now approached. She was flanked by a pair of Aradath Elves on either side of her. It was too late to turn around or call Aquila considering their close proximity to the shore. Arden also wouldn't risk calling Aquila with the Sluagh in the skies just above them.

There was no time and they were cornered with nowhere to run. The Sluagh in the skies above, evil elves in front of them, and a lake inhabited by spooky underwater fae all around them.

Chapter 9

SPLITTING UP

Arden's fingers were fast, and he swiftly drew his bow, but as he released the first arrow, he heard a devastating cry. It came not from his target, but from Arrae behind him. He spun around to see Arrae being tossed into the lake by the heavy claws of a glossy black-winged wolf hovering over his boat; the one that had escaped them in the forest. It had appeared behind Arrae while he was hurling his throwing stars at the enemies on the far shore.

Instinctively, as Arrae saw it, he started shifting into his animal form, but halfway through the process, the ferocious wolf hewed his body into the air. Arrae's body splashed into the depths of the water. As his body sank beneath the surface, lianas sprang from Gwen's hands and dove with force into the waters after Arrae. Gwen's lianas had her very essence running through them, so they understood the urgency of the mission. She foraged the waters for him, and thought she almost had him, but her concentration was disrupted by a sickening groan next to her.

Eliza had been watching Arden closely from the moment he had released the first arrow at their foes on land. She saw how the lightning-fast arrow was stopped midair by the lifted hand of the fae leading the pack, and when Arden's attention went to his cousin behind them, Eliza saw how the sinister faery twirled her fingers around elegantly, turning the arrow back in their direction. When she flicked her fingers, a visceral feeling told Eliza that this was it. As the arrow headed for Arden, she impulsively sprang from her seat and leapt in front of him. All she felt was a sudden burning sensation that rapidly pierced her stomach, setting it afire. She heard herself utter the sickening groan, a groan that called both Gwen and Arden's attention, but not fast enough. Eliza's arrow-pierced body toppled off the canoe so quickly, she felt herself falling once again, but this time the all-consuming waters of Mirror Lake enveloped her like a blanket, and she went deeper and deeper, with no reaching hands to save her this time.

GWEN

As Eliza fell deeper in the waters of Mirror Lake, Gwen frantically launched ropes of lianas to rescue her best friend. Arden dove into the water after Eliza, and as Gwen waited for him to surface with her friend, she could hear the sound of her frantic breathing as she reached for Eliza with one hand of lianas and Arrae with another. As the seconds wore on, the panic took hold of her. She tugged and tugged the yards upon yards of foraging lianas extending from her hand, but felt no weight pulling in.

In the waters of Mirror Lake, the lianas moved with great life in search of Arrae and Eliza. The surface of the lake remained deceptively calm with so few ripples it was as if nothing untoward had even happened. The canoe suddenly rocked forward as it hit something, and Gwen lost her balance and fell backward into the bottom of the boat. She peered out over the edge of the boat and saw that the boat had run aground.

Her hands still gripping the lianas, she slowly picked herself up, sensing a towering presence over her. Gwen reluctantly looked up to see Lady Sorcha's blood red lips curving upwards into a fine, cunning smile. Her pale skin was a stark contrast against her fire red hair, pinned up in a high beehive shape and lined with fine jewels. Her heart-shaped face was highlighted by her deep-set, rounded blue eyes, which were topped by slender eyebrows that curved upwards. Gwen clenched her jaw and her hold on the lianas tightened.

"Uh-uh." Sorcha shook her head at Gwen and then nodded to one of the two Aradath Elves on her right.

A muscular elf the colour of midnight blue bared his teeth at Gwen and laughed. With little effort, he gripped her arms, locked them behind her back, and lifted her from the canoe. The strings of lianas slid from Gwen's hands and flailed like fish out of water. The elf dropped her on her knees before Lady Sorcha. Gwen's head hung low as pain engulfed her. Not physical pain so much, but emotional pain. She subtly looked toward the lake, hoping to see Arden emerge with Eliza in his arms, but there was no sign of either them, and she couldn't see Arrae either. The winged wolf continued to hover over the waters looking to Lady Sorcha for direction.

"Find them," Sorcha uttered in a strong voice.

The four Aradath Elves looked to each other uncertainly.

"M-m-my fair lady," one of them stuttered while bowing in obeisance, "this is Mirror Lake, and...."

"And what?!" she growled through her teeth, her thin lips barely moving.

"These waters hold very powerful magic," he said, cowering in fear.

Sorcha looked upon the elf in disgust. She breathed

in deeply, closing her eyes and dragging her nails along her neck as she pondered on something. Without warning, her right hand made a subtle upward movement, and her energy drew a curved blade from the belt of one of the elves. Her hand quickly swung left, and the dagger floated in the air, aiming at the face of the elf who had dared question her orders.

Gwen looked on in shock, her heart racing from a dozen emotions that consumed her. The blade slowly moved in on the elf, the very tip of its sharp edge barely touching the elf's upper lip. He trembled and pulled his head back slowly to avoid the metal.

"Do-not-move," Sorcha ordered. Slowly, she made a circle around him, as if in deep thought. Again, without warning, her right index finger made a quick downward motion, and the blade pierced the elf's skin above his lip, making a downward slit across his lips. As blood appeared on and around his lips, he screamed in agony, sending it pouring down his face.

Gwen looked on in horror. What was this sinister faery going to do to her?

"Now. You were saying something about Mirror Lake?" she asked rhetorically in a whisper. The bleeding elf shook his head frantically, agony etched on his face.

"Hmm. Thought so," Sorcha said, satisfied, before nodding to the other three elves.

As the three elves dove into the lake, Arden's head emerged on the surface. He bore a wretched look upon his face, and Gwen received further confirmation as he staggered out of the waters empty handed. He ignored Sorcha and her company, looking only to Gwen with brimming tears as he dropped himself on the land.

"I'm sorry," he whispered with his head hanging low, trying to catch his breath. "I've searched and searched. I don't know how she or Arrae could have gone so far, but I searched in vain. It is difficult to see anything but shadows in these waters. I'm afraid our loved ones are lost to the lake, Gwen," Arden said.

"Lost! Ha!" Lady Sorcha blurted out. "What a worthless faery you are. Drwyrwen should bear shame calling you hers. My...."

Arden interjected. "What would a treacherous fae like you know of my mother?"

Sorcha bent over, hands on her knees, to bring herself to eye level with Arden. "

More than you might think, young fae." she smiled, the word 'think' rolling off her tongue.

She stood up straight. "I bear sincerest apologies for the loss of your faery kin. I never mean to hurt my own kind, but he"—she paused—"got in the way. I normally bear no reservation in harming a human, but I didn't mean to hurt the girl either. You should have never, ever drawn an arrow at an elder. That aside, when we recover the human's body, I will have my latest piece of evidence, and you two will be duly punished for your crimes."

"Crimes?" Gwen laughed sarcastically. "We've committed no crimes!" she shouted as a rage grew in her, threatening to burst through. She felt Arden rest his hand on her back in comfort.

"Oh, but you have!" Sorcha sung in a feigned innocence. "You've stolen The Key. You've conspired with the humans to wage war on our realm. You've committed"—she paused, widening her eyes—"murder."

Gwen's eyes widened in horror. She felt the shock of Sorcha's words lingering about in her head. She loathed this histrionic character.

"Murder?" Gwen whispered.

"Yes!" Sorcha grinned theatrically. "The Council shall charge *thee*, and *thee* with the wrongful murder of one Arrae of the Great Eastern Forest," She clasped her hands together in delight.

Arden sprung up in a rage and plunged at Sorcha with a

fierce roar. He had barely touched her, when her strange, bold utterances flung his body back. The sound of rushing wind filled the air before he landed with a great thump.

"Uggggh," he groaned under his breath.

She flicked her finger at the winged wolf and the remaining Aradath elf, who both moved to hover above Arden and keep him in check.

Sorcha pretended to dust imaginary particles off her cloak.

"This is my very best cloak," she whispered at him accusingly. "I wore it especially for today."

"What are you going to do with us? You, you...." Arden screamed.

Sorcha ignored Arden's grievances as she continued dusting her cloak. "Never mind what I will do to you," she said in a matter of fact tone. "Mind what the Council will do."

Sorcha opened her mouth again to speak, but this time she sounded exactly like Arden's mother.

"Son, I just want to know why you would lay down your life for a human. They are the cause of our suffering. Our acceptance of them was the demise of our realm. We are here now because of them," Sorcha mimicked Lady Drwyrwen's voice eerily.

This faery was sick, Gwen thought. Sick. She had somehow found a way to control the very dangerous species of shape-shifters in an equally dangerous game, which no doubt had to be forbidden in that realm.

Sorcha turned and walked aimlessly in the other direction, her hands folded behind her back.

"You should have listened to your mummy, as the humans call them," she said to Arden. "Interesting word. Mmmummy. I learnt it from that little troll who keeps asking for her...mummy," she mocked.

"You have Emily?! Where is she?" Gwen interrupted.

"Oh, the troll has a name!" she spun around to face

Gwen and Arden and spoke fiercely to Gwen. "I know *not* how you could bear to live among such filth." She exaggerated the word 'filth.' "Such monsters who destroy their own realm, living meaningless existences, knowing not nor valuing the preciousness of time or devotion to their own."

Saliva had gathered on the corners of her fine lips as she spoke. She wiped it away ungracefully, smudging the red balm staining her lips. Disgust took hold of her facial expressions.

Gwen looked upon Sorcha, confused at her anger towards humans she did not even know.

"What ends do you seek? To hurt us and our friends in such a cruel manner?" asked Arden.

"Hurt you? But I haven't done anything to any of you yet," she said eloquently with a tinge of doubt edged around her words. She took a loud, deep breath. "When I hand you over to the Council, you, half-blood fae, you will wish I had dealt you a nasty fate instead. Because they will do to you what they did to your mother, that human-loving traitor," she whispered staring Gwen in the eyes.

From the tip of her toes to the crown of her head, Gwen felt a chill surge through her body, and she tremored as she listened reluctantly to the incendiary words Sorcha spurted at her.

"Death be unto you," Sorcha whispered in a coy smile.

Gwen realised she felt nothing at these words. She was now numb, and she wondered if it was because, deep inside, she believed Sorcha.

"This death is far worse than any mortal death you know," Sorcha continued, unaware of Gwen's apathy. "It is"—she paused for dramatic effect—"a death that will take hold of you internally, ripping you apart from everything that is dearest to you." As she spoke, her hand reached out as if squeezing the life from an imaginary heart in her grasp.

"You probably don't know," Sorcha began whispering again, looking Gwen intently in the eyes, "but your mother is a bit of a legend here," She laughed wryly. "They say there was nothing she wouldn't do for you *or* your human father. They could have killed her for jeopardising our entire realm, but that would have been too easy a price to pay, so they banished her instead. Not from our lands, but from the very things she so loved. Spells so powerful were conjured to cage her, to ensure that if she was even foolish enough to be tempted, she couldn't come close to those most precious to her. Well, she could try,"—Sorcha smiled widely, eyes popping open as though she was wishing it true—"but not without causing physical harm to herself, and to you, and your father." Gwen could feel her trembling lips, moistened by the stream of tears that had silently spilled over her cheeks, onto her lips, and past her chin.

"Niada was offered reprieve in a rare gesture of kindness if only she would renounce you and your human relative. But she *so* famously quipped that she'd rather die a thousand faery deaths," Sorcha rolled her eyes. "As for the Council being inane enough to grant citizenship to rhwoskis like you, soon, my lovely, they will see what a grand error this was.

"Part fae?" She shook her head negatively, "it doesn't count. Your blood has been sullied." The words were like a sharp sword cutting Gwen slowly. She felt scorned. She suddenly had a different understanding and appreciation of the issues Eliza had had to confront in her own homeland—and in the faery realm as well. During their short time together, Eliza had spoken little of Trinidad, but Gwen had managed to overhear snippets of encouraging words that Rosie had offered to Eliza. She must have been so tormented, Gwen thought regretting her failure to notice Eliza's inner angst. Wishing she had realised how hard it must have been for Eliza living with the constant burden of not being whole enough, pure enough. If only they had had more time together, she could have been there for Eliza.

"Ohh, don't look so dreadful! You're only going to be condemned!" snickered Sorcha, who was about to force a dramatic laugh when her concentration was broken by the emergence of two of her three subjects from the waters of the lake.

"Where is she?" Sorcha blurted out in anger to her subjects, who were as empty-handed as Arden was when he rose from the depths of the lake.

"My fairest lady, these enchanted waters are treacherous and conceal their contents well," one of the elves managed to spit out while catching his breath and looking to his counterpart. "Where, where is Oriedon?" he asked the other elf, whose gaze had focused behind them.

Sorcha closed her eyes, letting out a frustrated sigh.

"My lady, shadows lurk in these murky waters. I think they have taken my brother," the elf lamented, as if expecting sympathy.

Sorcha rolled her eyes again. "Hush. Hush, my faithful," she said in a less than genuine tone. "His sacrifice will not be forgotten. It was in the name of our struggle. There was no sign of the human either?"

"No. I do not foresee recovering the human's body unless there is some magic that could aid our cause, or if we seek the dwellers of the lake," he said.

Sorcha's mouth twitched. "Back to camp until I figure out what we do about the human. The dwellers of the lake help no one and I need that body to add to my collection of evidence." She turned to Gwen and Arden. "Whichever of *you* has The Key, hand it over now," she ordered through her teeth, extending her left hand.

Gwen looked to Arden, and then back to Sorcha.

"We don't have it, my lady," Arden imitated her elves.

"It lies at the seat of the lake with our beloved human friend."

Sorcha tipped over into an immediate fit of rage, and from her mouth bellowed a frightening, shrill scream that echoed far beyond the vicinity of the lake. She held her pale hands to her face and dragged her long nails downwards into her flesh, in frustration, grinding her teeth. Turning her blood-scarred face to Gwen, she marched over and grabbed her by the throat, lifting her off the ground with one hand.

Gwen gasped for air, gripping frantically at Sorcha's hand, trying to loosen her tight grip. She kicked her dangling feet about and struggled to no avail. A faint feeling beset her and soon she could barely hear Arden's frequent pleas in the near distance, as she looked upon Sorcha's blurring face of malevolence.

"Change of plans," Sorcha muttered while still dangling Gwen in her hand. "Time to pay the Council a visit." She smiled, relishing the moment.

Chapter 10

THE COUNCIL

THE COUNCIL HAD RECONVENED YET again to discuss the threat facing the realm. They were in the middle of hashing it out again when the quiet Sylph interrupted.

"We have visitors," she said in a musical voice that bore a wind-like timbre about it. The pale-skinned air faery spoke so few words and only with absolute necessity that when she did speak, her fine voice penetrated even the noisiest of arguments around the table, bringing a sudden quietness as all listened.

Eolande hesitated, looking around the table. "But today we hold no public hearings," she said doubtfully.

No one paid her any mind, for even the most dubious among them knew that the white-draped Sylph had a quiet wisdom about her, tending to know the strangest of things.

Moments after her proclamation, the tall and heavy gilded doors slowly pushed opened, hinges creaking loudly in protest.

"Someone please mend the door," the stocky gnome grunted below his breath, his cherry red nose twitching uneasily at the sound.

As the space between the double doors grew wider, the

black velvety sleeves of Lady Sorcha's cloak became evident. She stepped forward elegantly, bowing demurely, and was about to begin apologising profusely for interrupting the Council.

"It is not open court today, citizen. How did you get past our guards?" Vonroth grunted rudely, inspecting Sorcha from head to toe.

She took tiny, graceful steps with her chin high in the air before speaking. "I am Lady Sorcha, your greatness," she answered, overly confident. "And your guards? Well, they understood the importance of my ill-timed visit."

Emryees's eyes narrowed in suspicion, as did many others around the table. The guards high in the Lordly Mountains of Eversong were anything but sympathetic. They were among the fiercest guards of that region and belonged to the race of Lamassus. These cousins of the winged, human-faced bulls, however, didn't bear wings as their relatives. They stood grand, their stone bodies warding off evil and chaos with their strong presence when awakened by such. Their spirits bound the rules of the Court, making it virtually impossible for one to break most rules, such as barging into the courts when one had no business there.

"You are Lady Sorcha of...?" questioned Emryees.

"Just Lady Sorcha, your eminence," she answered with a smile.

"Lady Sorcha of nowhere? You must come from somewhere," said Hiatar.

"I represent our realm, our peoples and our interests. Does it matter where I hail from?" she asked.

Sorcha nodded over her shoulder, though there was no one there to nod to, but soon her subjects appeared with Gwen and Arden in tow, pushing them forward and dropping them to the ground in subordination.

Around the table, chairs shuffled as many stood up defensively, alarmed at the Aradath Elves in their midst.

"Do not be alarmed, and please lower your weapons. These are our friends." Sorcha reached her arms out towards the elves behind her.

"You bring enemies of our state into the very seat of justice. Yet you call them friends. Yours they may be, not ours," Vonroth said in a rage.

The table waited in silence for a response.

Sorcha had expected this reaction. Of course, she knew that Aradath Elves had long been enemies of the state. A race of rebels who marauded their already ravaged lands in the period after the Plague. They exploited their rare abilities as shape-shifting elves with the help of dark arts, as they now did the forbidden: disguising themselves as fae and other beings of the realm to deceive and manipulate. Other times, shape shifting into the most abhorrent of beasts for the sole reason of driving fear into communities. Of course, Sorcha knew these things.

"We must unite to save our realm, your eminences. Our Aradath brothers and sisters seek the same as we, peace for our realm," she said firmly.

"If we have an enemy, it is not the Aradath Elves. It is them," she said, pointing to Gwen and Arden kneeling on the floor.

Eyes narrowed around the table, and the tension was thick as all listened intently.

"You know not who I bring before you?" Sorcha asked.

She walked around the two prisoners and, lifting her right hand delicately, she motioned as if presenting a trophy before the Council.

"My lords, I give to you Arden, son of Lady Drwyrwen, leader of the forest fae of the Great Eastern Forest,"— she paused, her intonation going upwards—"and Gwen, daughter of the traitor of traitors, the exiled Niada."

There was a chorus of gasps and whisperings around the table as disbelief and shock echoed at the truth behind the rumours that had been spreading.

After a considerable pause, Vonroth slowly parted his lips to speak, and all wondered which pressing question he would pose first.

"You have done well," Vonroth said to Sorcha, who nodded demurely. "Our guards have been seeking out these individuals."

"Do you have The Key?"

"No...."

"And what of the human?"

"I have failed in both regards, your eminence," Sorcha said regretfully. "I caught them plotting against our realm. The human escaped to a watery grave during a fierce battle on Mirror Lake, but not before she murdered the brother of this Aradath elf. While this young fae has betrayed his own, murdering his cousin Arrae, who tried to stop him from colluding with the human and this rhwoski to wage war on our realm, with the human world. There are many of them. I am afraid," she said, false tears welling in her eyes.

All eyes were on Gwen and Arden as Sorcha told apocryphal stories about them.

"We know of this young fae," the gnome informed Sorcha. "His mother dutifully reported his actions to us."

"And you, rhwoski," added Eolande, looking to Gwen in anger, "after we granted you citizenship this is how you return our kindness?" "Shame," the gnome muttered to himself as he cast a sidelong glance at Arden, "such a promising young fae."

"Let us not forget the accused are yet to face trial," Emryees said.

"Whose side do you sit on, Emryees?" Eolande replied.

Urhouri the Salamander butted in. "Emryees is right. We are not sure of their guilt."

"Neither are we of their innocence," Eolande snickered.

Urhouri ignored the comment. "What are the humans

planning?" she asked, looking back and forth to Arden and Gwen.

"They plan nothing. They're being set up," answered Arden in a firm voice before glaring at Sorcha. "This faery lies."

"I do no such thing!" Sorcha answered in feigned alarm. It was convincing. She held her hand delicately to her face tracing the lines of dried blood. "You scratched my face as I sought to protect my friends from your thieving human lover."

A gasp went up around the table.

"Yes, my brethren. They were lovers. All part of a grand scheme, begun by Niada the water nymph and *her* human lover," Sorcha shouted.

Gwen gasped in disbelief and uttered "no" shaking head.

The Council ignored her.

"What scheme?" Vonroth asked the burning q now on the edge of every tongue at the table.

"The birth of this rhwoski was no mistake eminences," Sorcha proclaimed. "She is only many hybrid children the humans aim to prod kin. We wait for a war in the fields tomorrow was come to us yesterday. With the birth of Sorcha whispered dramatically pointing *love* for our kin is stained by corruption magic. Greedy as they are, they desir their insatiable thirst for supremacy n their histories. They decimate their c a thought. Decimating us is no pro humans. They begin a war not with us down. *We* are too powerful for they begin a war of genetics. The our bloodlines," Sorcha clenche

"To weaken us, and level their gain, because they will

child, gifted with the powers of our realm, and who will fight in the honour of humans," she added.

Emryees could hear his own icy breathing amidst the deafening silence. The allegations were grave.

Vonroth's heavy voice cut into the quiet. "How do you respond to these allegations, young fae?" he asked.

"She lies. I've told you she lies!" Arden said pointing to Sorcha. "The humans...." he started but was interrupted by a slew of questions from the eager council members, now anxious about the outrageous allegations.

"You bore no love for the human?" Urhouri tilted her head in curiosity.

"I did, but...."

"So you admit to breaking the laws of the realm?"

"No, it's not like that."

"You associated with a human," said Urhouri.

"Did the human possess The Key?" Eolande intervened.

Emryees was growing impatient at the constant questions levelled at the accused, giving them no chance to answer. "Can we please let him answer?" he shouted.

The table went silent.

"So," Emryees asked, "did the human possess The Key?"

"No," Arden said confused.

"Hmmm" Eolande went loudly.

"It wasn't Eliza," Gwen butted in, speaking to the council directly for the first time. "The humans bear us no harm. I was the one who had The Key. I found it...."

"He doesn't hide the truth, your eminences!" sputtered

"Found it?" asked Eolande.

"I found it in our realm. Someone from your realm lost it in our seas," Gwen explained.

"You speak of both realms as though you belong to both, Child of Niada," Eolande pointed out.

"Both are my home," Gwen defended.

Her response ushered in confusion amongst the Council. Even Emryees found it unusual at how the young girl could consider herself family to both faeries of the realm and humans.

"And what of your cousin?" Eolande turned to Arden.

"We were attacked by Aradath Elves and this Sorcha at Mirror Lake. She killed him. She tried trapping us first in the Dark Forest and then...." Arden tried explaining.

"What were you doing in the Dark Forest?" ask Urhouri. "All know of the evil it harbours."

Arden sighed heavily, realising how everything he said probably sounded to the sceptical Council. He stuttered out his words in frustration. "We were trying to escape Aradath Elves in our path. Eliza wanted to return The Key and go home. That's all. I promised to help her deliver it and get her and Gwen home safely." Stillness took over the room again.

"You shall have a fair trial," said Vonroth to murmurings at the table, "but we cannot ignore your own admission to breaking laws related to associating with humans."

"The allegations Lady Sorcha bears against you are grave. Should they be true, the implications are great for our people. Whatever the truth, we have lost more of our kin and The Key, which could take more eons to replace, if the dwarves will even bother to craft another. Until your hearing, this council will vote to keep you and the rhwoski under our watch. Aye aye?" he asked, to which there was a resounding echo of agreement.

"One thing bothers me," said Emryees lifting a doubtful hand. "If the human was evil, why did our motherland bestow upon her a gift given only to the most extraordinary of faeries in our realm?"

There was no answer, but no one could deny it was indeed a valid question. A puzzling one at that.

"Dark magic can achieve many a thing, my lord," Sorcha

spoke up. She hadn't thought of that ever-important question.

"There should be an investigation prior to the trial. During which the answers to these elusive questions will be sought," the Sylph spoke, her fine voice soothing the others.

The council members looked to each other for signs of agreement or disagreement to the Sylph's suggestion.

"Agreed," said Emryees, to which Hiatar nodded strongly.

"So be it. All in favour of an inquiry?" asked Vonroth.

"Aye," the table responded in unison, and it was on that note that the formidable stone guards were summoned from their still form to escort Arden and a tearful Gwen down to the cold, dark cellars deep beneath the mountains.

Chapter 11

A LONESOME JOURNEY

When Eliza's arrow-pierced body plummeted through the cold, shadowy waters of Mirror Lake, that was not her end. Of course, both Gwen and Arden had not known this and neither had Eliza. As her consciousness faded, she felt an uneasy certainty that this time would not be like the others. Every other time, against the odds, she had somehow been rescued, by fate or friends that she had found in the most unlikely of places.

Now was not one of those times. Not this time. Because even if by a stretch of her imagination there might have been a rescue, she couldn't see how. As her body plunged into Mirror Lake, the waters cloaking her moved like a living thing, folding around her continuously, as though they were wrapping her tight so she couldn't get away. Dark, intertwining shadows danced around the lapping waters, which pulled her in deeper and deeper. She could feel every inch of her body fighting fiercely, pushing hard against the waters, to get herself back to the surface. But her efforts bore little results. The burning stab of the arrow in her chest had spread to her arms and legs, crippling her movements and sucking her energies dry. As her consciousness ebbed, a small part of her waited for a reaching hand beyond the dancing shadows, but it did not come. In no time at all, a vast nothingness swept over her, filled her up, and her last bit of awareness was consumed.

Eliza was being slowly drawn from a long slumber, if we can call it that, by an immensely annoying plopping sound right next to her face. Plop, plop, plop... it sounded. It was so getting under her skin that she wanted to scream her head off, but even more annoying than the constant plopping were the rhythmic sprinkles of cold water that would splatter onto her bare face at the very sound of every plop. She could do with a good scream. If she could wake up. Was she dreaming? Or was she dead?

Dead?

Why would she be dead? A sudden fear had snuck up on her consciousness.

Was she really dead?

How? Why?

She searched her blind consciousness vigorously but nothing came to her.

A strong realisation hit her hard.

She didn't *know* anything and that was all she knew. She didn't *know* if this mental conversation was happening because she was asleep or dead. If she was dead, she didn't know how it happened. She couldn't remember anything or anyone, though the memories felt like they were lingering somewhere near enough yet irritatingly too far for her to recall.

"Eliza?" a familiar voice called.

Her consciousness jerked, and she tried hard to shake it into action. She wasn't sure exactly what she was trying to cause, but any reaction would be better than listening to herself while staring into the void blackness of her mind.

Wake up, wake up, wake up! Argggghhh!

Nothing.

"Eliza?" the musical voice beckoned again.

Gasp.

Arden? She heard the voice in her head question.

Who is Arden? She answered herself back dubiously.

"Wake up, Eliza. You must wake up now."

Suddenly, the eyes of her consciousness opened, and as the great curtain of blackness lifted, in her mind's clouded eye she saw the most beautiful face before hers. She knew this young man, this grey-eyed ethereal beauty, but who was he?

Whoever he was, he was propped up over her as she lay flat on her back unable to move a muscle. She looked around them. Everything was a blur. Well, mostly everything, as things tended to appear in those hazy kind of dreams.

"Eliza," he whispered her name from his pink lips, his breath fresh as the morning breeze brushing against her face.

"Look," he said, his eyes moving upwards to a rain of bubbles floating down towards her from the heavens. "See how insubstantial, fragile, and temporary they are? Yet, each has its own purpose." He smiled as a huge, wobbly bubble settled onto Eliza's nose.

"Just like you have a purpose," he added.

Somewhere in her consciousness, Eliza heard another of those annoying plops, at the sound of which, the bubble on her nose burst into a million drops of cold water that splattered onto her face, simultaneously jerking her from her unconsciousness, and sending a flood of memories rushing through her mind.

When she awoke from her oblivion, the first thing Eliza noticed was the heavily moistened crystal chandeliers hanging from the roof of the cave. It was quite peculiar. Intricate and unique shapes of the dazzling crystal formations hung in stark contrast to the roof and walls of the cold cave she lay in. She gave her immediate surroundings a quick scan.

Plop.

Grrrrrr. She grumbled as a cold drop of water from a spiky crystal star above her dropped to the ground right beside her face, splattering all over her nose and forehead.

So you're the culprit, she thought to herself, wiping the water away from her face and quickly resuming the scan of her environs.

A mysterious green glow lit up the damp cave and reflected off the crystal formations everywhere. The cave was winding, and Eliza could see the surreal crystal walls in both directions curving around corners. Mounds of crystals formed giant plant-like blocks spurting up from the ground. Somewhere nearby she could hear a body of water flowing with life, like the energies of tidal waves creeping up against a still coastline only to recede again. Besides that, there was no sign of life.

She tried to sit up when an uncomfortable, stinging pain reverberated in her chest.

"Arrrrrghhhh." She writhed in pain, grabbing her chest in a gasp before laying back down.

She could hear her hard, rhythmic breaths bouncing around the walls of the cave. She waited for the pain to subside before propping herself back up on her right elbow. Hesitantly, she pulled the front of her cloak aside to look down at her chest. A purplish bruising covered and bordered a deep wound.

She ran her finger over the bruise lightly.

"Ahhhhgg."

Of course.

She had been hit by an arrow. Yes, she remembered now. She had taken an arrow for Arden, but where was he? Where was Gwen and the arrow? She looked about her on the ground for it, but it was nowhere in sight.

Shock gripped her as she recalled the last moments of consciousness in Mirror Lake. In a bout of fright, she peered around nervously. Where was she and what had happened to her friends? How did she survive? Was it because of that *light* inside of her?

This was one of those very rare moments when Eliza would gladly trade her current snafu for her usual complicated life, back on the racially charged island she called home.

A wet, ominous, dragging sound broke Eliza's concentration.

She sat nervously as she struggled to hear the sound against the near flow of water.

Besides the constant dripping, she could hear something heavy dragging through water.

Gasp.

Eliza soon realised that, very slowly, the sound was becoming louder and louder. Someone, or some*thing*, was coming.

A great fright gripped the inner walls of her stomach like a firm hand and wrung it, rendering her body inert and causing her to hyperventilate. Without thinking, she forced herself up, clenching her jaw through the staggering pain until she was on all fours. Slowly, with great effort forced into every movement, she crawled to one of the mounds of crystal spurting upwards from the ground. When she got behind it, she rested her back against it heavily. The mound towered over her head just enough to keep her from sight, but in her position in the winding cave, she had to hope that no one would approach from the other direction, which she was now facing sat against this rock.

The wet, dragging sound echoed with a kind of eeriness that Eliza imagined would have played during a tense scene in a horror movie. She felt like an unwilling participant playing out a scene in her own horror story. As the sound neared, Eliza could hear more water dripping. Whoever or whatever it was was now a stone's throw from where she sat.

Then, the sound stopped and it was quiet again.

Eliza listened and waited, and waited and listened, but she heard nothing more. Taking a quick gulp, she cautiously inched to the rough, right edge of the mound, and slowly peeped over the edge to see where the visitor had gone. Her eyes swung left and right. There was no one. She sighed heavily in relief, but then three heavy droplets of water plopped onto her left shoulder from above, and suddenly the fear returned. She dithered, and as her teeth started rattling against each other, she reluctantly looked up to see where the dripping water was coming from.

Huh? Nothing. That was a surprise, to say the least and Eliza was so stunned, she gripped the edges of the mound and pulled herself up onto her knees. Looking behind the mound from where she swore something or someone had been, but there was nothing. She dropped her weight back down on her legs and turned back the other way.

A scream burst through her lips when she saw the huge green eyes staring at her intently. She pushed herself back against the crystal mound, tilting her head away in fright. In the circumstances, anyone should understand why Eliza had screamed. Sheer fear, of course, but otherwise she had no reason to scream. The faerie stooping before her certainly didn't warrant a scream. Loridel was neither frightening nor ghastly in appearance—quite the opposite in fact. The pale-skinned fae stared back at Eliza curiously, and after a brief pause, an unexpected hearty laugh escaped her lips. Not a brief, superficial laugh, but a full-bodied, unfettered guffaw that showed no sign of letting up. Loridel threw her head back, and held her torso as the laughter shook her slender frame. Eliza wanted to be horrified, but instead, she found herself most confused. What was so funny?

The faery, whose white hair was styled in a crown of plaits circling her head, seemed different from the others of the realm Eliza had encountered during her stay there.

Refined and delicate were the words that came to mind when Eliza thought of her beauty, but her guttural laugh seemed most incongruous with her delicate appearance. Her dress echoed that of the Tudor fashion, making her appear an anachronism, even for a realm of magic and wonder, but this was the common dress among the Gwragedd Annwn.

The long, wide sleeves of her royal blue velvet frock hung gracefully off her arms, almost covering her hands, and her low square-necked bodice was bordered by the most dazzling embroidery and enticing jewels around its edges. Her bodice fitted tightly down to the waist, at which sat an enviable golden chain girdle, designed with an alternating pattern of purple stones, followed by gold stones, and then by fine ivory pearl drops. From her waist, her layered overskirt flowed down with a slit in the middle, revealing a white kirtle beneath. The kirtle spilled onto the ground with the same excess length of the velvet overskirt. Eliza couldn't help but notice how dirty the edges of the faery's skirt were, splattered with mud and soaking wet. As Loridel's laughter wound down, she noticed Eliza's intense inspection and stopped chuckling altogether.

"You must be hungry," she said, producing a round, golden fruit with its broken stalk still attached.

Eliza heard her stomach growl in encouragement, but she looked back up to faerie suspiciously.

"Take it, it will not harm you," assured the eloquent fae.

Almost without thinking, Eliza took the fruit in her hand and very briefly marvelled at the fine pores on its golden flesh, soft to the touch like a ripened apricot might feel. She bit into it and closed her eyes as she savoured an explosion of flavours that burst into her mouth, tantalising her taste buds like no fruit she'd ever tasted. With a few bites, a feeling of fullness settled in her stomach, which she hadn't even realised had been protesting in hunger.

"Thank you," she said to the faerie.

"You haven't eaten for some time," Loridel replied with a smile. "I am Loridel of Mirror Lake. I have been taking care of you. Human."

Eliza wasn't sure if she should smile back or be concerned after Loridel made it a point to call her *human*. After all, she was an enemy of the realm. She swallowed and placed the bitten fruit onto the ground next to her while at the back of her mind admiring the way the faerie spoke.

Loridel smiled. "A few bites of the Golden Dew can fill even the hungriest of beasts," she said looking to the fruit.

"You're one of those water faeries from Mirror Lake. The Goog-something," Eliza whispered in askance recalling the brief stories she had heard while on the boat across the lake.

"Yes. We are the Gwragedd Annwn," she said assuredly. "But who are you? Do you know?" she asked, and Eliza wondered if the question was genuine or rhetoric.

"Come," said Loridel helping Eliza up until she was propped against the fae's wet, slender body.

"Your wound is not yet healed. I will attend to it and you can tell me who you are," she said, leading Eliza away from that area of the cave.

As they walked around one of the corners, the sound of the moving waters drew nearer. Eliza marvelled at how the greenish glow reflecting off the crystal formations in the cave gave it an enchanted ambience.

"Beautiful, aren't they?" she said of the clear crystals hanging about. "We call this place Crystal Cavern, a fitting name, don't you agree?" she asked.

Eliza nodded in agreement. She felt so calmed by the sound of the nearby waters, which were almost musical.

Loridel led her to a vast space in the cave where an

underwater cave lead out into Mirror Lake. The shimmery, turquoise waters bubbled and churned, and when she looked closely, Eliza could have sworn she saw the waters twirling about. As Loridel sat her down against a crystal mound near the waters, Eliza crawled to the edge of the opening, putting her face near the waters as she listened to the hollow yet musical echo it produced.

"What...?" she began saying something, but her voice trailed off when she noticed Loridel, now sat close to her emptying a pouch of strange-looking pieces of plants.

"Where's my pouch?" she asked as she suddenly remembered seeing Loridel's.

"Do not trouble yourself, your pouch is safe," Loridel assured her, and Eliza believed the fae's words.

Without warning, Loridel suddenly burst into a stream of tears like a weeping child, which seemed genuine enough, though Eliza hadn't the foggiest idea why.

"Why...why are you crying?" Eliza asked very stunned, as Loridel threw herself to the ground, her face in her hands in the unexplained mourning.

"You, you..." she uttered in between tears, "you thought I stole your pouch." Her voice trailed off in a dreadful moan as she dramatically dropped her head back into her folded arms.

Eliza found herself stuttering in a defensive bid to assuage Loridel's upset.

"No, no, no, not at all. I am sorry if it sounded like that, Loridel. I just remembered I had a pouch, and there's something important in it, and I...." her voice trailed off realising that Loridel was so far impervious to her explanation. She paused, and searched for the right words to say what she meant. "Loridel, I'm *really* sorry, I know you didn't steal my pouch. You're a good faerie...."

Loridel lifted her blank face. "I am?" she asked dubiously, staring with her wide, teary eyes.

"Yes, yes...."

"But how could you know?" she asked as if it were a trick question.

"Well, you saved my life. You can't be both bad and good." Eliza smiled, as she found herself searching for the exact words so she didn't accidentally offend Loridel further.

Loridel looked at Eliza and smiled with sincerity, feeling touched by the human's words.

"No... no being in all these lands," Loridel sniffled and gesticulated with her slender fingers to emphasise the vastness of her realm, "has ever said a thing so complimentary to me or any of my kin before. They call us strange." Her tone was questioning and Eliza realized these fae may only be misunderstood, and beings in all of the realm did find the Gwragedd Annwn strange. Loridel's kin were special and gifted in many ways, in all things medicinal, for instance, and in being amazingly adept at swimming, given that they dwelled in vast underwater villages disguised to other eyes by magic.

However, the Gwragedd Annwn had a flaw that made them 'strange' even for creatures of Annwn. They had the most unexpected or contrary emotional reactions to situations, and when their emotions were right for the situation, they were often exaggerated. This couldn't be helped, of course, being a trait that they were born with.

In the short space of time she had been conscious, Eliza was learning this very quickly.

Loridel had quickly gotten over the misunderstanding and was gleefully crushing plants that she had gathered to tend to Eliza's wound. While she did this, Eliza told Loridel how she had come to Annwn, and all that had followed after. She found that Loridel knew nothing of what had become of her friends at the lake.

"Though, you were not the only one to fall into our lake," she said, to which Eliza's eye bulged with shock.

"Who...?"

"Two others. A most muscular forest faerie and an Aradath elf," she said.

"Oh no, Arrae," Eliza whispered wondering what had happened to him at the lake. "You have to save him," she said gripping Loridel's shoulders. When she caught herself, she inspected Loridel's face for any onslaught of emotions but none came, so she calmly pulled away, remembering the need to be sensitive.

"Please, can you save my friend?"

"Eliza, my kin typically do not get involved in affairs that do not concern us. Those who fall through the veil of our waters never leave. Unless they are like us, they will die," Loridel replied.

"Why then did you save me? Why didn't you let me die?" Eliza found herself getting emotional at the thought of Arrae dying while trying to help her.

Loridel paused to think looking at the churning waters beside them.

"I've seen humans from afar, but not up close, like you. I suppose I was most curious, also, you are different. For certain. This must be why Annwn gave you such a rare gift. I didn't know it when I saved you, but I could see something in you," she whispered, resting her hand on Eliza's chest.

Eliza put her hand over Loridel's, and searched deeply into her eyes. "My friends have risked everything to help me. I am indebted to them as I am now to you. Please, if you can help Arrae...." she trailed off.

Loridel listened to Eliza's heartfelt plea, and though her kin had kept themselves safe from the troubles of their beleaguered realm through extreme measures, isolation, and autarky, she knew that the times were different and Eliza was different. She was only a mere human girl facing great odds in their vast realm just to save the people she loved. What struck Loridel even more was not only Eliza's frailties as a human, but also her determination to try despite the overwhelming self-doubt that dogged her. Even Loridel could see it. Eliza wore her insecurities on her sleeves and if the Gwragedd Annwn could not relate to anything else, they could relate to devotion. It was really devotion to her own driving Eliza, just as it was devotion to protecting their own kin that kept the Gwragedd Annwn bound to their extreme rules and lifestyle.

Loridel smiled. "I will help you," she said. "My sisters are about seeking this Arrae."

Eliza was about to ask Loridel how she had known this, but the peculiar faerie answered before she could even ask. "You will see soon."

"So this key opened the doorway that you came through?" Loridel continued the conversation as she began applying the crushed plant paste to Eliza's wound.

"Ahh," Eliza muttered in pain to the light touch.

Loridel took one of the many leaves scattered about the ground from her pouch and folded it before pressing it lightly over the paste on Eliza's wound. The leaf stuck against Eliza's skin, and she felt a tingling sensation on the inside of her wound, as the medicine took root and began its work.

"You have a strong spirit for a human," said Loridel in admiration. "Your life was as sure as over with that arrow, an arrow carved by faerie hands, with only the strongest metals and magic of the realm. By some uncanny twist of... providence, you landed here, in deceptive waters with a mind of their own. Doomed to sink with no chance of release, still, you were damned to the one place that's home to the most skilful healers of the realm. Is there such a thing as chance?" she asked.

Loridel wasn't just being boastful. The Gwragedd Annwn could never falter with their innate talent for all things medicinal. This was why Eliza's bad luck was actually most lucky.

It might have seemed quite unfavourable that she fell

twice into Mirror Lake, and thrice unlucky that this lake harboured reclusive and mistrustful faeries; it was the one place she could have been saved from the lethal arrow to her chest.

Eliza realised she had much to be thankful for. Her luck in what had seemed a most tragic circumstance had been forgiving. Still, with everything going on, the heaviness in her heart had never left.

"What troubles your heart, Eliza?" Loridel asked, noticing the smallest shift in Eliza's mood.

Eliza remained mum.

"Ahh... uncertainty of the future makes you despondent."

Eliza looked to Loridel as something dawned on her. She remembered one of the first questions she had meant to ask but had never gotten around to.

"Loridel, is it true these waters can tell one's future?" she asked.

The pale faery smiled. "In no realm that I know of, neither yours nor mine, can the future be foretold with surety. None know our future better than we ourselves, Eliza. What we make of our present will determine what comes tomorrow."

Eliza looked at the churning waters beside them and wondered if what she had seen in the reflection of the lake was true. Maybe she was supposed to be on her own. Maybe only she could cross the bridge. Maybe if they hadn't been cornered and Arden and Gwen had made it to the bridge with her, she would lose them forever. Maybe, maybe, maybe.

She let out a heavy sigh, slouching back on the crystal mound behind her.

"You know Eliza, Mirror Lake cannot show you a sure tomorrow, but it can show you what is," Loridel said.

Confused, Eliza looked to the waters and then back to Loridel.

"What do you mean?" she narrowed her eyes in confusion.

Before Loridel could answer, Eliza eagerly asked, "Can I see my grandparents?"

"Choose wisely. You may only ask one thing of the Mirror," Loridel warned.

Eliza nodded. She wanted to know what had happened to her friends, but she also needed to see that her grandparents were alive and safe. Instinctively, she looked to Loridel knowing already what her difficult decision would be.

Loridel smiled and turned to the bubbling waters, which soon evened out into a calm surface much like the reflective one Eliza had seen just before she first plunged into the lake.

As the shimmering particles gathered about here and there, they soon formed the familiar faces that Eliza so longed to see. She cried with a smile on her face as she saw Rosie, Indira, and her grandfather in the little cottage on Abbeydale Road as night fell on the community. Her smile faded as she noticed their sleepless eyes, and as Indira broke down calling out her name.

"Eliza, my Eliza! Come home, my Eli," Indira cried, and Eliza found that her happiness at seeing her family didn't last as she now felt their suffering. The image started blurring, and Eliza stretched outwards to touch the waters in desperation, "Wait! Wait! Let me look at them just for a little longer," she pleaded, but Loridel held her hand back from touching the waters.

The images changed, and in a blur she saw a flash of scenarios in the English community around Abbeydale Road, the numerous *Missing Person* posters flying about the dark streets, the ghostliness of the community, and a sudden picture of a doorway at The Tor, which she now knew hid the main gateway between the realms. A picture of black, shaggy cats lingering in the shadows of the streets irked her, and she clenched her teeth at what she had come to recognise as the fearsome phookas terrorising the town. They were lingering in her world, on a street near her family. As the images faded away in the waters before her, and her inner anger raged, she noticed Loridel staring quietly.

"Eliza, when you return The Key, how will you get home?" Loridel asked, but Eliza had a sinking feeling this was one of those questions that Loridel already knew the answer toAnd it was. If all she had explained to Loridel earlier was true, then, if she successfully returned The Key to The Sacred Valley, restoring it should immediately close the main gateways between realms. How would she return home if the doorways were now closed? How would Gwen make it home? If she could find Gwen, and even if they could somehow return home, could they make it back to a doorway unharmed with the Council after them, and with so many evil forces on their trail? The sinking feeling made her stomach feel hollow. Would she ever get home? The wretched realisation manifested itself on her face, and she looked to Loridel in horror.

"I can't go home, can I?" she uttered despite already knowing the answer.

Loridel tried very hard, and managed to stifle the laughter that was brimming within her. She looked away not to cause any offence to Eliza. Eliza saw Loridel's efforts in trying to contain the true essence of her emotions, and knew the faerie's efforts were in recognition of the horrible truth she had just confronted. She would probably never make it home.

In charge of her emotions now, Loridel looked Eliza in the eyes intently. "Eliza, you know The Key, I am told, was crafted to control the only two gateways which have been recognised for many eons as the main entryways between our worlds. It does not mean that these gateways are the only ones."

Eliza instantly understood what Loridel was saying, but how would she find another doorway without her friends? How was she going to survive a minute beyond that cave without any help in that parlous place?

Loridel continued. "There are many holes between our realms. Difficult they may be to find, but they are there." She inched in closer to Eliza, narrowing her eyes and lowering her voice. "We have one in our waters." "A gateway to my world? Here in these waters?" Eliza asked excitedly looking to the bubbling waters again.

"Yes, it may not take you exactly to your village, but it will take you back to your world safely."

Eliza was now confused. "But if The Key doesn't control this doorway or other ones, then my world will never truly be safe from the dangers here," she reasoned.

"Holes between realms are incredibly difficult to find, Eliza. The one at the Tor is huge, while the one beyond The Sacred Valley is most conspicuous. That's why all creatures of this realm know of them. If those two doorways are closed, your realm should be safe again. None except my kin know of the gateway in our waters, because as you have seen, unless you are one of us, you cannot find your way to our village. And we are hardly a threat to your world."

"I can take you to the gateway in our waters if you wish," Loridel said.

Eliza's heart almost skipped a beat with excitement but then reality came back, as fast as it had departed. "I must put things right first, Loridel," she said, pausing to search for the right words to say, what she knew she wanted to say but couldn't somehow. "My grandparents, they've protected me all my life, and now I have to protect them. That's what you do when you love someone. And my friend is out there," she said turning her head with her teary eyes away. "She came here to save me when I was kidnapped by a phooka. She's out there because of me. if

I go back now, I would have failed everybody I love. I have The Key. This gnome, we saw this gnome who insisted Gwen give me The Key some days ago. Now I have it. It is my burden to carry. I am the only one who can put this right," she managed to utter before the harsh reality consumed her, and for the first time, since she had left her home, Eliza let everything go. Everything.

And she cried.

She cried shamelessly, letting the innermost sadness that she had safely tucked away somewhere unreachable inside come to the surface and spill over.

"Fret not, Eliza!" Loridel said with great alacrity, wiping the grin off her face to look as solemn as she could despite being unable to help her awkward emotional self, so she let her giggles escape, and Eliza couldn't help but smile. Somehow, the flaw of this peculiar and socially inept faerie had managed to put a smile on her face even though she was hurting so badly. It was strange to Eliza how even a trait seen as a flaw could achieve something good.

"All is not lost, Eliza," Loridel continued. "There is always a way. This is a realm of magic and you have magic in you. In here." She touched Eliza's chest again, gently. "This is a realm of possibilities, a dangerous place, but still a realm of possibilities, and if you cannot find your way back to this cave at your journey's end, then we will help you find a way home. However, you have to believe, Eliza. Believe that all things are possible. Believe in yourself. For all the evils here now, our realm is very much like your world. She is kind and giving to those who are kind and giving to Her. When you believe, you attract all the good from Annwn to you, and She will help your bidding. If you find you cannot trust what I've said to you, trust in the love you have for your kin. Let that love guide you."

The words struck a chord within Eliza, and she knew what she had to do. Just as she had realised when she first became conscious, she realised again that she wasn't sure of much. She wasn't sure of how she would get home, if she would at all, and neither was she sure of what she would encounter on the lonesome leg of her journey. She wasn't sure of how she would overcome any attacks on her own, or how to channel the odd powers the realm had gifted to her. She was unsure of many a thing, but Loridel was right. If Eliza was sure of one thing, it was the love that bound her to her grandparents and to her friends.

Chapter 12

UNDERWATER

"Get in!" demanded Loridel tugging at Eliza's arm.

Eliza shook her head frantically, pulling her weight back. Enough time had passed for her wound to mend, and she could now move about with much more ease and less discomfort than before. Eliza welcomed this. What she did not welcome was the reality that it was now time to leave the safety of the cave and go out on her own.

"Can't you come with me?" she asked, already knowing the answer but needing to ask just in case.

"No, I cannot. I've told you, water is the essence of my life. I will suffer away from it, if I am gone for too long," Loridel said, still very annoyed and tugging away at Eliza's arm. She let go and stared at the delicate girl crouched on the damp ground of the cave, staring into the churning waters.

"I'm afraid of this water," Eliza carped on.

"You are afraid of many things."

"Yes, but...."

"You were afraid of me before you knew me," said Loridel.

"Well, yes," Eliza mumbled. She knew she couldn't win the argument, but she still hesitated.

"I can't swim," she said, getting annoyed at her own incessant complaints. She thought Loridel was doing quite well, in fact, in dealing with her stubbornness.

Loridel folded her arms.

"I can't breathe underwater like you, Lori" Eliza added, satisfied there could be no decent comeback for this.

Loridel's eyes twitched in guilt. "I've already cured that," she said.

"What do you mean you've 'cured that'?" Eliza eyed her suspiciously.

Loridel swam back from the edges of the opening and motioned for Eliza to look in the waters.

With her forehead furrowed in suspicion, Eliza crept closer to the edge, ready to resist any sudden tricks by Loridel to pull her into the mysterious waters.

She glanced up at Loridel and then back at the reflective waters. The image of her face drew her in closer to the water's surface. Her jaw dropped and she gripped her face, aghast at her reflection.

"What did you do!?" she blurted hysterically, inspecting the gills on her cheekbones. "Ahhhhhh," she murmured in a shrill, musical moan, touching them.

Loridel felt a good cry coming on. She resisted it easily, still feeling mostly annoyance at Eliza. Her time with the human had so far been teaching her to control her overpowering emotions.

"They will not last. The effects of the golden dew only last several days at most," she said. "You will be able to swim too, once you get in the water. But you will not see what I mean sitting over there."

Fine. Eliza supposed she couldn't resist it forever. She didn't want to leave, but she knew she couldn't stay either. Eliza edged closer to the waters, and slowly put her feet in.

"Come." Loridel beckoned her.

She eased herself into the cold waters, feeling her hairs

rise and an intense shiver run through her whole body. She moved towards Loridel's outstretched hand.

Loridel gripped her hand and nodded with a smile. Instinctively Eliza took a deep breath. Loridel grinned at her, and they dipped under the surface of the water. As soon as her head had gone under, Eliza noticed many things. Still holding Loridel's hand, she realised she could now see clearly under the waters and that, strangely, she was swimming with great ease.

"It's because you've also been endowed with those," Loridel said.

Eliza could hear Loridel's voice in her head! The shock of this stunned her momentarily, and it took a few moments for Loridel's words to sink in.

To her surprise, she noticed that the tips of her feet had been elongated to form thin flippers. She marvelled at them before looking to Loridel in fascination. "The golden dew did all this?" she asked.

Loridel smiled back and encouraged her to swim on.

As they swam on through the underwater cave, Eliza also noticed how effortlessly Loridel manoeuvred through the water, even in her heavy dress.

Once the novelty of her newly acquired but temporary abilities wore off, Eliza began to marvel at the beauty down below. She saw the energies in the waters twisting and twirling, and flipping and folding in every direction, like a life force moving within that space.

"What makes the waters move like this?" she asked.

"These are living waters, Eliza. As alive as you and me. What you see is the very essence of its life," Loridel answered.

Engulfed by her amusement of the wonders around her, she let Loridel's hand loose and twirled around gleefully, examining the life force around her. She delighted in the weightless bounce her body bore in the water, and for a fleeting moment, Eliza experienced happiness.

Eliza marvelled at the crystal flowstones spread across the cave's floor amongst crystal columns stretching upwards like leaning buildings in a concrete jungle. Mossy drapes hung from the ceiling, flowing like her grandmother's kitchen curtains in the cool Caribbean breeze.

They swam deeper into the cave, and eventually made their way through to the vast lake.

Ooohhhh, Eliza thought in wonder, as the cosmic waters lay before her waiting to be explored. The lake was far more colossal than it appeared to be from the surface. Far more than any being of the land could fathom or speculate on. Its far-reaching depth and space could never truly be known to those outside of the Gwragedd Annwn.

Colours exploded in the vivid landscape of the lake, with bright reds, greens, yellows, and pinks in the soft, swaying corals and other thriving fauna, and in the unique inhabitants that lived there.

The most unusual of creatures patterned by fusions of dazzling colours, stripes, and amazing textures swam about paying no attention to Eliza, as though she were one of them. She looked past a gigantic rainbow-coloured jellyfish to a single line of iridescent fish whose colours changed as they swam, then onto a gorgeous golden-haired water faery who looked much like Loridel, and was dressed similarly too. Eliza gazed at her dress fluttering about in the water gracefully just like her hair.

"Greetings, Loridel," the faery said never taking her eyes off Eliza.

"Hello, Ipsy," Loridel answered.

"You may do well to take your friend away soon. Her presence is already causing great unease among some," Ipsy said as though Eliza wasn't even there.

Eliza frowned.

"Do not fret, Eliza," Loridel said quickly, looking to Ipsy. "We will not be here long at all."

"What trouble will she bring us?" Ipsy interjected, genuine worry written all over her beautiful face.

"Be about your business, Ipsy. This quarrel has already passed," Loridel said with authority, to which Ipsy bade her farewell.

Eliza and Loridel swam off, and Eliza hesitantly looked behind to see Ipsy floating motionless, staring at her.

They made their way into a fluffy white cloud that turned out to be a field of gelatinous, flower-like creatures once Eliza could see them up close.

"We are almost past the Jelly Floats" Loridel encouraged, leading Eliza by hand through the sheets of fluttering white.

Eliza attempted to push the creatures out of her way with her hands as she followed Loridel, and when they broke through the last layer of Jelly Floats, Eliza gasped at the sight before her. A thriving underwater city.

It was like nothing she could have imagined. Hard, gigantic corals formed great architecture in the most vibrant colours—azure, lavender, and salmon among others, in the underwater city. No two structures were alike, and adding to its lure were the countless Gwragedd Annwn and other creatures bustling in and about the city. Loridel held Eliza's hand tightly and led her into the dreamy city, where eyes everywhere were turning to the human in their midst. At first, Eliza noticed how quickly those who saw her turned away or vanished inside the towering structures. Others she saw stared brazenly with wide eyes whispering amongst themselves.

What she noticed next spooked her a great deal. The unabashed laughter, the sorrow, the exaggerated horror was all too overwhelming for poor Eliza. She was so shocked she hadn't even noticed that her hand had slipped out of Loridel's so she could spin around towards the glaring faces.

"Eliza, come on," Loridel said encouragingly, just a few paces ahead of her,

but Eliza didn't move a muscle. The oddities and frightening realities of this realm had a way of incapacitating her, but any human would be terrified faced with a chorus of maddening laughs, cries, and screams aimed at them in a strange place. The strange beauty of the place captivated Eliza, but Annwn's haunting uniqueness and charms were also its terrors.

A group of inquisitive water faeries had encircled her and touched her curiously like she was a toy sent for them to play with. One ran her fingers through Eliza's curly strands, one traced her fingers along Eliza's face before being bumped aside by another for the chance to examine Eliza's face. Another poked Eliza's hand to see what a human's skin felt like.

Loridel unceremoniously parted them and pulled a stunned Eliza along.

"I thought she'd be stranger," Eliza heard one of the Gwragedd Annwn say behind her.

"No, she's beautiful. In a most peculiar way of course," another chimed in.

Eliza glanced over her shoulder, still stunned, as Loridel tugged her along through the waters, leading her inside a salmon-coloured building. They entered a small room with many bright fixtures about it, some clearly to sit on and huge sponges that Eliza imagined were for resting.

Loridel swam in front of her and held her by the shoulder. "Do not be bothered by them. They mean well, I am sure of it. It's probably their first sighting of a human. Stay here," Loridel said, sitting Eliza down on one of the spongy chairs.

"I will be with you again shortly," she added before swimming through a hole in the coral.

Eliza couldn't sit still. She wanted to know what all the commotion was outside.

"Faster, my fins, faster," a high-pitched voice ordered.

She got up and swam to a hole on the other side of the room, poking her head out carefully to see without being seen. A short distance away, pairs of Gwragedd Annwn ran strings and strings of decorative flowers outside and through the different levels of a towering mauve coral. At the highest level, a delightful water fae peered through a hole and issued order after order.

"Don't knot the flowers, my fins. These took moons to grow," she said. Eliza looked on, still so taken with this dreamy world.

As she leaned her nose against the looking hole, a golden-skinned sea horse suddenly appeared from nowhere, poked its tuberous mouth through, and touched her nose.

"Whoa!" she pulled back in surprise at the creature that sniffed around for a bit before swimming off. She watched it swim away, before resting on the huge patterned shell just beneath the hole. It moved up suddenly, and Eliza found herself rolling over and off the fixture. When she caught herself, she noticed a head emerging from one end of the shell.

"Oh, gees, sorry. I thought you were a, a thing to sit on," she said to the sea turtle slowly swinging its head about to see who or what had disturbed its rest.

"Neverrrrrrmind. Common missstakeeeeee down hereee," it answered. "You be the humannnn all the finnns been clamouring about lately?" the turtle asked.

"Yeah, I guess so," she answered.

"Seaweed?" the creature offered as he slowly munched on some algae growing through a crevice in the coral.

"Um, no thank you," she said.

"Sooooo, how's you liking it abouts the town?" he managed to ask, his words slowed down even more by his chewing.

"Well, I never like being the new girl in town. Everyone

talks about you and looks at you funny, and... Let's just say I wish I had a shell like yours," she said.

"Ifff it's any consolation, I've lived here all mi long lifes, and everyone still talks about how slooooowwww I am," said the turtle.

Eliza chuckled.

"Here we are," Loridel's voice echoed through the hallway just before she appeared through the same hole through which she'd left.

"Ahh, I see you've met Turtle." She smiled at Eliza. "Sit down. Let us talk."

Eliza was about to sit on the moss green fixture when Loridel sprung up and pulled her forward, and placed her on a protruding bit of coral.

"Don't want to wake the Crab. He's very snappy in his sleep," Loridel said, gesticulating with her fingers in a snappy motion like a crab's claws. "I've something for you."

Loridel presented Eliza with the pouch that held The Key.

"Ohh, thank you, Loridel!" she exclaimed throwing her arms around the blushing faery.

"Little bright bulb you are for using a waterproof pouch," Loridel exclaimed, brushing her index finger lightly against Eliza's nose. She asked Eliza if she knew the way onwards to The Sacred Valley.

"Ahh, rats! I don't have a map," she said. Arrae and Arden had held the only copies.

Nevertheless, Loridel had figured that much, having already inspected the contents of Eliza's pouch.

"My sisters have been across the mountains before," Loridel said. "I can lead you to the foot of the mountainside. From there, you must climb up to Misty Bridge. You cannot, and must not, cross the bridge without the bridgekeeper." Eliza smiled fondly at the memory of the bizarre gnome,

Skoran, who had given her the same warning just a few days ago, though it felt like a lifetime.

"Loridel, do you know what questions the bridgekeeper will ask of me? We were supposed to get some kind of payment for the bridgekeeper, but we never figured out what it was," she said with concern in her voice and worried she was. If she hadn't the payment for the bridgekeeper, she would have to answer a riddle and Eliza rightly reckoned that any riddle would challenge her knowledge of Annwn, of which she had very little.

"What of this payment do you know?" Loridel enquired.

"Well this gnome who was helping us said that it has something to do with 'that which rolls on the grounds of living waters,' but he didn't know...." Eliza's voice trailed off as she realised something. Living waters? She had heard that description before. From Loridel of course, when she described the very waters Eliza was now in.

"Getting your payment will not be difficult at all," Loridel said.

Eliza was in awe at her luck.

"You will have your payment, and as I said, you must not under any circumstances attempt to cross Misty Bridge alone."

"Why do they call it Misty Bridge anyway?" Eliza asked in sudden curiosity.

"The bridge connects the Mountains of Mirror Lake to the Great Mountains of the Never-Ending East. It crosses over Doom Valley," she said, fixing Eliza with a stern look. "Be wary and follow all instructions with great care. The bridgekeeper belongs to a race unlike any other in these lands...." "*Every* race is unlike any other in all these lands," Eliza quipped not intending to be rude though it sounded that way.

"Little Eliza!" Loridel raised an index finger at her. "Listen. The bridgekeeper's people are called the persecutors of all creatures. All. They help *no one*. If you fall, a hand will not be extended. If you offend, forgiveness is unlikely. So be wise. It is your only way through those mountains and to the other side. We know nothing of the passageway inside the mountains, but my sisters say once you pass through. you will see The Sacred Valley ahead. You cannot miss it."

She handed Eliza an item wrapped tightly in a plastic-like material. Eliza unravelled it to reveal a smoothly carved wooden ornament with deep engravings about its surface.

"Oh it's lovely, Loridel. What is it?" she asked eagerly.

"A blade," said Loridel. "A gift from Mirror Lake. You may or may not need it, but I hope it serves you well."

"Ohh," Eliza said, bringing it closer to her face, and squinting her eyes as she inspected it. "How do I open it?" she asked.

"Ahh... you can't," said Loridel. "The blade opens only when you need it."

"Well, I kinda need it to open now, so I can see it," Eliza said in her usual feisty manner to which Loridel laughed.

"Not like that, my child. It will open only when you really need it to. Lies and deceit will not work on it, so you cannot pretend to need it either," she smiled, anticipating any possible playful trickery from Eliza.

"So how does it work?"

"Magic," Loridel answered in delight, always wanting to have the chance to say that.

"Okay!" said a satisfied and grinning Eliza, looking at the blade's handle for the last time before tucking it away safely in the pouch.

Loridel got up and as she had done since leading Eliza into the waters, extended her hand to lead the girl away. Eliza clasped her hand into Loridel's and bade farewell to the turtle, who wished her a happy adventure and safe return home.

As they left the coral, Eliza noticed many of the Gwragged Annwn had congregated nearby.

"They want to wish you a safe journey home, Eliza," Loridel said.

The human looked to their faces wishing she could read their expressions or hear their conversation.

"Goodbye, and thank you for the gift. I am most grateful and I will never forget your kindness," she said, to which many of the Gwragged Annwn seemed pleased, in their own strange way of course.

"You see? They like you. They were just worried, and rightly so. Your perception of our rejection was merely that. Perception. We are not all the same in this world, Eliza," Loridel said.

As she bade them goodbye, the golden seahorse appeared again, sniffing about her as it swam circles around her.

"Hop on," Loridel said, guiding her onto the creature and placing her hands around its elongated neck. "Better reserve your energy for the rest of your journey." The seahorse zipped along behind Loridel, who led them away from the underwater city. They swam through a deep hollow and came out in an even more ghostly area of the waters. There wasn't a fish in sight, but down below them, at the seat of the lake, Eliza could see a circular stone monument in which the waters within held a certain light and reflection about them. Around the monument, Eliza saw a couple of mermaids swimming about. She became worried recalling the spite of the mermaids she and her friends had encountered at Mermaid's Lair, and Loridel could sense her fear.

"They are unlike other mermaids you might have met, dear Eliza. Rest your heart," she said and continued swimming on.

They swam down to get a closer look, and Eliza found that once there, more mermaids appeared from all about and joined them. From the bottom of the lake, their collective silvery-scaled tails descending towards the water monument was a most beautiful sight to behold. As the congregation grew, their faint song became more prominent.

The song filled up the waters, echoing and consuming Eliza and Loridel. It was mellow and haunting, but above all else, it was sad. For all its melancholy, though, all they wanted to do was sit and listen to it. Eliza swore that she could almost feel the emotions of the mermaids swimming about her. Such breathtakingly beautiful creatures singing such a beautiful song, yet they were so sad, and Eliza wondered why.

"They lament the wrongs of our realm," Loridel explained. "But for them, there is always something to lament."

"But why?" Eliza asked.

"Isn't there always something to lament in your own world? Well, so it is here, so they lament. That is what they do," Loridel said watching the mermaids.

It was hard not to feel sad when surrounded by such despair.

"Why did you bring me here?" Eliza soon asked.

"That," said Loridel pointing to the bare ground, but all Eliza could see were swaying shrubs and flora.

Loridel pulled her hand and dipped it into the reflective waters of the monument. At the bottom, Eliza could feel smooth stones against her palm. She grabbed a small handful and pulled her hand out. Captivating teardrop-shaped crystal stones lay in her small hand. For a moment, Eliza felt the tiny stones drawing her in, much in the way she had felt just before picking the Gift of Annwn.

"They have a way of affecting beings," Loridel said in response to the longing in Eliza's eyes.

Eliza looked to her and back at the stones. "Where did

they...?" she was about to ask when Loridel turned to look at a mermaid sitting by them.

Eliza followed Loridel's gaze and saw a tiny tear roll off her cheek and solidify as it wobbled in the water before settling to the lake's floor.

"The tears of these mermaids are very powerful. It should be no surprise anyone would ask them as a price, but he who knows the worth of sorrow held within a single teardrop would know that even one tear is one too many," Loridel said in a sombre tone.

Just then, a loud blast shook them from their reverie, followed by a vast reflection of light from somewhere beyond and strong ripples that reverberated throughout the lake's strong waters.

"Stay here," Loridel warned, as she swam back through the hollow with great speed Eliza had not seen before. In no time, she reappeared, a sense of urgency about her and worrying concern etched on her youthful face.

Beckoning the seahorse, she hurried Eliza onto it.

"Someone is trying to break through the veil of our waters, no doubt using dark magic," Loridel said.

A sense of panic beset Eliza, and regret too for bringing trouble to the doors of those who had helped her, just like Loridel's sister Ipsy had warned.

In her signature demeanour of calm, Loridel shushed Eliza's apologies. "Our waters are strong. We are protected. We do not fear for ourselves, Eliza, we fear for you. We must go," she said.

At this, she took the three teardrops from Eliza's hand and placed them safely in the pouch slung across Eliza's shoulder.

They sped through the waters at an alarming rate, giving Eliza a bad case of vertigo, though the seahorse looked like he was enjoying it, playfully bouncing about like he was racing Loridel. They swam a different way from the one they came, to a different region of the lake and up through a small hole which could only fit one at a time.

They emerged in another underwater cave, smaller than the one where Eliza had woken up. At the top of it, the surface was small and circular, bordered by some rough, stones of different shapes and sizes that looked like they had formed an imperfect circle around the waters only by chance. When Eliza stepped out of the waters, she rubbed the seahorse's head gently and said thank you. She was certain he nodded back at her before swimming off. When Loridel lifted herself out of the water, its depth suddenly appeared shallow, and soon the entrance to the city below seemed nothing more than a large puddle of mud and water mixing about in the tiny alcove. Loridel reached behind a rock and pulled out Eliza's boots. It was then that Eliza realised her webbed feet had already quietly changed back to their natural shape.

"Come, we are a long way from the perpetrators still. I will show the way up to the mountain, dear friend," Loridel said to Eliza, touching her face tenderly. In the short time she had nurtured Eliza, Loridel had become fond of the human girl, finding what she was certain to be a lifelong friend. This she hadn't said to Eliza, but even Eliza was aware of this new bond. In so short a time, Loridel had built her up, teaching her to put away, even if temporarily, the uncertainties and self-doubt so courage and resilience could move in. It was this fortitude that Eliza would need to take her through to her journey's end, all by herself.

Chapter 13

PRISON

Deep underneath the Lordly Mountains of Eversong, a cheerful whistle echoed through the corridors of its dismal, cold prison against the rhythmic sound of heavy footsteps. Dim light from the glowing stones set atop wall sconces cast intimate shadows along the walkway. A subtle fragrance drifted through the air as the footsteps and whistle grew louder. When the bulging-bellied, patched-eye gnome reached the last cell in that corridor, he continued whistling as he opened a small section of the bars and slipped a small basket of ripe popidops through.

"Thank you," Arden muttered with a doleful face, hastily grabbing the basket as the guard's whistle faded up the hallway. He lifted it up towards Gwen. "You should eat something."

Absentmindedly, she dangled upside-down from a swing she'd made of lianas in the corner.

"Gwen," Arden said in a firm voice.

She stopped swinging and looked at him. "What?!" she snapped.

"You need to eat something," he moaned musically in frustration.

"Why?" she flipped herself off her home-grown

hammock in petulance, ran a rough hand past her fringe, and through her blond-white bob that had grown long and untidy.

Still seated against the wall, Arden fixed her with a stare.

She looked away feeling slightly embarrassed and regretted casting her irritation against him. She knew he was only being kind.

"Arden," she sighed, "what does it matter if I eat or not?"

"Because you can't give up."

She paused with wide eyes. "I don't... exactly call this giving up. Don't you see? Matey, we're done for," she said matter-of-factly.

"Is this how you honour the memory of our friends?" Arden asked rhetorically.

"Arden...." she shook her head wishing he knew how much she wanted to avenge Eliza's death. "Arden, I loved Eliza. I still do and more than anything, I want... I wish I could make this right. I can't bring her back. I can't... bring her back," she whispered as if in a deep trance. She had cried all she needed to cry, and was just about coping. Just about. "I want to make them suffer for it and I want to give my friend what she wanted. I want to make her family safe again, and my dad safe again. I've lost my mum and my best friend. We've lost Arrae! I don't want to lose anyone else, I don't have much else to lose...but you know we don't stand a chance of a fair trial. You saw the rubbish the Council listened to from that red-haired skank," Gwen ranted.

Arden looked away. How could he argue with her? Then he grew angry at her apathy and shot back fiercely, "We have to try to get them to focus on Sorcha and what she's hiding, and if that doesn't work, Gwen, we *have* to believe help will come." He had said it with confidence, trying to encourage Gwen, trying to make her believe, but also trying to convince himself. Arden knew Gwen was right, but he couldn't admit it because it would mean that he failed Eliza, Arrae, and so many innocent humans who had gotten caught up in the madness. His own heart ached from the losses. His beloved cousin who was more like a brother, who always stood by his side and he ached for Eliza, the human girl he had risked everything for. He closed his eyes and tried to picture her smooth brown face and her gorgeously long, but unruly and thick, curls. He longed to see her blush again, the girl of opposites—feisty yet uncertain, strong-spirited yet shy.

Gwen observed his quiet, his pain. She grabbed up the basket of popidops and planted herself next to him against the wall.

She tossed one of the ripe red berries in her mouth and placed the basket on Arden's lap.

"So, why do you care so much about Eliza anyway?" He looked away, remaining silent, so she continued. "You never told us why you've been helping us." Gwen nudged the basket of fruit against him in encouragement.

He obliged and popped a handful of berries in his mouth.

"Firstly, I care about you too," he said with a full mouth. "I could tell you were speaking the truth about all that has happened in your realm. I did what was right. Isn't that reason enough to support you and Eli?"

"Yes, yes. That's admirable," Gwen nodded, "but what you did was more. Arden... you disobeyed your mother, broke the law, and risked your life and that of your relatives to help us. I'm sure there's more to it," she said.

He dipped into the basket of fruit again before passing it back to Gwen. He took a long pause, and nervously tugged at the blond plait flowing over his shoulder.

"I..." he paused with a shaky voice.

Gwen could feel his nervousness. "Hey, no pressure, take your time. I mean, we've lots of it right?" she smiled.

He turned his face to Gwen and she looked up from the basket to meet his piercing grey eyes. "I love Eliza. I've loved her even before I met her," he said, and his breathing grew heavy and loud.

Gwen looked away, trying to keep a neutral face. That was not what she expected to hear. She had suspected there was some kind of attraction, but not love. At the same time, she wasn't sure of what she'd expected Arden to give as his reason for helping them.

"I know how it sounds, but you're half-fae. Think about it. I met Eliza in one of my dreams. The first time I saw her, I knew I loved her," he said, picturing their first meeting. "In that dream, I saw something in her. I felt it too. The pull was so strong I didn't want to wake up, and I used any chance I had to sleep hoping to see her again and figure out what the vision meant."

Gwen was starting to understand. From firsthand experience, she knew faeries sometimes had prophetic dreams about the people who would appear in their futures. After all, she too had dreamt Eliza in her future. She gave Arden a sympathetic smile and passed the basket of remaining popidops to him.

"Of course no one would understand. She's human, but I told one of my elders in confidence, and, surprisingly, he told me to follow my heart but be wise. He knows your innocence, Gwen. You see, Eliza and Arrae's deaths won't be in vain. Word will travel. Someone will come. Someone has to," he said assuredly, and Gwen found that, although reluctantly, a small part of her believed him.

"Arden," she said with urgency breaking the brief silence between them, "what else did you see in your visions of Eliza? What if we've had help all along?"

Arden stared at her curiously, wondering where all this was leading.

"Back in the human realm, Eliza told me about a recurring dream she was having that I think might have been a vision. It's crazy, I know, but she said she comes from a family of dreamers. They usually see things and have to interpret them, but Eli saw the future clear as day. She had a premonition of the beast in the lake. She saw two friends on land watching her as she picked the Gift of Annwn. She saw the darkness following her. It was obviously a warning, but even though she tried to avoid reality unfolding that way, it did. What if the dreams have been sent to guide us? So we could prepare? I don't know what Eli saw in the waters of Mirror Lake, but whatever it was, I'd bet it means something."

"Gwen...I don't understand," Arden said, confusion written all over his face.

Gwen knew he wouldn't get it until she finished explaining, so she nodded and kept on at it. "Well, when I dreamt of Eliza, I knew she'd be my best friend. I knew we would be here in Annwn together. That's all happened already, but there was something else, something I couldn't tell her about. I saw her cutting through a swirl of darkness. It's confusing. Tell me what you saw in your vision of Eliza," she urged him on again.

Arden obliged. He closed his eyes and concentrated. As he related the story to Gwen, vivid images of his dream emerged in his mind. Eliza's face was there again. They were holding hands amid a rain of floating bubbles near Mermaid's Lair. Her smile pulled him in, and then the vision blurred. He was now shielding her from something strong and sharp. When it passed, their eyes locked and their faces were drawn together.

A sharp, sardonic voice cut through Arden's retelling of his vision. "Both far more ignominious than I'd imagined," Sorcha snickered from outside the bars.

Arden and Gwen sprung to their feet in a rage. In a flash, Arden rushed to the bars to grab at her throat, but she stepped back and smoothly bared her teeth in an evil grin. His weapons had been seized, but what Gwen had couldn't be taken from her. Instinctively and with unprecedented speed fuelled by her rage, she sent two ropes of lianas flying through the thick metal bars and around Sorcha's neck. Firmly, they rung around like two snakes tightening around their victim before a kill. Sorcha lifted her neck and stared at Gwen all gimlet-eyed.

"Let-me-go," she managed to utter, unable to fight back, since all her weapons had been taken prior to entering the holding area.

Gwen didn't even flinch.

"Ha," Sorcha uttered, tugging at the lianas with her hands to lessen the pressure against her neck. "Don't tell me you're still mourning over the human. It's just flesh. I can find you another one to play with." She grinned.

Gwen gritted her teeth, tightened her hold, and pulled her arms forward, trying to crash Sorcha into the metal bars. Sorcha barely had time to lift her hands to conjure a wind force to prevent herself from slamming in. She pelted the wind towards Gwen, who planted her feet firmly, determined not to move despite the force hitting her body.

"This way. I believe they have another visitor who should be leaving about now," a heavy voice echoed from around the nearby corner.

In surprise, Sorcha dropped the wind force, and Arden urged Gwen more than once to drop her lianas as well in caution. Soon, the stocky gnome reappeared with one of the council members in suit.

Emryees was clearly surprised to see Sorcha visiting the prisoners, and didn't pretend to hide it. As he approached, Gwen could feel a slight chill in the air.

"Why, what business do you have down here, my Lady?" he asked.

"Oh," Sorcha uttered innocently, folding her palms demurely in a return to her pretensive behaviour, "I just wanted to be sure that the prisoners are well secure. I know what they're capable of."

"And what's that?" Emryees asked, raising a brow in curiosity.

"*Oh.* Were you not there when I presented my case some days ago, your eminence?" Sorcha asked rhetorically.

Emryees stared at her intently. "My lady, I assure you the prisoners are secure, and if I'm not mistaken, I believe your visiting time has passed." He tilted his head.

"Yes, my Lord." She bowed in feigned obeisance and walked out without even casting an eye on the two prisoners again.

Gwen scrutinised Emryees impolitely. His white tunic almost glowed against his pale, icy skin.

He turned to them and nodded in greeting. "I am Emryees. I sit on the High Council. If I recall well, it is Gwen and Arden?"

Gwen stared at him wide-eyed and felt a bit irritated when Arden answered.

"Yes, my Lord."

"What do you want?" she butted in.

Emryees smiled. "Your help."

She narrowed her eyes at him and so did Arden.

"With *what*?" Arden chimed in.

Emryees reached into the right pocket of his tunic and pulled out a ripped piece of lush fabric dotted with some faint red stains. He extended it through the metal bars.

"What's that?" Arden asked.

"I'm hoping either of you might be able to tell me," he answered.

Gwen approached, never taking her eyes off his.

Taking the cream-coloured fabric from his hand, she brought it close to her face inspecting it carefully before closing her eyes and breathing in its scent.

"Where did you get this?" She eyed him suspiciously.

"What is it?" he asked eagerly, leaning in closer.

Gwen raised her brows at him. "First tell me where you got it."

"Okay I'll tell you, if you at least tell me what is on it?" he asked again, a sense of urgency in his tone.

"It's blood. Human blood," Gwen said, handing the fabric back through the bar.

Emryees seemed most bewildered as he stared the piece of fabric in his hands. He then looked down the empty corridor.

"Now you tell me where you got this," she asserted quietly.

He looked up at her reluctantly and hesitated.

"Well?" Gwen said emphatically as Arden listened attentively.

He waved his hand.

"Thank you. I promise I'll be back soon to explain everything," he muttered before walking off briskly.

"Hey!" Gwen shouted leaning against the bars.

"I need to check something first. I'll be back," he shouted, already at the end of the corridor, about to disappear around a bend.

Gwen's shoulders slouched as she looked to Arden curiously.

"What do you think it means?" he asked.

"I wish I knew," she whispered.

Emryees bolted through the winding passages in the underground prison. As he ran past the stocky gnome, it growled as the Ice Faery stirred up a chilly gust. He emerged at the entrance to the prison and into the round courtyard. His eyes trailed along the winding staircase running upwards along the grand structure encircling the courtyard, and carved into the colossal mountains. He lithely ran up the stairs and then hesitated and turned back.

"Ta chumah," he shouted, and one of the many huge, long-beaked birds in the courtyard swept up and landed for him to get on. It shook its feathers in a chill as he climbed on, and he patted it gently. He whispered his destination and the bird sprung up off the ground, straight to the very top floor of the Lordly Courts.

When Emryees arrived and hopped off the bird, he noticed the lean figure he was looking for, tilting over a circular banister just some feet away. He couldn't have missed her if he tried. Not with that head of wild, fiery red hair.

He approached with caution and cleared his throat nervously to get her attention. "I've been looking for you. Thought I'd find you up here. Alone."

She spun around swiftly with a less than amused look on her face.

"Emryees," she whispered.

"Urhouri," he responded with a childish smile that he couldn't help. "I was beginning to think you were avoiding me."

The Salamander furrowed her brows and wrapped her arms around her pale yellowish skin in a light shiver. "How can I say this...mildly?" she smiled cheekily. "You know you put out my fire," she said, eyeing his icy skin.

He chuckled. Urhouri had a flaming sense of humour, he thought.

Being a Salamander, which is the proper name for a fire faery, it would be natural for one to assume that Urhouri couldn't mix with Emryees, an ice faery, without much discomfort, but both were quite able to interact and live amongst other beings without affecting them greatly with their fiery and icy natures. Urhouri's rhetoric was not literal at all, but Emryees knew this, having heard it every odd moon or so.

"Whatever it is, the answer is no. *As usual,*" she said seriously, yet her voice bore a light heartedness.

He chuckled again. "It's not that. Not this time, my sweet."

She looked at him in surprise, finding it unbelievable and also attempting to hide the fact that she was flattered by his latest name for her.

"What then do you seek, Mr Ice?"

His banter and demeanour took on a serious tone that Urhouri noticed right away as Emryees slowly pulled the torn piece of blood-stained fabric from his pocket.

"What is this?" she enquired.

"It's human blood. There," he pointed to the dots on the fabric.

"*Human* blood?"

"Yes."

"Where did you find it?"

Emryees paused, and Urhouri sensed there was some complication or ugliness in the answer.

"It's from Lady Sorcha's dress," he said, swallowing a gulp.

Urhouri looked him directly in the eyes and then at the fabric again, before he began explaining how he came about the odd item.

It was an unusual find. A piece of fabric tainted with human blood, torn from the dress of a main witness in the upcoming human trials slated for the coming days. Whatever it meant, it was new evidence for the investigation that was going on prior to the trial.

"So take it to the guards. It must be lodged as evidence," Urhouri said, trying to let the little voice of reason in her head overpower the voice of suspicion.

"Urhouri," Emryees complained, "You know I can't do that."

She folded her arms but didn't argue, because she already knew why he couldn't.

The investigation had been ongoing, and the witnesses and accused had been questioned individually, while official court enquirers had been sent to gather any evidence they could find on the ground. There was a growing mass of witnesses who had claimed to have seen the accused wandering through the realm, killing anyone who challenged them. They would all appear at the trial, which had been causing a commotion in the lands. Anti-humanists groups were stirring in the lead up to the trial and trouble was to be expected.

Still, beside the wilted, dead Gift of Annwn, and a map that were seized from the two accused, there was little solid evidence from either side. All they had were the accusations. Accusations of who stole The Key and why, but there were no dead bodies to prove the accused stole The Key, murdered anyone, or plotted against the realm. At most, Arden could be implicated for aiding a human. Gwen's case was a bit more complicated given that she was part human, and therefore application of the law seemed, well, irrelevant. but something more was obviously going on. Somehow, the high court's enquirers had so far been unable to find anything, including the bodies of those who had been reportedly murdered at Mirror Lake, and the human accused of doing the dirty deed.

Something was amiss, but at these times, with rumour after rumour, Emryees remained uncertain of whom to trust. His friend Hiatar the centaur had been snooping around as well, but unsuccessfully. They were just two and needed help, so he was taking a chance on Urhouri, the Salamander with whom he shared something deep, but unacknowledged.

"What can I do?" she asked dubiously.

"I need to find out how there came to be human blood on Lady Sorcha's clothing, but there's not much time," he whispered.

She looked around them nervously and leaned in. "This is interfering in the official enquiry, Emryees. There will be trouble for this," she said.

"I know," he admitted bluntly. "But we can't just keep accepting theories of what's befallen our realm because there's no better explanation, Urhouri. What if they're innocent?" he pleaded.

"We might not ever know," she said.

"We can try," he answered, looking into her amber-ringed eyes to beg, but getting caught up in his emotions and gazing at her longingly instead.

She turned away swiftly, her fiery skin growing just a bit warmer, and leaned back over the banister, staring out at the picturesque lands that seemed to go on forever. From the tower of the Lordly Court, everything looked so peaceful. The verdant mountains surrounding them eventually evened out into flat lands as far as the eye could see. In the far distance was The Sacred Valley, and faintly visible behind that, the Great Mountains of the Never-Ending East stood like miniature peaks touching the neon pink skyline.

"You can travel much faster than I can, Urhouri. This is for our people. Someone must take the risk. If not us, then who?" he asked.

She turned her head and sighed.

"Very well, Icy," she said, taking the fabric from his hands. As her hands lightly touched his, he felt his icy insides tingle, and an urge swelled. He grabbed her hand in his.

"Emryees!" she said, nervously looking around. "Let go."

He looked down at her hand in his, a sudden lugubriousness wiping across his formerly calm visage. "Urhouri...." He suddenly sounded desperate and his lips quivered.

She shook her head in a frantic panic, but didn't let go. "Don't. We've been through this. I thought we had an understanding?"

He looked down, writhing in an emotional pain that had gripped him for too long, threatening to tear him apart.

"Why...?"

"You know why."

"We don't have to give in."

"Yes, we do, or we don't and then we get excluded. From our own," she looked away as hot, brimming tears filled her eyes. Roughly, she pulled away her hand with the fabric in it. "You know why. You are an Ice Faery, and I am a Salamander. We do *not* mix. Ever. It is not allowed. For certain, we will be kicked out, humiliated, and *punished*, no different from how those *pitiful* prisoners are being treated for associating with a human," she said as the tearfulness in her voice edged around her words. "There is no *we*, Emryees," her voice suddenly became sympathetic. "Look for one of your own."

He couldn't look her in the eyes as she repeated the familiar retort that stung his ears. He didn't want to hear it. He hated it, and he hated the damned rules. The formal ones, and the unspoken ones. He hated them all, damn it.

"Urhouri," he wanted to say something more to her, but she had already transformed into a ball of blazing fire and lifted off into the air.

Chapter 14

MISTY BRIDGE

From midway up Mirror Lake Mountain, Annwn looked anything but precarious. The lands were lush, spotted by large dots of bright blooming trees and flowers. It felt different too. The air was crisp with a hint of what could have been lemongrass, and the minuscule faery flies flitting about made it seem magically wonderful. It was easy to get caught up in the wonders of such beauty, but Eliza didn't have time for that. She had stopped briefly just to look down at the cave she'd emerged from, to see if she could still make out Loridel's figure watching her, but she was too far up now. Everything below seemed so far away, and the idea of sinister enemies behind her, trying to break through the veil of Mirror Lake was far from encouraging.

Loridel had said that few would try something as stupid as attempting to break the lake's veil—its strength and impenetrability were known throughout the lands. This was a sign of desperation. Whoever it was, Loridel had reasoned, was so desperate to get through the lake that they were resorting to forbidden dark magic. Their motive? It must have been to recover The Key and now that Eliza was making her way up the mountains with that very item in her pouch, the thought sent a shrill coldness through her. She needed to move quickly.

The climb had started out fairly easy, but now halfway, she floundered, stymied by exhaustion and gripping the mountain wall for support. It was difficult to ignore the reality of her aloneness. Besides the singing winds, there was quiet. No Gwen, no Arden, no Arrae. No Loridel.

Loridel.

The water faery had told her to keep her eye on the goal, and to remember her motivation when she faced these moments of aloneness. *Believe in yourself, Annwn believed in you,* Loridel had told her. *Trust in the love you have for your kin* and Loridel was right. They were the reason why Eliza was facing the challenge alone. It sounded easy enough, but for Eliza, the sensation was heightened by her surroundings.

From up in the mountains, the world around her seemed so big and she felt so small. Small and alone. To her ears, the singing winds had formed a gigantic clock that was ticking away sluggishly. She could count the seconds as they wore on painfully slowly. Believe, believe, believe.... Arrghhh, damn it!

No matter how much she spoke sweet words of encouragement to her inner self, a tiny part of her couldn't help but wonder why she, of all people in the land, would be given a gift so special. If she was so special, why hadn't anyone else noticed? Back home, she was considered the opposite of special. At best, she was an anomaly... an aberration to more people than just the purists.

The slower her pace up the mountain, the faster her thoughts raced, and soon her mind wandered to her friends again. Would she ever see them again? Her beloved Gwen, and beautiful Arden—he had risked so much to help them, though she wasn't entirely sure why. Then there was poor Arrae, lost somewhere in the magic veil of Mirror Lake. This whole thing might have been easier if she'd only known how to channel the powers she got from that flower. She paused and stared at her hand, her soiled, fragile, human hand. The hand of a girl unaccepted. Maybe Annwn had made a mistake, her mind wandered away again.

When she finally reached the top, she was completely out of breath. Her lungs felt restricted and she dropped herself flat on the ground in weariness. Laying on her back, she gazed into the neon pink sky and could almost glimpse little twinklings somewhere up there. It looked so much closer now, yet still too far to touch. Somewhere across from her was a movement, and she quickly got up remembering the need for caution.

The mountaintop was hazy, and as she headed toward where she hoped to find the Misty Bridge, she understood the given name. Quite fitting, she thought, because Misty Bridge was just that—so completely enveloped by thick blankets of mist that she couldn't even see the bridge itself. If she gazed hard enough in the distance, she could get a quick view of a bit of the wooden handrails before they disappeared into the mists again.

As she ventured gingerly towards the start of the bridge, a hooded figure stepped out of the mists, its hands outstretched towards Eliza.

The hands looked delicate and youthful, and were stained by incredibly elaborate designs of red ink that stretched down each finger. Still, the being's hands were nowhere as captivating as her face when Eliza finally saw it. Under the hood, the bridgekeeper's natural beauty was further enhanced by ornate jewels embossed in her skin. A line of shiny gems bordered her forehead from one temple to another. Fine-coloured studs lined the exterior of the bridgekeeper's eyebrows, and on the outer area of her eyes, they formed coils. Her long, slender nose was pierced by a diamond hoop whose chain disappeared behind the thick hood of her cloak.

Eliza thought the heavy jewellery seemed almost a

fitting tribute to something so strikingly beautiful. She wasn't aware that she was gawking with her mouth open until the bridgekeeper extended a hand, palm up, and waited in silence. She was confused in that minute, until she snapped out of her little daze and fumbled through her pouch for the teardrop stones from the bottom of Mirror Lake.

The bridgekeeper wrapped her long fingers around the gems tightly, before walking towards the bridge and Eliza couldn't help but notice the ease with which she walked. Almost as if, she wasn't walking at all.

"Wait! I can't see the bridge, how will I cross?" she ran behind the figure a bit shaken at the idea of not seeing anything past the mist.

"Follow the light," were the bridgekeeper's only words, uttered in a deep, feminine whisper.

Just before they stepped onto the bridge, a strong wind blew past them, and the ends of the bridgekeeper's dragging cloak ruffled lightly, revealing the tip of what appeared to be an amphibious tail.

A bout of fright hit Eliza, and she stopped abruptly in terror looking on. The keeper stopped at the start of the bridge and turned back to stare at Eliza as if telling her to catch up. Without uttering a word, Eliza ignored the tightening feeling in her chest and carefully approached the start of the bridge just behind the mysterious keeper, who belonged to the race of nagas.

As the bridgekeeper stepped onto Misty Bridge, Eliza noticed a bright light emanating from just below her cloak, no doubt at the end of the keeper's tail. With this in sight, Eliza too stepped cautiously onto Misty Bridge amid the thick haze. As she did this, the fog thickened and all around them turned dark, like someone had flicked a great light switch off. She could see nothing at all, except for this little ball of a light rolling on the floor of the bridge before her. Her heart was thumping so fast and so hard, she was afraid it would beat right out of her fragile chest. Misty Bridge seemed sturdy enough, but when the wind blew too hard, Eliza could feel a slight swaying movement and she gripped the wooden handrails so tightly she thought the wood might snap from the force. Though the mountains were far from each other, the way across was shorter than she'd imagined. She was quite relieved, to say the least, when she saw the other side of the bridge. It was windier over there and the air smelled somewhat older, if that's possible. As the bridgekeeper stepped off ahead of her, and the fog slowly started to lift, Eliza caught a most terrifying glimpse that could have sent her fainting. The naga had an immensely thick tail that was coiled up neatly like a cinnamon bun, well, not half as neatly. Instead of fainting though, as she stepped back onto solid ground in the slowly lifting fog, she spun back to see what she could of the bridge she'd just crossed.

Behind and below the bridge, where the blackness still was, mysterious glowing eyes peered at her hungrily. Terror struck her, yet again, and she stumbled back against the mountain wall and watched as the darkness lifted and light returned, leaving only the grey, cloudy mountain mists. Still, she couldn't see the bridge and then, the bridgekeeper was gone. Nowhere in sight, like she had just taken the fast train back to the other side. Eliza felt an intense shiver that definitely did not come from the chilly air around her.

She walked along the mountain until she came to the entryway of the well-known Mountains of the Never-Ending East. There was sign posted on the wall beside the large, rounded opening. On the first sign was a picture of Arden and Gwen with the word 'WANTED' in big, bold letters. The rest of the words were in a language she didn't understand, but she was sure it must have been saying something to the effect of 'human and half-faery also wanted in connection with stealing The Key.' Her jaw tightened as she clenched her teeth.

Next to the poster, carved into the mountain walls was more of the language she didn't understand with an arrow pointing left.

Great. Directions that she couldn't read.

As she stared hard at the oddly shaped signs, she found herself stepping back in surprise as they began moving around magically, until they eventually formed letters that she could read.

'TO GET TO THE OTHER SIDE' was the first heading, and below it, directions said that those interested in making it to the other side of the mountain should stay on the straight path regardless of what they see or hear. She creased her brow, wondering what on earth one could possibly 'see or hear' in there. Below it, the other heading read 'TO GET TO NEVER-ERY' and the directions said that anyone interested in getting to this place, whatever it was, should take any path *but* the straight.

Fine, simple enough, she thought to herself. How hard could it possibly be to stay on a straight path? Eliza ventured past the entryway and after lifting a light off the wall scone, she trotted on through the opening and into mountain.

An earthy smell permeated the inside of the mountain, and shadows danced across the walls from the dim light of the handful of wall sconces along the wide hallway Eliza walked down. The 'straight' passageway wasn't exactly straight—it twisted and turned countless corners, snaking through the mountain, but it was easy enough to follow. Many, many other passageways looking exactly the same with dim lights, and nothing that could be used as landmarks, sprouted from the main hall.

Eliza found it most unwelcoming and as she wore on

through the mountain she began listening intently to her own footsteps.

One, two, three... she started counting every step as she paced carefully. It was all she could hear in this vast mountain with so many spacious corridors.

The quietness was too loud.

Then she focused on her breathing, which grew heavier and heavier. These mountains were supposed to be safe, yet her eyes continually scanned the path far ahead of her, in anticipation of something that might pop out and scream a dreadful surprise.

When she could bare neither the silence nor the anxiety anymore, she started humming the up-tempo melody of *Twist and Shout*. Her grandfather had played the tune so much on his record player that it had been etched in her mind forever. Humming took her back to their living room, where her grandfather had so many times lifted her off her feet in an impromptu outbreak of dance, much to her grandmother's dismay for fear they'd break a vase or something valuable. She knew her grandmother secretly loved it when they did that.

Reminiscing on it lightened her mood, and she started singing the familiar melody.

Well, shake it up baby now,
Twist and shout
C'mon, c'mon, c'mon, c'mon baby now
Come on and work it all out

She'd hardly sung the first word of the second verse when a sudden noise cut her off. She thought she'd heard an echo. Except it was not her voice. She stopped walking and looked around suspiciously. After listening to the silence intently for a moment, she started singing again, this time in softer and far slower.

An unfamiliar voice somewhere beyond her repeated a

single line of the song. She spun around swiftly in a full circle, looking for any signs of another, but there was none. Then, she heard more voices singing the full verse and chorus she'd just sung during her happy transportation back to her family living room. She pressed herself against the mountain wall in a panic. After a few long seconds, the singing stopped and one of the voices called out, "We mean not to frighten you, fair one."

Another continued, "Only to keep your good company in this lonesome place."

"So where doth the fair one head to?" another asked.

Slowly, Eliza moved away from the wall and started walking briskly along the straight path, ignoring the voices. The onslaught of questions and meaningless banter continued, until she shouted back.

"Don't talk to me!" in a right fit of rage.

Her little outburst did well to shush the voices altogether. She stopped and looked around, feeling satisfied with herself, before resuming her brisk walk, but the voices started back again after some minutes, and she became annoyed. Nonetheless, she decided on a different strategy, which was to ignore them entirely. She slowed down her pace and casually strolled through the tunnel as if she were most comfortable and unperturbed. Sure enough, the voices became softer and softer until she could hear them no more. She smiled.

Too soon after, something else made her concerned. She could hear footsteps, coming from behind her. They were not very loud at all, but in mountain passages so quiet the slightest movements were easy to hear. She picked up pace as quietly as she could and soon realised the footsteps did same.

Someone was following her.

A panic rushed through her body, and she began to run through the winding passages. As she ran and the footsteps sounded closer and closer, the voices began talking to her once more. This time, encouraging her to take the approaching corridor on the left to escape her follower. Mentally, Eliza rejected the idea, intent on following the mountain directions, but as the footsteps behind grew louder and appeared closer, and the voices whispered to her assuring her safety if she hid, she gave in and ducked into the corridor on the left, off the straight path. She tiptoed alongside the walls of the side corridor and stooped between lights in an area of darkness. She waited, and then, realised the footsteps had stopped. Whoever it was had clearly been thrown off, but she waited some more, just to be safe.

"S'not too uncomfortable in 'ere, is it?" one of the voices whispered to her. It sounded like it was coming from the wall opposite her.

She crawled over and pressed her ear against it.

"The fair one should stay here with us, just for her safety," another added.

The voices were coming from the walls.

"I will, just until that person is gone," she whispered back, grateful for their help.

' No, no, no... the fair one will never be safe out there!" disagreed one of the voices. "Fair one must stay with us... forever."

"What?" Eliza asked in shock.

"Fair one is safe as long as she lives here with us," responded one of the voices.

Eliza's forehead furrowed in disbelief. She was quiet for a few long seconds, thinking. Had she been duped? She listened intently. No footsteps or sound of anyone else in the passages. She let out a long, heavy sigh. Okay. She'd been duped. She edged to the end of the corridor leading back out to the straight path and peaked out. The way was clear, the only problem was, this was *not* the straight path. Where had it disappeared to? In sheer disbelief, Eliza ran out onto the corridor and sprinted along its winding path on and on and on, and then when she still hadn't found the straight path, she took another corridor and continued searching desperately, but couldn't find the way she came. Every winding path led to another and another, but the main passageway was nowhere to be found.

She was stuck in Never-ery. Great.

"S'not so bad in e're fair one! We'll keep your company!" one of the walls jovially said.

Eliza didn't answer. She was upset with the voices that had tricked her, but more over her stupidity. All she had to do was follow the instructions. The simple instructions outside the mountain, but no. Now she was stuck in a place that she didn't know how to leave.

She tightened her grip around the light and resumed walking through the meandering passages. She walked until her feet ached and until she was tired of seeing the same scenery every time she turned another corner or stepped down another passage. She knew she was going nowhere fast, but she kept walking and walking and walking.

Hours had passed, but Eliza never stopped. When she began staggering, she sipped water from the bottle in her pouch, but it didn't rejuvenate her. Her knees were buckling, and before she knew it, she'd collapsed from sheer exhaustion.

When she woke up, Eliza was uncertain of how long she had been out. Hours? It could have even been a day, but when she awoke the despondency finally set down on her, like a heavy weight that she couldn't lift off. She sat herself up against the wall and propped her chin onto her knees watching the bare wall in front of her. They began talking again, about all sorts of things like famous beings that had passed through their passages, and they asked many questions of Eliza but when she didn't answer, they pretended that she had and answered back with their chatter. They were right flibbertigibbets.

While she sat, Eliza noticed a lump of something on the bare ground some footsteps from where she was sitting. If not for the emptiness of the tunnels and the absence of anything, she might have missed it. She crawled over lazily to inspect it. As she moved her light in closer, she threw herself back in a scare, dropping the light when she made out the skeleton and lump of dirty belongings.

She suddenly felt her lower jaw trembling uncontrollably and her eyes started spilling out unceasing tears that appeared without warning. She skirted around the skeleton and wept until her insides felt so drained she found that she had no more tears left. The voices of the walls faded into the background as she wallowed in sadness. She would probably die in these passages like that traveller, whoever he was. Whether he was faery or human, he must have had a family to go home to, just like she did.

She pressed her face against the ground and closed her eyes tightly wishing it could all go away, and she could somehow be back in her house near the lush mountains on the sunny island. Her grandmother in the kitchen cooking tasty delights and her grandfather happily complaining about and fixing odd things that didn't work in the house anymore. He was good at that—fixing broken things. As she lay there thinking of the lovely safety net her grandparents had fitted around her all her life, her memory threw her a past arbitrary moment whose significance she wasn't even sure of. Her grandmother was reading to her as she dozed off... "...suffering produces perseverance, perseverance, character, and hope."

Hope.

She was still alive, so there was hope. There must be.

She quickly wiped her tears away, and pushed herself off the ground, determined not to give up until she found her way out. If she never escaped the mountain, at least she would die trying.

As she set off with stronger resolve, it wasn't long

before she could hear footsteps again. Blasted walls, she'd not fall for it again, but as she walked on, she couldn't help but get that little, odd feeling that these were real footsteps. She knew better than to ignore her instincts. To be sure and safe, she pulled out the magic knife that Loridel and the Gwragged Annwn had given her, but it wouldn't flick open. She continued trying to snap it open, but it wouldn't. While standing there, she saw an approaching shadow coming from a passage connecting to hers. Quietly, she tiptoed the other way. She had to do something, so she doubled back on her location to sneak up on the being. Holding onto the wall and tiptoeing quickly, she'd soon snuck up on the individual who was draped in a dark cloak with a hood. Obviously, it was someone who didn't want to be seen, just like her. As the being stopped and tilted its head, sensing her presence, Eliza gave the knife one final flick, but it still didn't budge. She'd call a bluff. She had no other choice really.

"Do *not* move or I will hurt you," she said in the fiercest voice she could conjure up.

The walls broke into a sudden bout of laughter at her bluff, startling her and causing her to drop the knife. When it fell, it clinked when it hit the bare ground and the figure slowly turned around.

Cautiously, Eliza inched back as the figure stepped forward and pulled off its hood.

Chapter 15

SURPRISE

THE STRANGER LIFTED OFF ITS hood but kept its head down. In the dim lights, Eliza couldn't make out its face. And then, in very slow movements, it bent down and picked up Eliza's magical knife. Eliza was about to back up some more, but then the stranger extended the hand holding the knife.

It had picked it up for her.

Cautiously, she reached to the wall on her left and pulled a nearby light off its mount. She moved in closer to see the stranger's face. She almost dropped the light in shock. The person standing before her looked just like Gwen.

"You should arm yourself better, young one," said Niada in a full-bodied voice. Even without an introduction, Eliza was sure of it. There was no mistaking the striking resemblance. Her skin was as pale, her eyes were as blue, and the contours of her face—the high cheek bones, the upturned nose, the fine lips and hair—had Gwen written all over them. Eliza had always thought Gwen's blonde-white bob had been bleached, but clearly this was just something else she had taken from her mother. A heavy fringe hung low on Niada's forehead and the rest of her hair was pulled back and pinned by pliable preserved flowers.

It was like seeing Gwen from the future.

A series of emotions swept over Eliza—intense surprise, relief, happiness, sadness, but she struggled to make sense of it all. Ultimately, all she could come up with was,

"I wish Gwen was here to see you," in a soft whisper that cracked.

Niada smiled heartily and threw her long arms around Eliza in a warm embrace just like the ones Gwen had smothered her in. It was like hugging family, though they had never met. Eliza had many questions, but as she stood there hugging this long-limbed faery, she suddenly worried how she would tell Niada that Gwen had been taken away. She loosened on the hug and looked down searching for the words. She began to speak, but it came out like a murmur, which made no sense, but Niada had been a proper mummy to Gwen until she returned to this realm and she knew the signs of worry etched on Eliza's faced and her odd behaviour. She rested firm hands on Eliza's shoulder and encouraged her to look up.

"You must help Gwen and Arden...." she started saying when Eliza interjected.

"They're alive?!"

"Yes, very much alive, but maybe not for long," said Niada. "They are being held under guard at the Lordly Mountains of Eversong. They will face trial in a few days,"—Niada paused with a distressed look on her face—"They're bound to be found guilty for helping you steal The Key, Eliza, and for murder and treason."

"But I didn't...." Eliza started saying.

"Yes, we know you didn't steal The Key, but the Council doesn't. I'm not sure if they want to know the truth, either. Anti-human animosity in the realm is tipping over, Eliza. Many lobby groups will attend the trial. Someone must be punished for these crimes, and the Council holds the perfect prisoners," Niada said regaining her composure.

Eliza cupped her hands over her mouth in disbelief.

"What must I do?" Eliza asked suddenly.

"The one behind the mayhem is called Sorcha, a malevolent faery who embraces a dangerous, dark magic that is forbidden here. She is behind the kidnappings in your realm, though I do not know her reasons. She has been mind-controlling the dangerous phookas to carry out her work. I know where two of the human victims are. You must take them to the Council as proof of Sorcha's deeds, but you have to do it during the trial so the public can bear witness," said Niada.

"Okay...but how...?" Eliza started uttering, thinking many a thing, like how exactly she was going to rescue the two human victims and then burst into the seat of the council amongst skilled and gifted beings of the realm who could take her down before she even blinked.

"You mustn't worry over that yet. Before going there, you must exonerate yourself from the accusation of stealing The Key. This is at the heart of the trial, and an added excuse for much of the anti-human antagonism. You must return it first to The Sacred Valley as you planned before becoming entrapped here," Niada said.

She then sat Eliza down and fed her like she was a little child, hushing the many questions that Eliza wanted to ask. Niada told her they would have much time for questions once they'd left the mountains, but first, Eliza needed to rest for the journey ahead. It would be stressful and perilous, and now, there was more at stake—her friends' lives. As Eliza drifted off to sleep on Niada's lap she uttered incoherently, "How... how did you find me?"

Niada tilted her head as she stroked Eliza's thick, black curls.

"Dear child," she whispered, "not even banishment will keep me from my Gwen. I have been closer than you both know." With those words, Eliza drifted off to faraway, happy place in the first peaceful sleep she had had since entering the Mountains of the Never-Ending East.

When Eliza opened her eyes, she found Niada sorting through tiny parcels of old plants, stones, and dust. An afternoon and night had passed, but Eliza would have never known inside those passages, which stayed dark with each passing day.

"What are you doing?" she said while stretching off her sleep.

"Planning," Niada whispered with a smile, not taking her eyes off the parcels.

"For what?"

Niada looked up and bent over towards her, whispering even softer. "Our escape."

As with any place so old, with so much history, there was a story behind everything in Annwn and bearing her trademark smile like all was well and they hadn't a care in the world, Niada began to explain the difficulties they would now encounter in the mountain passages of Never-ery. Now, compared to the many other parlous places that the realm had to offer, one could argue that Never-ery wasn't that bad at all. The only downside? The walls—they loved company, as you might have noticed and they often resorted to trickery to trap beings within their dim passages. Once stuck there, few, if any beings at all, were ever able to find a way out. Often, travellers went insane in there, not that that mattered to the walls. They didn't mind insane company, as long as that company stayed.

"They will not be pleased," Niada whispered of the walls to Eliza. "But every trickster can be out tricked." She smiled and quietly relayed their plan of escape.

"Once you step off a corridor, the winding passages change. We have to find a corridor with a wall at the end or a wall between corridors, like at an intersection," she whispered. "Then we'll blow it up."

"Sounds doable," Eliza said.

"Yes, it is, but when we find the wall, we must blow it up before crossing the end of our corridor, otherwise the paths will change again."

"How do we know when a corridor ends?" asked Eliza, trying to recall if she had noticed any.

"Yes, that's the hard bit. I'm uncertain, but it seems impossible to find the end of curving corridors, so we might as well spend our time looking for one with an intersection or one which ends when the path is broken by an off-shooting passageway on either side," whispered Niada, pulling Eliza off the ground.

They strolled through the passages, not wanting to alarm the walls with any frantic searching, but as a couple hours wore on Eliza's impatience began to set in. Her right eyelid was now jumping profusely, and she began tapping her index finger against her pouch.

Niada grabbed her hand and halted their walk. "Be calm and steady, Eliza," she whispered with that infectious smile and glow in her eyes and strangely, Eliza felt a sudden calmness wash over her, reassuring her that everything was going to be ok.

"How did you do that?" she asked, looking at Niada curiously. "Did you use a spell?"

"I am a mother, I have many powers." She beamed, which made Eliza giggle, and they set off again.

Another two hours must have passed when Niada held her arm out suddenly in front of Eliza, who had started walking without paying attention, due to tiredness, or boredom perhaps. Maybe a combination of both.

They'd stumbled onto a rarity—an intersection. The path they stood on ended shortly from where they were at, forming a T-shaped junction with a wall smack in the middle.

"This is it," Niada said with what sounded like a tinge of hope and uncertainty muddled together in her voice.

She slipped a hand into her right pocket and pulled out one of those little packets, which she had filled with a careful mixture of her old plants, dust, and stone. She walked ahead of Eliza very cautiously and stopped at the very end of the corridor. Then, she threw the contents of the packet into her palm.

"Shundo uiam facio," she uttered, blowing the mixture off her palm towards the wall in their way.

She quickly ran back to where Eliza stood and covered her protectively. No sooner had she done this, there was a little rumble, and then, a huge blast that broke a hole in the wall. A stream of blinding light pelted its way through the opening, striking their eyes, which had grown used to the darkness. As Eliza shielded her face with her arm, Niada urged her out quickly. As they rushed to the hole, the walls beside them began closing in with great speed, amid a cacophony of the walls' upset voices. They'd barely made it out, and both fell outside the hole, rolling down the mountainside. It was lush, but stones and boulders made the rolling painful.

"Arrghh," Niada groaned as they came to a sudden stop where the ground levelled out briefly, before declining again.

"Are you okay?" Eliza scrambled over to her, examining the minor gash on her cheekbone.

"I'll be fine, once I apply a little..." but something just behind them drew Eliza's attention away from Niada's cut. Out of the mountains, a vast green boulder was slowly and quietly making its way out, towards them.

"Ummm..." Eliza stuttered.

Niada spun around and looked back to Eliza alarmed.

"Run!"

They took off as fast as they possibly could, but they were high up in the mountains and the descent was becoming steeper. The boulder started tumbling faster and faster, and the noise became louder like a thunderous rumbling as an avalanche of green boulders burst through the tiny hole Niada had made in the mountain wall.

"Faster, Eliza, run faster!" Niada screamed frantically at her from behind. The faery could easily outrun Eliza with her lithe movements, but she stayed behind to ensure the human's safety.

Niada was screaming something at Eliza, but she couldn't hear what it was with all the noise and there was no way she could stop to ask. The land on the vast mountainside was uneven, and as the boulders moved in closer on their trail, Niada took a chance. She ran up to Eliza, and pushed her hard, throwing their bodies with a force, far, far left where the slope wasn't as sharp. The push was tough against Eliza's fragile human body, but Niada wrapped around her taking whatever of the fall she could. Just for a brief moment, the boulders had continued rolling the other way, but as soon as Eliza and Niada had come to a halt and picked themselves up, they had to scurry off clumsily. They were able to get only a quick glance at the boulders diverting to their new path along the slopes, and that wasn't all. There was a reason why it had been getting noisier. The green, earthy boulders were growing as they tumbled down the mountainside towards them. The new path Niada had taken them down was easier for Eliza to run on without hurting herself, and she pushed so hard until a fire lit her lungs and she had nothing more to give towards the work her legs were doing.

The monstrous boulders began to cast a shadow ahead of them, and as they rolled up on the two, Niada pulled Eliza again to their far left, giving them just a little edge on the boulders, which took time to turn even slightly. During that time, Niada screamed something else to Eliza. In Eliza's head, she could have sworn she'd heard Niada say they had to jump. Like *jump off the mountain. How crazy was that? So of course Niada couldn't have said it,*

Eliza thought as she ran, but as Niada continued steering her left, she realised she could see the edges of the mountainside.

Niada ran up to Eliza. "We have to jump!" she screamed.

"Nnnnooo," Eliza mumbled not loud enough for Niada to hear, but Niada knew what she was saying.

One of the monstrous boulders was just toppling onto them and Eliza couldn't run any faster. Niada pushed her out of the way and uttered a spell, causing a little earthy hill to emerge from the ground to stop the boulder. It held, but not for long.

As they ran alongside the edges of the mountain now. The boulder broke the stopper and escaped and in a desperate bid to catch them, another rolled onto it, then another, and another merging into an even more devilish problem. *The mother of all evil, giant boulders*, Eliza thought.

"We won't make it, we have to jump!" Niada screamed.

Eliza knew Niada would push her off if she had to, but she didn't want to jump. They were so high up and she hadn't a clue what lay below. As she pondered this, she realised she didn't have much choice. Niada was now running next to her, and the boulder was on their heels. So dangerously close that it gripped the ends of Eliza's cloak, and as she barely managed to slip her arms out of the garment, setting herself free, she gave Niada one last look and they jumped.

Chapter 16

THE SACRED VALLEY

As they plunged off the towering mountain, everything suddenly transformed into a hazy blur. They were falling fast. Before Eliza could look down to see what fate would meet them below, the feeling of an encroaching presence began to cast a shadow over them. Literally. The colossal boulder had leapt off the mountainside after them. They'd probably die before even hitting the bottom, whatever was there. In truth, they were falling into a gorge with a deep ravine. They were so high up that even if the boulder somehow missed them, the impact of the fall was very well likely to do the job. Before either eventuality could happen, Eliza felt a sharp sting on her arms as her weight was suddenly lifted with mighty force, followed by an unexpected burden pulling her legs downwards. It happened so fast it took a few long seconds for her to realise what had transpired.

Arden's eagle, Aquila, had caught Eliza with her strong talons, and Niada had just managed to grip onto Eliza's legs. Great eagles were among the strongest and noblest of creatures in all the land and they were eternally loyal.

The bird belted a long squeal, which echoed in the high winds, and Eliza shut her eyes and mouthed a soft *thank you* to the massive eagle.

"You're welcome," Aquila answered in her language.

I can understand you! Oh my! Eliza thought in surprise.

"It appears you can," Aquila answered.

The shock didn't last for long, as Eliza recalled hearing the thoughts of their wolf assailants in the Dark Forest. It was obviously part and parcel of her newly acquired *gift*.

"For many days, I've scoured the lands seeking out my Arden," Aquila said, sounding distressed, as they flew over many magnificent ridges.

"Where is my Arden? He hasn't called me or answered my calls in days. Eliza, where is he?" moaned the eagle.

Eliza hated having to give bad news.

"Aquila, Arden is being held captive," she said and the eagle's talons tightened.

"Ouch!" Eliza exclaimed in discomfort, to which Aquila quickly apologised.

By the time they had flown over the many Mountains of the Never-Ending East and several other ridges, she had told the eagle the entire story, and was just finishing as Aquila landed them safely at the beginning of The Sacred Valley, where Eliza would have to restore The Key.

Aquila would stay with them until the end, she vouched to Niada and Eliza. The eagle was obviously revved up by anger, and when she committed to the task at hand, her usually neat feathers ruffled. Though hesitant, Eliza lightly rested her hand and face against the eagle's side in a comforting gesture. Aquila squealed in thanks.

Eliza couldn't help but feel very anxious now. She'd thought returning The Key would signal the end to her story in Annwn, but how things had changed, and changed quickly they had during her time there. Restoring the queer ornament in her satchel would not only ensure her family's safety and make the human realm secure again, but now her friends' lives were resting on that; partially at least. Returning The Key would only be the first part of bringing this entire mess to an end.

She thought about how she couldn't wait to be rid of the dreaded thing. *Dreaded, trouble-making thing. Dreaded, abominable, piece of bad luck. Dreaded....*

"Point taken, Eliza," Aquila interrupted her suddenly.

Right.

She forced an embarrassed half a smile.

Until she learnt to separate her thoughts from what she meant to say to animals of the realm, she needed to be mindful of the thoughts she kept.

She looked towards the vast valley that lay before them. A massive conical forest spread out at the heart of the valley, in the richest dark green she'd ever seen. There was a light, calming wind whistling faint songs in the valley, and her heavy curls blew against her face. It reminded her of spending peaceful Sundays enjoying the fresh morning breezes near the mountain range where she lived back home. Alas, there were few things peaceful about or in this realm, she thought. Pity, because it held so much beauty therein. She pulled the unruly curls back, and looped them into a single, thick plait, with a fixed steely gaze.

"Let's go," she said.

The three of them ventured in carefully, and Niada began explaining the need for caution in returning The Key.

"There is an infamous lone guard that lives within this valley," she said. "It has been placed here to protect The Key."

"But we're returning it, so it should be okay, right?" Eliza asked.

Niada didn't answer half as quickly as she'd hoped.

"I said, *right*?" she said in a feigned laugh, which went as fast as it had come out of her mouth.

"It may hardly matter that we're returning The Key, so extreme care is necessary," Niada eventually said. "But you are not alone. Aquila and I are here." Aquila squealed in agreement.

"What sort of creature is the lone guard?" Aquila asked Eliza, who translated for Niada as not all faeries are learned in the tongue of eagles, like Arden.

"I do not know, but whatever it is, it was meant to protect The Key from every possible kind of thief. Therefore, it must be adept at many kinds of attack. I do not know which creature is a master of the many skills there are to know in these vast lands," answered Niada.

They navigated through the many towering, thick trees until they could see a marble platform just ahead.

"That must be it," Aquila squealed and they continued.

Eliza's eyes roamed around them and she listened intently but could hear nothing besides the travelling songs of the winds. She felt a slight tension in Niada's body next to her as they approached the bottom of the marble mount. There were about nine steps leading up the entire platform, and at the top, at the very centre, stood a sculptured pillar.

She looked Niada's way. Niada had drawn a dagger and was spinning around them frantically.

"Why are you...?" she started saying before she stopped abruptly.

A deep hiss echoed loudly in the valley, riding on the singing winds, yet she felt it pass through her ears with a jarring sting. She tilted her head and writhed in pain. When it stopped, she swivelled her head around, and searched for the beast it had come from.

"What the hell," she uttered.

It was the hiss from her dreams; but Arden had slain that monster at Black Lake. Well, not slain, but de-eyed it. It was a water monster, so how could it have travelled so far on land? There was no way, no....

As questions rushed through her mind, they were soon

answered when the utterer of the hiss emerged from trees somewhere behind the platform.

At first, all they saw was the upper body of a fair, beautiful being, neither faery nor human, emerging unhurriedly at the top of the platform, as it moved up the stairs from the opposite side of the forest. The colour of his skin was a deep blue, he was bare-backed, and atop his head sat a tall, turban-like crown that appeared most unusual and far too big for his head. Once he appeared from behind the platform, his eyes fixed on Eliza and never shifted, not even once.

Niada took notice and pushed Eliza back. "He knows," she whispered.

As he moved up the final stairs to the top of the platform before them, it struck Eliza—the ease with which he walked was like he wasn't walking at all. Because he wasn't walking. He was a naga just like the bridgekeeper she'd encountered at Misty Bridge. Sure enough, as his lower half became visible, there were no legs attached to his waist. Only a thick mass and length of snake's tail, which eerily slid him closer to them. Eliza could also now see the distinctive red ink stains forming intricate patterns on his hands and tail just as they had on the bridgekeeper's. She stood unshaken and unfazed, though still slightly jarred from the penetrating hiss in her ears. The naga was now coming down the other side of stairs towards them, never once picking up speed. Eliza didn't move when Niada tried nudging her back more, she kept her eyes fixed on the naga which slightly towered above them.

He stopped mere inches from her, eyes still locked into Eliza's but almost looking past them, like he was trying to steal a peek into her soul.

"I've come to return The Key to you," she said in a low voice, which she found surprisingly steady, but the naga didn't respond, he just kept staring into her eyes, and before she knew it, she felt an oddness becoming more apparent on the inside of her. She was going to reach for her satchel to pull out The Key, but instead found her hands reaching for her stomach. She touched it lightly and looked down at it, and then back at the naga.

"Eliza, what is it?" Niada urged her.

"I...." was all Eliza could manage to stutter out, before she gripped her stomach with tight hands and bent over towards the ground. The oddness was becoming more than that.

"What are you doing to her," Niada screamed, tightening her grip around her dagger, not wanting to act hastily, but the naga didn't answer or move. He just stood there with a neutral look on his face, arms at his sides and far behind him, his tail lightly tapping the ground like he was enjoying whatever it was he was doing.

Aquila was trying to speak to Eliza as well, but she could hear little of what the eagle or Niada were saying now. Their voices were slowly fading into the distance. A vast emptiness slowly consumed her, like a lethal poison working its way through her system steadily. She could feel it working, and as it passed through her, her insides began turning numb. The poisonous hand of emptiness stretched its fingers through every corner of her being, until she felt devoid of anything good. She could feel only bad things, things she didn't want to feel. The absence of goodness, of love, made the presence of negativity more prominent. Bad things like fear, insecurity, and self-doubt.

Aquila and Niada launched a fierce attack on the naga. Aquila lifted off the ground and pounced from above with her talons ready to grab the naga, and Niada aimed for his midsection with her sharp dagger, but before they could deal any considerable damage, the naga's immense tail flew up in the air, and in one massive strike, blew them both aside in a strong lash. They landed a good way off with a heavy thud on the ground.

The naga remained motionless, still staring at Eliza.

By this time, she was past bending over, and had fallen to her knees as the emptiness drained her and made her weak. She tried mentally to lift her arm to signal to the naga, but the hand just flapped about lifelessly like it belonged to a rag doll.

When they got up from the harsh fall, both Niada and Aquila pelted towards the naga again, but again didn't get very far. As they approached the creature, for the first time it turned its focus away from Eliza. The naga snared at them, and as it bared its teeth, its turban crown lifted off swiftly and six hissing snakes emerged from the crown of its head. Whatever it was doing to Eliza it had started on Niada and Aquila. Though the naga was clearly focussing its energies on Eliza, its impact on Niada and Aquila was just enough to keep them at bay. Aquila squealed in agony.

Like Eliza and Aquila, Niada had her own pains to bear. Pain that wouldn't leave, so she had to store it away. Among this pain was that of her banishment separating her from the two people she most loved. How the naga had been able to access pains they'd kept secret, safely inside their hearts, she didn't know. Until she noticed the symbol on the back of its tail.

"Fight it," Niada dug deep to find just enough energy to grimace to Aquila and Eliza, as she gripped her head with her two hands.

"I know what you are," she uttered through her teeth to the naga, before looking to Eliza, crouching on the ground. The girl's eyes were beginning to roll back.

"Eliza!!!" she urged in between heavy breaths, "Fight it! You must...must fight whatever it is you are facing. Your enemy is not the beast before you. It is the one in-inside you. The beast is using your deepest fears and pains to harm us," she said staring intently at Eliza.

Slowly, through the intense pain Niada began crawling

towards Eliza. She felt like a newborn babe crawling against a vicious wind.

Eliza's consciousness was fast fading as the emptiness crept up on her and her spirits drained. Black began closing in, and she lost sight as her eyes rolled back. All there was in the enclosing blackness was a faint voice somewhere far off.

Still shackled by her own inner darkness inflicted by the naga, all Niada found she could do was beg Eliza. She begged her, pleaded with her to fight. She begged until tears spilled out. All along, she'd been fumbling and struggling just to get to a bit of faery dust from her bag.

"Eliza, please, fight it. You have the power in you, fight it," she begged and as she begged, the naga shifted its motionless stance and settled in for the kill.

Three of the hissing snakes on its head wrapped themselves around Eliza's midsection and slowly began tightening their hold.

"Elizaaaa!" Niada screamed, and with what little energy she had, she blew the dust towards the naga and uttered a charm. The ground shook violently, and then mounds of earth around the naga began springing up, up, upwards aggressively, like green earthy snakes forming thick prison bars around it. The naga resisted, and lunged its body against Niada's earthy prison trying to break free. Its tail and snakeheads managed to remain outside the prison, and their hold on Eliza never loosened. Niada had fallen flat on her face just steps from Eliza, her hands stretching towards the girl she was failing.

"Eliza," she continued her plea, uttering it like a mantra, her eyes closed as she tried to reach Eliza's dreams, to touch her mind to Eliza's. "Eliza, you must be the one to defeat it. You can and you must. Find that power in you. It's there, just find it, believe in it, and use it," she said.

In Niada's cry of desperateness, some little remnant of goodness left somewhere in Eliza's inner self started surfacing in the sea of emptiness that was consuming her, but the naga was also trying to reach Eliza's dreams at the height of the internal battle, and had already gotten there. As it reinforced Eliza's inner fears and pains, it dug up that agonizing recurring dream of a past memory, which set in on her fading consciousness. A recurring dream that never, ever finished since her mind had started recalling the seven-year-old memory.

She was back on her sunny island, in her nine-year-old body skipping three houses away from her own to the tiny shop converted from the front of a neighbour's house. She bounced in gleefully, about to pick out her favourite sweet, when the drunken shopkeeper emerged, wielding a bottle of rum clumsily like a weapon. His words stung her like poisonous venom; just like the one that was consuming her in Annwn.

"Get out of here, you little blithe!" he shouted at her with a heavy tongue and slurred speech, but Eliza didn't understand. "What's blithe?" she asked innocently tilting her head of curls.

He chuckled. "Blithe? That's you and your dirty blood. Your dirty, diluted, contaminated blood, you bastard," he sputtered out, before continuing in a foreign dialect, saliva spilling out at the corners of his mouth.

The words were like a knife, ripping her insides out. She'd heard them before. *Dirty blood. Mixed blood .Bastard.* She dropped her four quarters, and they hit the shop floor with heavy clinks. She backed out the shop clumsily, almost falling over the edge.

"And you tell those reckless grandparents of yours to keep their shameful racial transgressions from infecting the community!" he pointed a rough finger at her before she staggered off in tears.

She ran home crying, with every sharp-edged word replaying itself almost on purpose in her little mind.

This was where her dream always ended, where she'd

wake up with the fresh pain of societal rejection, and a lack of self worth sinking its claws into her flesh.

But for some reason, that little remnant of goodness left inside her managed to pull the rest of that memory from wherever it had been tucked away. The dream went on.

In her last moments before her life would be plucked away by the strangling naga, as Niada urged her to fight, Eliza Aurelio heard the voices of her consoling grandparents.

"Why yuh crying, chile?" her grandfather hushed her, as she sat on his lap.

"But he called me dirty blood, and impure, and bastard...." She didn't finish before she sank her crying face into her grandfather's floral shirt. Her weeping grandmother sat beside them and stroked her hair.

"Eliza," her grandfather said, before lifting her face out of his chest.

'No" he shook his head. "No, Eliza, he wrong. He damn wrong. You eh none of those things. What you are is a sign of love, a beacon of change to come. There are those who believe the races will *never* come together, because daz how they want it, but your existence proves them wrong. Very wrong. You my girl, you're a bright star amidst the bigotry and disharmony. Never, ever let them define you. *You* define you, no one else. If you let others define you, you will never realise your greatness. And you are great," he looked into her eyes. "Realise yuh greatness, chile" he said.

The words were like two prodigious, celestial hands lifting her up, high up above the sea of emptiness, and above any rejection, and fear of not being whole or pure. Why hadn't she remembered her grandfather's words? They were words of truth and words that lifted her from the brink of death and defeat.

Though Niada and Aquila had thought Eliza was gone,

she was not. Her eyes remained rolled back, but there was a rumbling inside her. Yes, she was struggling as the snakes on the naga's head restricted more and more air from her lungs, but as they tightened their hold on her, her right hand slipped its way stealthily into her pouch, and she reached for the magic knife that Loridel and the Gwragged Annwn had given her.

She was weak, but as her grandfather's words lingered over all other words of self-doubt and fear and bigotry, she found inner strength where she had none physically. With potent confidence, she slipped the magic knife out, and flicked it open! At last, it opened! As did her eyes. Her hand went quietly below the snake's encircling bodies around her, she turned the long blade upward, and in a swift, single movement, she fiercely sliced the snake heads wrapping around her. The naga hissed in pain, and in a massive thrust, it finally broke through the upper barriers of Niada's earthy prison. It was surprised to say the least that Eliza had sliced off its entangling heads.

Eliza found that as she began to believe in her inner worth, power and wholeness, strength unlike any she had known crept upon her. She pushed herself off the ground, though still physically weak and gripped the magic knife firmly.

The naga bore a devilish sneer and to everyone's surprise, the snakes atop the naga's head began growing back in pairs.

"Believe, Eliza," Niada urged, as the effects of the naga's spell began wearing off slowly on her and Aquila and she did. She believed in her grandfather's words. She believed in her greatness, and her wholeness, and in love. She was love and she was loved and despite what anyone in her racially divided land had said, her mixed race wasn't a curse, it was a gift.

The naga lifted its giant tail high up in the air, and as it came down, it brought a heavy wind lashing towards

Eliza. Her instincts told her to run, and fast, but Eliza felt the magical energies inside her resurfacing from somewhere deep, stirring like a wildfire trying to escape and suddenly rushing towards her palms with more force than she could manage. She thrust her hands towards the naga's landing tail and explosions of light burst from it.

The impact threw her back and blood spurted from the naga's tail as the devastating blow made contact. It hissed in anguish, but soon became enraged. The snakes upon its head began lunging at Eliza simultaneously, but as she slowly lifted herself off the ground, she fended them off with continuous bolts of magical energies. The naga tossed her weak frame forcibly to the ground, and they wrestled. Eliza was pinned beneath the naga, pushing her palms against (the) its enraged face, but the naga's snakes soon tied Eliza's hands back as it pressed the rest of her body against the ground. Unable to move any of her weakened muscles, Eliza focussed. She focussed on her grandfather's words, and then screamed in a fit of rage and that was when the fight came to a sudden and unexpected halt. A blinding explosion of magical light burst through her chest, pushing the naga away, and bringing its life to an end.

When the fight was all over and the effects of the naga were totally undone, Niada and Aquila rushed over to embrace Eliza. She'd done it. She'd believed in herself, and in her worth.

She walked up the nine steps of the platform and rested The Key in the socket atop the sculptured pillar. It released streams of coloured light high into the skies, which sent reverberations in the air in all directions as it locked the doorways between realms. That was it, Eliza thought, and she felt the load on her shoulders was somewhat lighter, though not gone.

She limped off the platform aided by Niada and Aquila, and as they rested, she could feel the current of magic flowing through her body. Niada fed her water and held her face delicately.

"I am proud of you, my child. You have restored The Key, and now there is but one thing left to do. I know you are weak, but time will not wait on us."

Aquila squealed anxiously, to which Eliza nodded tiredly. The trial of Gwen and Arden would be starting any moment now, and there was still much to do. Niada told of how she had discovered where the evil faery Sorcha had been hiding humans kidnapped from the human realm. She had hidden them first them in the Dark Forest, and now that she seemed to have the trust of the Council, she had moved her last victims where no one would suspect—in the very seat of justice: The seat of the Council, high up in the guarded Lordly Mountains of Eversong. Niada had learnt of these secrets through friends far and near, and through her own prying.

"So we have to sneak into this place first, find the victims without getting noticed. If we can manage that, and then take them all to the trial? How?" Eliza said in one go.

Niada sighed.

"I'm sorry, I should have more faith." Eliza smiled faintly.

"No," Niada responded quickly. "It's not that, Eliza, I cannot go with you. You must do this just with Aquila."

The shock was sudden. It was not what Eliza had expected to hear.

"What, what do you mean you can't go with me? Don't you want to see Gwen? Aquila and I can't do this alone," she said.

"I'm sorry, beloved. My banishment is bound by a powerful spell that bars me from getting within close distance to Gwen or her father. I watch them from afar, I speak to them through dreams, but I cannot be near them. To do so is to risk bringing harm to them. It is a risk I can never bear to take," she revealed.

Eliza sunk into her place in the ground, feeling hurt for Niada, and for her Gwen. She was suddenly less worried about going into the Lordly Mountains of Eversong with Aquila.

"Do not worry." Eliza smiled at Niada. "We'll do everything possible to save Gwen and Arden. For love," she added, to which Aquila squealed and stomped her heavy right foot in agreement.

Niada grinned at Eliza's brave heart, a human girl empowered more by love than the magic flowing in her veins.

"My dear Eliza, when you and Aquila go, be discreet and take care. We've won half the war with the return of The Key. The other half begins the moment you step into those mountains. I will watch you from afar and do what I can to assist you, but danger will be ever present. You will face anti-humanist groups, the Council guards, the Council itself, and above all, Sorcha. You are an enemy to all there, but Sorcha... She will do anything to stop you. She fears you," Niada said.

"Me? But why?" asked Eliza, confused.

"You are gifted by the motherland Annwn. Our motherland makes no mistakes, and every choice of Hers is made with great reason. You are now one of Annwn's chosen, and your gift is more powerful than any dark magic there is. It is made strong by the love in you. Love is light, and light expels darkness," Niada explained.

It was more responsibility than she'd ever had, but Eliza decided then and there that she would embrace her gift and take charge. Niada was right. She had been given the gift for a reason. She didn't know what that reason was, but the gift helped her to return The Key to make her grandparents safe again and now it would help her save her friends.

"Can we defeat her?" Eliza asked.

"Even the strongest wall can be brought down, Eliza." Niada moved in closer. "Find her weak spot, and hit her hard," Niada said making a fist.

As they planned their entry into the seat of Annwn's judicial system, a light wind rustled through the trees, and a furious roar echoed through the valley. They were met by an unexpected visitor.

Chapter 17

THE TRIAL

Horns sounded from the Lordly Mountains of Eversong, echoing far and beyond. At their jarring resonance, a flock of impressively large scarlet birds lifted off from the roof of the grand structure carved into the extraordinary mountains. Their long wings fanned out far, and from below, the flock looked like an ominous blanket of red blood spreading over the High Court and its environs. A blanket that forebode what was to come on this day. Emryees looked up at it on his way into the premises and he found that he couldn't shake off the bad feeling it had passed onto him. His stomach churned uneasily.

He was about to enter the side gate into the High Courts and paused to observe the snaking, intractable crowds waiting to enter through the grand gates. A particularly unruly section of the crowd had broken off and was chanting anti-human sentiments, demanding the deaths of the accused, and insisting that they saw firsthand the recovered body of the human offender. Anti-human antagonism was rife and threatening to spill over into violence and in a realm of extraordinary creatures; such violence could end only one way. It would be a tragedy of phenomenal proportions. The tension was airborne, and one could sense the apprehension of those races deemed too apathetic about the humans.

It was judgement day—the trial of the half-faery, Gwen Callaghan, and Arden of the Eastern Forest. It was *their* trial, but the implications of it would extend to the wider realm. Emryees just knew there was more to the story than was told to the Council and the beings of Annwn. Something inside him told him the accused had been truthful, but he had to be sure and the official inquiry into the events surrounding the theft of The Key had found nothing substantial to quell the brewing anarchy. If the trial was fair, the result would be an impasse, but with suspicion and anti-human tensions this high, the Council would undoubtedly be under pressure to deliver guilty verdicts, and harsh punishment to the accused. There was no way in Annwn such a trial would be fair.

He hoped that whatever it was Urhouri had found would be good enough to prevent the disaster that he could feel slowly unravelling in the realm. All they had was a piece of blood-stained cloth torn from the dress of the faery Sorcha. A bizarre find, considering it was human blood and that Sorcha had turned the prisoners in and accused them of stealing The Key. She had told the Council that the humans were driven by their insatiable desire for power, had discovered Annwn, and wanted the powers of faeries. Such powers could only be given to the human race through miscegenation with the faeries of Annwn. Everyone knew Niada had done just that—cohabited with a human, producing a mixed blood faery, the accused Gwen.

The half-fae's existence alone had been enough to stir underlying anti-human sentiments into raucous calls for humans to be banned from the realm; particularly after the unexplained events of The Unknown Plague. Humans had been outlawed, and not too soon after, The Key that sealed the two known doorways between the realms, was stolen. A great feat that was, given that The Key was so well guarded. That humans were capable of this at all was ludicrous. Their guns and weaponry would serve no good in Annwn, but there was no other explanation for the missing Key, and why it had been stolen.

There was no one else to blame, no one else with a motive, and the beings of Annwn were anxious for justice; especially since rumours had long spread that humans were to blame for their realm's beleaguered state, and misfortunes, for The Unknown Plague, and for their missing King. The theft of The Key was really the straw that broke the camel's back.

Urhouri had been reluctant to snoop around and interfere in the official inquiry. Their realm was one of austere rules now since the advent of the Council, which they both sat on. They would get in trouble if found out. They might even be accused of being pro-human, but Urhouri had agreed to help him, wanting to do good by their motherland, even if they were among the few committed to ensuring that good was done and upheld.

After days of searching, she'd sent word that she'd found evidence implicating Sorcha. Her note had sounded grave and worrisome. Like she'd uncovered the kind of thing that could make their kingdom topple over with laughable ease.

Emryees thought on these things while making his way to one of the private rooms, high up in the Lordly Mountains of Eversong. He made haste, as they had little time before the start of the trial in the opened arena.

As he approached the isolated room, he made out his secret sweetheart by her fiery red hair practically glowing in the dark. Her back was facing him as she leaned over a table.

"Urhouri," he whispered to the Salamander as he walked into the room.

The doors closed in behind him.

Emryees spun around in surprise. It was the Council chair.

"Vonroth."

"Hello, Emryees," Vonroth answered with a nod, hands folded in front of him. "Urhouri tells me she has evidence against the faery Sorcha," said the wizard in his husky voice.

Emryees looked to Urhouri suspiciously. She still hadn't turned around. He looked back to Vonroth but kept his silence.

"What is it that you have found, Urhouri?" asked Vonroth. Three worry lines appeared between his bushy black brows as he paced about the room. "And more importantly, why didn't you report it to the inquiry?"

"Vonroth," Emryees said lifting his hand defensively, before Urhouri could answer. "It wasn't...."

"No," Urhouri interjected, spinning around. She didn't look at Emryees at all. He stared at her intently, but her eyes didn't waver. He wondered if it was because she felt guilty for betraying him by going to Vonroth first. Instead, her eyes were fixed on Vonroth, and she didn't look very happy at all.

After a few long seconds, when she did eventually manage to look Emryees's way, the air between them was intense. It was as though time had stopped in sombre acknowledgement of a wrong committed between two who loved. It was just the two of them, alone in the room.

Emryees looked her in the eyes, in a way that only she could understand. It was a look that begged the question of *why*. Why had she betrayed his confidence when he had asked her to keep the matter between them—a matter of national importance with grave implications for all?

Now, not only could they face the Council's swift and callous hand of punishment for interfering in the course of justice, but this was playing out at a time when they knew not who they could trust. (But) As he looked deeply into her amber-ringed eyes, he read them the way no one else could. Time resumed, and his stomach churned in warning. The revelation behind her soul's windows removed all doubt: If there was a betrayer, it wasn't Urhouri.

Footsteps came from an adjoining room.

Lady Sorcha.

Silently, she walked over to Vonroth's side, with over-exaggerated poise.

He felt his body hardening to solid ice from the shock.

"What's going on?" Emryees uttered beneath his breath.

"Oh, lighten up! Errr... Omrose? Umriss?" Sorcha flung her hands about dramatically and looked up at the ceiling in pretend wonder. "Whatever!" she emphatically brushed his name off, and beamed with a wide grin that stretched her thin, blood red lips from one corner of her face to the other.

Urhouri slowly began to edge towards Emryees.

"Uh-uh-uh," Sorcha raised a cautionary finger and ticked it back and forth in time to her mocking staccato tone, still grinning.

"It's them, Emryees," Urhouri said in a shaken voice, tinged with disgust. "The rumours of an infiltrator are true. Vonroth is *the* infiltrator. He serves that lowly one. They framed the humans. They stole The Key, and they opened the doorways so they could kidnap humans. For experiments of some kind."

Sorcha and Vonroth laughed amusingly.

"Very good, Urhouri," Vonroth mocked, clapping his hands and stepping towards her. "Now where is this evidence?"

Emryees moved in his path.

Sorcha feigned a hearty laugh, and then looked back and forth at Emryees and Urhouri in disbelief.

"They have... that thing, that... lll...lll"—she pushed her tongue forcibly to get past the unexpected stutter—"Love," she eventually sputtered out. "What's worse is they've been infected by the humans. They sympathise with them."

Sorcha's disbelief was incredible. To her and Vonroth, humans were good only for one thing, which she duly explained to the pair. To her, humans were weak and welcoming them into Annwn was a terrible mistake, but she'd found that they were good for one thing. Power. She'd made a most remarkable discovery, and subsequently embarked on ambitious experiments to conjure a very, very dark magic, one forbidden in the realm for good reason. In the course of these experiments, she found that by sapping the emotions and life force of humans, she was able to produce a magic darker than the realm had ever known. Such magic is not easy to come by and, as such, required a sacrifice. Hence, humans.

"So you see," Sorcha said nonchalantly, "The Key is long gone. And with the doorways permanently opened, more humans will *accidentally* find themselves here!" she had an outburst of giggles and twiddled her fingers childishly. She suddenly grew serious and folded her hands.

"With the *unfortunate* heightening anti-human tension, we shall be cornered into drastic action. We must protect our people," she said with feigned alarm. "Dear, oh dear... We shall have to create human camps." She flashed that evil grin that suited her so well. "More humans equals more power, get it?" She bellowed a laugh filled with excessive snorting.

Emryees looked to Urhouri in shock. He was greatly perturbed by everything he'd just learnt, including the vileness of the character that was the faery Sorcha. "Exactly how long have you two been experimenting with dark magic?" he asked.

"Long enough to see its worth and potential," answered Vonroth in a practical tone.

Emryees narrowed his eyes at Vonroth. The wizard who chaired the Council meetings and whose 'wisdom' was often sought, was really a monster at best. Emryees felt sick to the core.

"You are hurting innocent human beings," Emryees said, gnashing his teeth at Vonroth in suppressed rage.

"We know," Sorcha said with gleeful abandon, tilting her head.

"Vonroth, do not let this evil, evil darkness take hold of you. Those two faeries out there, Gwen and Arden, they've suffered for the sake of our home. Their human friend died trying to right your wrong. Innocent...."

"Enough, enough!" Vonroth grunted impatiently.

"It is a price they are willing to pay, Emryees," Urhouri said calmly. "Vonroth is beyond help and reason now."

Emryees scoffed. "If you are willing to sacrifice the innocent, including our own, to what end will you go to gain this evil power?"

Vonroth gave Emryees a dry, bored look, tired of the conversation since Urhouri was clearly not going to reveal what evidence she had against them.

"Okay," Emryees whispered. "Answer me this, this last question. Your... it was your dark magic that caused The Unknown Plague... was it not?" Emryees said sceptically, staring at the two traitors. "Was it not?" he shouted, and sharp ice splinters crashed from his fists in anger.

Vonroth flashed a sly grin, while Sorcha uttered a low laugh.

"What are you going to do?" Sorcha quivered in pretence. She pushed her two fists outwards dramatically, conjuring black balls of magical energies, which she juggled about carelessly. "You cannot stop my magic and, who will believe you? The *dangerous* culprits who collude with humans are about to go on trial," she smiled, feeling satisfied that she was unstoppable at this point.

Emryees lifted his icy hand.

"Eh!" Sorcha warned him, extending her black magical

energies in Urhouri's direction. "One wrong move from you, and she gets it."

Emryees had had it. He swivelled his head towards Urhouri. She subtly shook her head knowing the high impossibility of the two of them being able to take down a faery dabbling in such dark magic, but Emryees maintained his stance. He twitched his left eye at her, and she noticed the slight movement in his chest as he filled his lungs with air.

He spun back around at Sorcha and Vonroth and blew a strong gust of icy wind onto them, hardening them into icy sculptures. Urhouri hesitated, but when the first crack sounded from the icy forms, she hurriedly reverted to her other form, folding into a ball of fire. With a loud crash, she broke through a nearby window, flying out in a burning whiff.

Emryees flexed his muscles and braced himself for Sorcha and Vonroth. They needed to be captured alive. He channelled his inner energies towards changing into his ice form, just as the two traitors broke through his ice.

Sorcha bared her teeth at him and signalled to Vonroth to wait.

"You foolish block of ice," she snickered at Emryees before pelting him with a bolt of black energies. His transformation to his ice form was almost complete when the black magic splashed across his form, and snake-like living black weeds started digging into his icy skin.

"Arrgrghhhhh," he screamed in agony at the fiery pain, but he flexed his muscles and the purity of his ice burst through, kicking the black weeds out from his skin. During his brief distraction with this though, Sorcha lifted the heavy table high up behind Emryees and dropped it on him, with such force it knocked out the poor ice faery.

"Very good, Sorcha," she praised herself, shaking off the melting ice from her hair. "Imprison him. And make sure that ball of fire does not make it to the trial," she now said to Vonroth.

"Of course, my lady." Vonroth bowed, taking her hand, which now showed visibly blackened veins.

"Let us be quick about it," she snapped staring at her hand as he kissed it. "The guilty need swift justice. And I need to feed!" before swinging her heavy dress back and walking out the room.

The sudden light of day stung Gwen and Arden's eyes as they were escorted out of the dark underground prison into the centre of the vast oval arena. The many tiers of seats were already filled with spectators who became noisy and agitated as Gwen and Arden entered. At the heart of the arena sat a circular bay barricaded by The Sluagh, which flew around it continuously with great speed. Their distorted black shapes swirled angrily in the wind. The Council initially knew not what to do with them except use them for its own bidding. The Sluagh parted as Arden and Gwen were led into the bay and closed the gap again after they passed. Gwen looked around them anxiously, first at The Sluagh, which she'd never seen that close up, and then at the panoply of beings from the realm sitting in the stands. She could see many forms and shapes and colours of queer beings she'd never even encountered in Annwn before.

"All will be well, Gwen," Arden rested a protective arm over her shoulder.

"Traitors!" a voice from the crowd managed to sound above all others and before they had time to brace themselves, a large rock was hurled directly at them. Gwen screamed as the rock approached their heads, but it shattered when it hit the whirling Sluagh barrier.

A chorus of surprised gasps and whispers rose up from

the crowd, and the formidable high court guards were seen forcibly removing the spectator who had thrown the rock.

"We're screwed," Gwen uttered to Arden who was still gripping her, looking to the stands.

"Have faith, Gwen. They can't hurt us in here," he said as he stared at his mother. Lady Drwrywen stared back at him from an area of the stands reserved for leaders of various races. Her face was cold and looked surprisingly aged, even from afar. Arden broke his gaze and stared at the ground.

As other leaders and spectators made their way into the arena, the high court horns bellowed for a long few seconds. The guards silenced the crowds as the dignified council leaders entered the arena in single file, into their reserved quarters. As the council members sat down, the spectators waited silently in anticipation, but none rose to speak. Instead, loud whispers echoed from their section.

The council members eyed the two empty seats among their ranks.

"Where are Urhouri and Emryees?" asked Hiatar the centaur, looking about with great concern for his friend. "We must wait."

"No," protested Vonroth. "As Council chair, I advise that we proceed. The trial has much to cover." The trial soon kicked off with the announced charges of theft of The Key, aiding and abetting a human, murdering Arrae of the Eastern Forest and named Aradath Elves, endangering the beings of the realm, and lastly, treason.

Seconds turned into minutes, and minutes into hours, but as all sides passionately argued diametrically opposite positions, it became clearer and clearer that with no solid evidence, the trial of Gwen and Arden was going nowhere fast.

When it was Gwen's turn to speak, she pleaded with Annwn's residents to believe her. "Please, please, I swear we came here to help. We are not the enemy. My human friend was kidnapped, and I came here to save her. Sorcha stole The Key and planted it in the human realm. I don't know why, but she's up to something. My friend had the noblest and kindest of hearts, and for that reason Annwn gave her *the* gift. Tell me who can manipulate the higher powers of Annwn?" Gwen challenged.

"Sorcery!" a couple voices from the stands shouted before they were quelled by nearby guards.

"Mmhmmm," Gwen answered quickly, shaking her head. "You know better. Sorcery cannot touch the higher power that we owe our existence too. My friend died trying to save her family, by restoring The Key. It is she who was murdered and tossed to a watery grave at Mirror Lake. Where's the justice in that?" Gwen's voice cracked as tears spilled out over her cheeks.

All around, the stadium went silent until the adjudicator's throaty voice broke it when he called on Sorcha to testify and of course being the wicked, misanthropic faery that she was, she told lies. Beautiful lies.

"She says she's not the enemy, but can you trust her? Can you trust a mixed blood? I say unto you, fellow beings of Annwn, these traitors mean to relegate you, and you, and you by sullying the blood that flows through your lineage... by joining us with human beings." She dropped the pitch of her voice for effect, and it was to the sound of collective gasps among the spectators. "They are loyal to human beings and no one else! The human race is weak. It wants our gifts. The humans want stronger genes and the only way they can guarantee the survival and dominance of their race is through their children. Children they will have with us. Mixed-blood children who will recognise the human race as their own. Like she does," Sorcha said, pointing a long, wicked finger towards Gwen. "The traitor faery Niada loved a human, and pledged her commitment to their cause. Her rhwoski daughter now fights for the humans and him! Arden? He shames us by loving a human.

Together, they stole The Key to offer a permanent opening to our realm, so they could quietly infiltrate, and steal our hearts, our purity, and home," she boldly claimed.

"So prove it!" Arden shouted in rage at Sorcha.

"I don't have to," Sorcha snickered. "Everyone here knows the suffering we endured after The Unknown Plague. We won't risk another tragedy with our doorways opened, leaving us to the mercy of your human allies," Sorcha answered.

Sections of the crowd conceded with raucous shouts, and fists thrust high up in the air.

"We both know very well that humans didn't cause The Unknown Plague, Sorcha," Arden said through his teeth, but she ignored him.

"He murdered his own cousin! They murdered our brethren. They will be martyrs to the human race!"

"Oh shut up! You insufferable git!" screamed Gwen.

Sorcha paused and stood up in her witness box, leaning over the edge. Gwen could see a subtle smile emerging on her face.

"Angry, are we? It must pain you to know that you will never be one of us. You could never be a true daughter of this soil. You are rejected by the tainted half-human blood of your veins. Blame the folly of your mother. Not us. The humans are the only ones who accept you, and at best, all you will ever be, is part human and Annwn's bastard," Sorcha said plainly.

There was a pregnant pause in the stands as Sorcha pilloried Gwen and her mixed-race heritage. Though she had earlier wept for her lost friend, this caused fissures to appear in Gwen's sturdy, tough exterior. Tremors shook her frame, as the fractures spread slowly like a crack along a glass screen, until Gwen's outer shell had been completely broken. In a fit of rage, she lunged past the protective barrier of The Sluagh, meaning to break the neck of the disgusting wretch that had murdered her friend. If she didn't live for another day, at least she'd die avenging her sweet Eliza. Arden screamed and reached out to stop Gwen as she ran forward, but she pulled away from his grasp.

She never made it past The Sluagh barrier, though. When her body touched the mass of swirling black shapes around the oval, a haunting scream escaped her lips as the spirit held her inches off the ground, gnawing away at her flesh and draining her life force. Gwen's torso flopped over the edge of the oval, the excruciating pain rendering her inert. Arden rushed over to her and grimaced as he pushed his hands through the barrier to pull Gwen away quickly from the edge where the spirit stayed. Gwen staggered backwards in his arms, and the two fell on the ground. The crowd stared, silent and waiting, but Sorcha said nothing more. She had no more apocryphal tales to tell the spectators, because she knew she had said just enough to feed their fears. In a realm where interracial relationships (more so those with humans) were frowned upon and feared, it was inevitable that the few mixed-race children of Annwn would be marginalised. Fear of beings outside of Annwn was even worse after the events of The Unknown Plague, and to 'protect' the realm, interbreeding with humans was outright forbidden. In the following years, the fear bred prejudice, which bred bigotry, which bred racism. So what was left for the products of such unions? Such children were regarded innocent in the matter of miscegenation laws broken by their parents, so they were spared any punishment. Officially, anyway. On the surface of things, the beings of Annwn appeared to accept mixed faeries like Gwen, but underneath that, the hand of bigotry kept such children on the fringes of the society. Sorcha's sophistry fed the deeply rooted insecurities and prejudices of spectators sitting anxiously in the stands, speculating over Gwen and Arden's involvement in these worrisome events.

Fear is, after all, a great illusionist that distorts the obvious truth of reality.

The heavy silence was finally broken by clamouring in several sections of the stadium. There was no evidence, but the crowds had heard enough. Pandemonium broke out, and faster than you can say zi-pih-dee-zap, all sorts of objects were being hurled at the bay holding Gwen and Arden. The objects—rocks, bottles, logs, stones, among others—didn't penetrate The Sluagh barrier of course, but it was still terrifying for both Arden and Gwen, who remained crouched on the ground.

Violence broke out among different factions of spectators. The anti-humanist groups and those suspicious of humans and mixed fae greatly outnumbered those who weren't. The ones who didn't bear strong dislike towards humans were easily picked out—they remained quiet and unaccusing, so they were targeted. The high court guards moved into sections of the stadium to quell the turmoil as council members looked on in shock, some whispering among themselves. As Gwen and Arden remained only witnesses to the antagonism directed at them, it became more obvious than ever that this was their end. If they were not found guilty, disgruntled anti-humanists would probably find a way to end their lives. Now devoid of any hope, Gwen quivered in Arden's arms like a frightened child, forgetting who she was—the strong tomboy who never stood down. Arden, on the other hand, looked around them continuously at the many objects flying their way and crashing against the barrier. He analysed the faces in the crowd, and his lips moved robotically as he muttered barely above a whisper. Amid the madness in the stands, his eyes manage to find his mother. She had been callous in dealing with him after his decision to support Eliza and Gwen, but now she looked like a different faery altogether, her hands cupped over her mouth in alarm.

As the high court guards managed to quell the disorder,

in another section of the stadium a raucous chorus rose up.

"Guilty, guilty, guilty," they protested.

In the Council quarters, the nine present council members argued amongst themselves.

"We need to act quickly, before this violence spills over into the realm," said Eolande.

"Yes," agreed Hiatar, "but neither side has real evidence."

"We have no choice in the matter. The citizens of Annwn have decided," Eolande said.

The usually quiet sylph interjected and they went quiet as they always did when she spoke.

"We are the rulers of the realm. We have a choice, and we must exercise it wisely."

"Yes," answered Eolande, "We must choose to keep the peace and prevent possible anarchy. Look at them! There is only one verdict. And it is guilty." At this, the other members of the Council erupted in argument.

"A guilty verdict promises no end to this matter," said the wise sylph in a monotone voice, her huge hawk-like eyes turned to white.

"Ahh! Says the prophet," Eolande snickered.

"It is true," the sylph answered calmly as her eyes changed back to their natural colour of brown.

Eolande sighed heavily in frustration. "That witness will not rest until she gets justice. If we don't find them guilty, blood will rain on this realm and our hands will be stained," she said.

Hiatar snorted loudly in disagreement.

Vonroth raised his hand to speak, while bearing his trademark facade of neutrality. "I am afraid Eolande is right. The matter is out of our hands. Unless we see some evidence, the verdict must be guilty. As Council chair, I ask you to consider the future and state of order in Annwn as we deliberate. Shall we vote?" he asked, and tensions had hit the ceiling so hard in their confined space that they hadn't even noticed the armed guards had successfully subdued the disorder, and were waiting anxiously on them, as were the spectators.

Vonroth leaned forward and eyed Hiatar, the last council member on the end of their row.

"Not guilty," he said, followed by a continuous chain of individual judgements from the uneasy members.

Guilty, guilty, guilty, not guilty, guilty... it went on, and the fate of their prisoners was plainly obvious, even before the vote was over.

Chapter 18

JUDGEMENT

Gwen eyed Arden nervously as the high court's horns bellowed, calling everyone's attention to the Council. Vonroth was now standing, and she knew their judgement was coming. Arden tightened his grasp of her in comfort, his lips still moving fretfully. Neither Gwen nor Arden listened carefully to Vonroth's closing remarks. It was all muffled until their churning guts told them the important part was nigh.

"In the absence of any evidence, and in light of today's events, the Council hereby finds Arden of the Eastern Forest and Gwen the half-faery..." before Vonroth could finish, loud murmurs erupted from the crowds. He grunted impatiently, and was about to continue, but council members hushed him and turned his attention to the stadium, where thousands of arms were outstretched, pointing to the skies above.

A dozen balls of blazing fire flew towards the stadium and pelted the ground. The guards assembled in defence, but as the balls hit the ground, they unfolded into Salamander faeries, armed and ready to strike. Urhouri emerged from behind the group, gripping something unrecognisable in her hands. She motioned for the court guards to be at ease, and walked to the centre of the arena, near the bay that held the prisoners. The council members shuffled about uneasily at their colleague's sudden and ill-timed appearance.

"Citizens of Annwn," Urhouri eyed the crowd, trying to locate Sorcha and Vonroth. "You've been misled. We've all been misled." She looked to Gwen and Arden. "These two are innocent." Her claim led to murmurs and whispers in the crowds.

Another figure emerged from behind the group of Salamanders. It was Emryees. Urhouri had broken him out of prison.

"She speaks truth," Emryees said, and the crowd and council members stirred more as the other realm ruler appeared.

"You may be wondering why I am not sitting in my rightly place on the Council now. I was imprisoned because I learned the truth. I am ashamed to say we have placed our trust in the enemy. The Council chair, Vonroth the wizard, and the so-called witness Sorcha are the enemies," Emryees cried out.

Everywhere the faeries stirred at this new, confusing development.

"They are the ones who stole The Key and opened our doorways. Humans were never a threat to us," Emryees said.

The council members all stared at Vonroth anxiously, awaiting some immediate defence on his part, but it never came. Vonroth's face was cold, hard, and unflinching. The unexpected turn of events silenced him. Sorcha, however, grew tired of waiting for Vonroth to stand up, so she did.

"These are nothing more than allegations. What have the humans promised you for this betrayal of your own?" she said calmly, maintaining her veneer of innocence.

Urhouri stared at her unfazed, and began walking around the edges of the arena, close to the public stands.

As she walked around, she lifted her hand to towards the public, revealing the scrap of blood-stained fabric.

"In my hand, sisters and brothers, is fabric torn from the dress of the witness Sorcha, a dress easily identifiable to my fellow council members," said Urhouri. She approached the Council and openly asked which of her colleagues remembered the fabric. Recognition crossed their faces as they examined the material.

"The stains on this fabric are of blood. Human blood. Smell it, you cannot mistake the scent. This faery called Sorcha is not what she seems, my family. She is more than a misanthrope. She is an iniquitous practiser of forbidden dark arts. She experiments with it and has channelled a dangerous dark magic to gain unimaginable power, but we all know why dark magic is forbidden. It requires too great a sacrifice and she sacrifices human beings. This was why she and Vonroth stole The Key and planted it in the human realm, thinking it would be lost. They couldn't have known this brave faery Gwen and her friends would resolve to return it despite the danger they would face here," Urhouri said, her eyes still fixed on Sorcha, who was grinding her teeth.

Sorcha rolled her eyes and attempted to deflect attention from the cloth in Urhouri's hand.

"If I stole The Key, then where is it?" she challenged Urhouri. The spectators and Council waited anxiously. "There are few in this arena who could surely say they are not concerned about dangerous humans entering our realm with the doorways opened. We all fear the potential threat of more mixed-blood faeries coming to our realm."

The stadium stirred and potential chaos was quietly brimming again.

Emyrees hushed the murmurs. "That's not all. For centuries we lived in fear, not knowing when another plague would come. Her experiments with dark magic are what caused *The* Unknown Plague. She is the cause of our suffering. Not them," Emryees said pointing to Gwen and Arden.

The arena vibrated with commotion as the spectators began to whisper to one another.

Sorcha nervously pinched at the blackening and bulging veins on her hands. As she grew more and more petulant, the evil faery found it harder to keep up her charade. She belted out a nervous but exaggerated giggle.

"Okay! Okay! You win!" she grinned, tossing away the varnished layer of her *innocent victim* persona, and revealing the psychologically unstable character that she was.

"Yes! I stole The Key! But I did us a favour," she claimed, her arms flailing desperately around her.

The admission jolted the arena into shocked silence as the news sunk in.

In the Council booth after a few long seconds, Hiatar rose from his seat and shouted, "Arrest her!"

Guards began moving in towards the witness stand, but Sorcha was unfazed. She took on her full, truest form and jumped over the stand, gleefully dancing and twirling her long purple dress around her.

"It is too late! This shall be your cry, the moon turns dark, and you'll wonder why... Your Key is lost, more humans shall be my feed, and as the darkness rises, a miracle you shall need..." she sang as she pranced about carelessly.

As Sorcha danced towards the prisoner bay, council members ordered The Sluagh repeatedly to part so guards could escort Gwen and Arden to safety, but alas, the spirits would not move. Urhouri reinforced the orders, as did the guards, but the spirits just kept swirling around the prisoner bay.

"Fools!" snickered Sorcha. "Did you really think you could control something as powerful as my babies? You never had control over them. They only do my bidding."

The shocked council members were finally beginning to realise the folly of their ways to trust in something that came out of The Unknown Plague.

To prove her point, Sorcha uttered a charm and some of the black shapes twisted and twirled away from the prisoner bay and flew into her opened mouth, before she spat them out with a rage. She continued towards the prisoner bay as Gwen and Arden looked on apprehensively.

Urhouri called out, "You are far outnumbered by many powerful beings here, Sorcha. Give up and we will spare your life."

"Give up? Who, me?" she playfully snickered. "If a strand of hair on my head is so much as ruffled by any powers in this arena," she said as she walked straight through The Sluagh barrier without harm, "then your poor prisoners will be the ones to suffer first."

Lady Drwyrwen stood up angrily and shouted to the Council and guards. "Do something! My son is in there!" but everyone in the arena seemed confused as to what should be done next. Fed up, Drwyrwen was just the first of many faeries of the realm to take up either their rods or hands to direct their powers towards The Sluagh, but the barriers remained intact and impenetrable.

Sorcha looked on with a smirk on her face. She turned to Gwen and Arden huddled in the corner of the bay. As she walked closer to them, Arden stood up to protect Gwen who was still reeling in pain from her encounter with The Sluagh.

"First I will kill you, then I will,"—she paused twiddling her fingers—"Oh this is so exciting. I don't know which to embark on first.

"Oh, I know! She should have very interesting blood as a half-faery. I shall like to extract some of you. I need to feed anyway, I'm much too weak," she grinned at Gwen, too weak to meet her gaze.

"You will not touch her," Arden said as he hovered

around Gwen. Sorcha smiled and pulled a dagger from her pocket. Inspecting the blade, she ran her finger along its long edges right to the pointy tip.

"Then I shall mince you to pieces first," she said. The leaders of the realm tried many a thing to penetrate The Sluagh, and some of their magic seemed to bear some hold on it, but before they even made it halfway through the barrier their powers would bounce back out. The council members sought spells of yore that might weaken the spirits but found nothing that worked. They had welcomed into their high courts spirits they had no understanding of. Drwyrwen left the stands and rushed into the arena, but was held back by Urhouri with all others on the grounds who had been unable to help.

Sorcha lifted her blade to Arden who was still muttering something, and as her hand came down, he grabbed it.

"Your spells will not work on me, youngling," she grunted through her teeth as she struggled to cut him. When she tired, for she was long due for feeding and growing weak, she used her powers to fling Arden's body hard into the wall behind him, and she moved in on Gwen. Arden's body hit the wall with a heavy thud.

"I promise this will be painful," she smiled at Gwen who remained curled up on the ground.

As Sorcha was about to pierce Gwen's heart, an eagle cried out, distracting her just long enough.

"Aquila," Arden whispered as he tried to get up, but he immediately crumpled back to the ground in pain.

Aquila appeared in the skies above, circling the arena and squealing profusely. No one had seen the tiny sprinkles of dust she'd released from her talons all over the arena. In no time after, a ferocious roar filled the arena and a figure rode into the arena on top of a fierce sabre-tooth beast. Arden immediately recognized his cousin in his animal form, but it took a few minutes for his mind to believe what his eyes were seeing. Eliza sat tall on Arrae's back, her long, plaited hair whipping out behind her. Nearly hidden behind Eliza on Arrae's back sat two stunned and frail-looking humans gripping on for dear life.

Eliza jumped off of Arrae and ran towards the prisoner bay. A shocked Gwen muttered "no, Eliza, no" as Eliza threw herself towards The Sluagh, passing through it effortlessly. As Gwen looked in awe at Eliza running towards her, Sorcha shook herself out of her stunned stupor and stabbed Gwen in the chest. A devastated and enraged Eliza burst through barrier, knocking the evil faery over. Shock took hold of the arena again as a human made her way past the impenetrable barrier with seemingly little harm.

Sorcha and Eliza rolled on the ground fighting for a few long seconds, before Sorcha's wind force pinned Eliza into a corner. Sorcha wasted no time and aimed for Eliza's heart with the dagger. Eliza grabbed her hand and the magical lightforce exploded from her hand hurting Sorcha so incredibly that she screamed in agony before letting go in sheer fright. Anger and humiliation washed over Sorcha, and she lifted a dozen daggers from her heavy dress and pointed them Eliza's way.

As Sorcha was about to strike Eliza, an ailing Gwen issued the thickest strings of lianas she'd ever produced, which crept up on Sorcha and violently wrapped themselves around her. However powerful the wicked Sorcha was, it was enough to distract and hold her.

As Eliza caught her breath, she thought hard as Sorcha slowly cut her way through the lianas.

"Give up," she panted to Sorcha, still trying to figure out the faery's weakness. They were both exhausted, but Sorcha just kept cutting the lianas in a rage. Her hands went free and she approached Eliza who was still pinned to the wall by Sorcha's wind. The faery was visibly hurt and worn, the black veins on her hands had crept up to her neck.

This time she went for Eliza's throat. She grabbed it with one hand and in the other, she held a dagger, but Eliza could barely lift her arms with the wind force still pinning her down.

"Play fair," Eliza grunted, trying to give herself more time to think.

"There's no such thing as fair play," Sorcha replied.

"Surely you don't need your wind force to take down a human?" Eliza wound her up.

Sorcha looked around her at the hundreds of faeries watching their battle, and without thinking, she dropped the wind force.

Ready now, her grasp around Eliza's neck tightened and she moved the dagger into Eliza's face, irritable, tired of wasting time, and hungering for human blood to feed her powers.

Eliza gasped for air. Her feet were now dangling in their air. She grabbed the approaching blade heading for her face and reeled in pain as it cut into her palm.

"Aquila," she managed to whisper as she used her other hand to push Sorcha's face away.

Where's the magic when you need it? poor Eliza thought to herself, trying hard to channel the energies flowing within her.

As she pushed Sorcha's face harder, magical light escaped her palm burning a mark onto Sorcha's face. The stunned faery maintained her hold of Eliza but dropped the dagger in shock so she could touch her face.

"What are you? How did you steal The Gift?" she growled, her eyes looking like they wanted to pop out of her face.

Eliza wanted to answer, but she was thinking, thinking hard about something Niada had put into her head about looking for cracks in walls.

"Question is, if you were a wall, where would your cracks be?" Eliza croaked.

"What?" asked Sorcha, very confused about this human.

"Once and for all, let us end this," Sorcha said through her teeth, lifting her fallen daggers back into the air.

Eliza extended her arm but away from Sorcha and towards The Sluagh.

"What are you doing?" asked Sorcha.

Eliza focused as best as she could until magical light flowed out of her palms again, this time with force, hitting The Sluagh. With her other hand, she directed the magical light at Sorcha.

"Hitting your weak spot." Eliza smiled.

At first, Sorcha just started to look very uncomfortable, clumsily trying to control her daggers, but then it became more evident that The Sluagh was also growing fainter and fainter.

"Stop it," Sorcha grimaced before managing to send a dagger into the flesh above Eliza's collarbone.

"Arghhhhhh," Eliza dropped to the ground still throwing bolts of magical light at both The Sluagh and Sorcha. The dwindling spirit began to break apart, and when she realised she had lost the battle, Sorcha decided to flee.

The weakened faery stumbled about in pain and spun her cloak around, and The Sluagh folded into it, lifting her off the ground into the air. As the swirling black shapes lifted her away in haste, she managed half a smile, her lips parting as if to say something, but Eliza hit her with another powerful bolt of light, which tore her apart from The Sluagh and Sorcha fell to the ground with a thud. The troupe of Salamanders rained fire on her, wanting to take no chances, and Sorcha burned and burned in their magical fires. Before she was entirely gone though, she warned, "Declare your allegiances...." she said to the wider realm. "The king is coming," and with that, her frame crumbled and her ashes scattered into the wind, followed by the remains of The Sluagh that was part of her.

Chapter 19

HOME

In the moments following Sorcha's death, the thing that surfaced in Eliza's mind was that she never thought this was how her story would end. She had fallen to her knees calling her friend's name repeatedly, and in desperation, everything around them blurred into a meaningless haze. Gwen lay against the wall, motionless, blood seeping slowly from her chest. The voices around Eliza muddled into a cacophony of distant sounds, and she was unaware of even the sound of her own voice attempting to call Gwen back from wherever it was, she was off to.

When that didn't work, Eliza found herself shaking Gwen's limp body nonstop until she finally broke down caressing her friend's face. When she was gently pulled off Gwen, she looked on in a daze as Salamanders took her friend away from her hurriedly. She gazed into her blood-stained hands and became lost in them as the stains morphed into tiny living streams, which swelled and swelled beyond her hands, then they gushed around her before threatening to swallow her up. She was gagging when the sense of sound returned to her numb ears.

"Breathe," Urhouri urged her.

When she managed it, air surged through her lungs

and her body suddenly felt like she'd lived a thousand years in pain.

"You are hurt badly, you need care, come," Urhouri said with outstretched arms. Welcoming, but also ready to take Eliza if she would not willingly go.

Without thinking, Eliza walked over to the opened arms. She wanted to say something but couldn't think of what. Her attention, though, quickly shifted to the thousands of beings sat quietly in the stands of the arena beholding her like she was a spectacle. No sooner had she embraced Urhouri she broke free of the arms holding her and stumbled into the middle of the arena.

She spoke like a drunken madman, dazed by trauma and exhaustion. "You Key is restored and your doorways locked again. Go see yourself. But know that I did it for the people I love," she said intending to stop there when she remembered something more.

"Gwen called this place home. She sacrificed her life not just for me, but for you! And yet you bastardise her for the blood that runs,"—she paused hesitantly—"ran through her veins. You had no right... No right to punish her for being part faery and part human! That didn't make her less, it made her special. I, like Gwen, am not of pure blood as you say, yet your infallible Annwn gave me a precious gift that helped me to return your Key and I was helped by those you reject. The scorned are your saviours. Yet you will not see it. Your world is as broken as mine," she finished speaking just before everything became a blur in the matter of a few blinks, and a seemingly never-ending darkness followed.

A blinding white light permeated the room, and twinkling little particles floated about through the tall opened windows. When Eliza opened her eyes, she was lost as to where she was and why she was there. As her memory came back to her slowly, she thought she must have passed onto another life, but then a familiar squeal echoed from outside in the winds and soon Aquila the great eagle was sitting on the window ledge.

"How does Eliza feel?" asked Aquila.

Eliza managed half a smile before trying to sit up, but everywhere ached, her wounds were sore, and her skin burned profoundly. In fact, it had been left raw in many places from passing through The Sluagh.

"Easy," said a female voice from behind her, startling the living daylight out of poor Eliza.

Urhouri smiled at her yet there was an underlying sadness in her face. "You were badly hurt when you fought Sorcha, Eliza," she said.

Eliza had so many questions, but as she sifted through her mind still recalling all that had happened, a painful reminder pierced through her deeper than any of her inflicted wounds had gone. She winced in agony, and tears resurfaced. She clenched her teeth and began inching off the bed.

"You need rest," Urhouri said, but Eliza ignored her and continued pushing herself off the bed.

Urhouri outstretched her arms, trying to gently bar Eliza, now out of breath but still insistent on going somewhere.

"I want to see her," Eliza said under her breath and through her clenched teeth.

Emryees the ice faery stepped forward.

"You will not tell me that I cannot see my friend." She stifled back the tears that threatened to choke her as she gazed up at the two faeries before her. "So you either help me or you leave me alone."

Emryees looks to Urhouri and hesitantly she nodded.

Together, they helped a groaning Eliza out of the oval room leading out to a massive corridor lined by tall windows, which revealed the neighbouring mountains draped by the neon pink sky.

They stopped outside a door to the far end of the corridor, and offered a consoling smile to Eliza before proceeding to help her in.

Eliza's heart felt like it had stopped beating, when the door pushed opened and far away on the draped poster bed, Gwen lay like an angel covered in white. The streaming white light through the windows made it surreal, and Eliza wished it was all a dream. She pulled herself free from Urhouri and Emryees's arms and gripped her torso in pain, as she stumbled her way slowly towards the bed, never taking her eyes off Gwen's face. She looked paler and sick. Except she wasn't sick. If she was, she could get better.

Her trembling hand reached out to touch Gwen's face but got only as far as inches away from it. She couldn't. Instead, Eliza's hand pulled the sheet back from Gwen's chest, as she wanted to inspect the wound that her friend had taken. A flood of tears was on its way. As she began pulling the sheet back, the soft whisper of a familiar voice sank into her spirits sending a deep shock.

"Eliza," Gwen said, her eyes barely opening and Eliza barely got halfway through saying Gwen's name when the tears exploded from her eyes. "I thought you...."

Gwen smiled weakly. "Can't get rid of me that easily, you silly cow."

Eliza's laughter muddled into tears and she leaned over and gently kissed Gwen's forehead, her tears splattering onto Gwen's face.

The two friends laughed with each other, just they as had done not so long ago in happier times, and Eliza felt the blood slowly flowing back into her cheeks and through the rest of her. Though the sadness still filled her heart to see her friend in the state that she was in, Gwen could barely laugh without hurting herself. Eliza took Gwen's hand and lifted it to her face.

As they talked and talked of all that had happened when they'd parted ways forcibly, Eliza fumbled when she realised she had to tell Gwen a most important thing.

"Gwen," she said lifting the peridot necklace off her chest. "The gnome was right."

"What?"

"I know why your peridot glows sometimes," said Eliza, to which Gwen stared at her clueless.

"Gwen, your mum is alive. And well."

"What?" asked Gwen in shock. "How...?"

"She saved me and she looks over you with love and pride. She's so, so proud of you," whispered Eliza, feeling regret that Niada couldn't be there to greet Gwen herself.

Gwen sobbed as her best friend explained further her encounters with Niada.

"I knew it," Gwen whispered to herself in satisfaction, and before they could say another word, they were interrupted.

"Knock, knock," said Arden from the doorway.

Nervously, Eliza struggled to stand up. Gwen waved her hand frantically at Eliza, signalling her to stay put.

"Eliza," he said and bowed his head courteously to her. She blushed as she always did in his presence.

He looked worn, and bore many haunting scars of the trying days they had seen. Still, a noticeable lightless was visible on his face and in his demeanour. An expression they had seen little of since meeting him.

Arden filled the girls in on what had happened after the fight with Sorcha, when they both went unconscious. He said that Arrae had changed back faery form so the arena could see he was alive and well. Arrae explained it was Sorcha who tried to kill him, and then he brought the two frail humans forward. They were the only human victims who had survived after watching Sorcha sap their fellow captives of their life essence and emotions.

Arden and the girls talked, but he hardly ever took his gaze off Eliza. She couldn't have known though, because she firmly avoided his eyes. Until Gwen started yawning profusely. So profusely, in fact, Eliza shot her a hard warning stare.

"Boy oh boy, am I tired!" Gwen feigned, giving Eliza an eye back.

Arden stood up most promptly. "We will let you rest, Gwen. Later there is an official meeting in the Council chambers below. Our presence is requested, but we will come see you after," he said before taking his leave and stopping at the door, clearly anticipating Eliza's company.

"Go!" Gwen whispered to Eliza with a mischievous grin. Eliza fixed her friend one final look of disapproval and then reluctantly stumbled out of the room to meet Arden outside.

He looked at her with great sympathy as she made her way out the room wincing, and outstretched his arm to support her. A warmness shot through her body as his arm wrapped around her.

He led her to a vast, dreamy garden, in an area where a low canopy of trees, vines, and delicate flowers intertwined beautifully. The path was strewn with layers of bright-coloured cotton buds, which also glided through the air in the light winds.

"Here," he pointed to the hanging bench suspended from two neighbouring trees, and swiped the buds off for Eliza to sit. Then they sat in silence for a few seconds before Eliza opened her mouth to say something.

Arden had the same idea as Eliza and they both spoke at once.

They stopped and smiled shyly at the awkwardness.

Arden nodded towards her. "You first," but Eliza immediately shook her head. "No you."

Arden chuckled, and looked at her before shaking his head. He leaned forward and propped his elbows on his thighs, his head cradled in his hands, staring at an apparently interesting patch of grass before him.

"What?" asked Eliza curiously, inspecting the same patch of grass.

Without warning, he grabbed her hand in his and squeezed it gently before resting it against his cheek. A single tear trickled down his cheek, dropping onto her hand.

"Arden?" Eliza leaned toward him with concern.

He raised his face until it was inches from hers, and she could see the flood threatening to spill through his eyes.

She had heard her grandmother say that eyes are the windows to the soul, and then and there, she found the meaning of those words as Arden's soul lay bare before her.

"Arden," she whispered not knowing what else to say.

His lips trembled as he stared back into her eyes. With his other hand, he lightly traced the long purple scar on Eliza's forehead. The one she had suffered at the hands of the phooka in the Dark Forest. When his fingers reached the end of the scar, they continued down the side of her face until her cheek was cupped in his hand.

"Why?" she whispered to him without needing to elaborate on the question. He knew what she was asking.

"Because I've loved you even before I knew you," he answered, his thumb now tracing the outline of her lips.

"How?" was all she managed to mutter overcome in the moment.

"Your face first haunted my dreams many moons ago, but once I saw you, your memory has haunted my every waking moment. I've dreamed of being with you, and you're here, but you're hurt," he said struggling to stifle his tears, till Eliza could no longer understand what he was saying.

She thought he was trying to say it had been his fault. She rested his face on her shoulder and embraced him, feeling his tears soak through her white cotton dress.

"Arden, none of this is your fault. I wouldn't have made it without you. Gwen wouldn't have made it without you. Okay? You've protected us as best as you could. And... At times, along the way, you've been my sanity," she said lifting his face up. Now she was holding his face in her hand.

She could drown in those grey eyes of his and she gazed into them, and before she knew it, his lips were pressing against hers, between hers, and caressing hers with an undeniable urgency. She'd never kissed someone before, but she found her lips moved with a mind of their own, in sync with his. She was suddenly aware of his embrace, getting tighter, and somehow their kiss growing more passionate and urgent. When she pulled from him, it was with great reluctance, and only because she needed to breathe. As she gasped for air, she felt the warmest tears on her own cheeks. Not tears of sadness, tears of something else. Joy maybe? He wiped them away with the back of his palm, and pulled the stray curls from her face. There was something between them too great to ignore anymore, and whatever it was, it made her happy. As happy as she knew it made him....

"Put it on, yuh silly cow!" moaned Gwen, still reeling in pain, but not even that could stop her from getting into true character.

Eliza frowned as Urhouri awaited her approval.

"Ahh." Gwen scowled again. "Put it on before I come put it on for you!" Gwen meant business as she grimaced while edging off the bed.

"Okay, okay, I'll wear it." Eliza frowned again. "Stay put before you hurt yourself."

Smiling, Urhouri rested the glittering halo of beads on the crown of Eliza's head. It was a fine complement to the flowing silk dress and the glittering dust that had been powdered onto Eliza's skin. Standing in the mirror, she stared at the girl looking back at her.

"You are beautiful," said Urhouri, and Eliza looked back at her in disbelief that a creature so unfathomably lovely could call her that.

"Thanks," she said unconvinced, but as she stared back at the girl in the mirror, she secretly marvelled at how Urhouri had transformed her into someone so pleasing to the eye. However, even the transformation couldn't hide the long purple scar on her forehead, shouting at her, mocking her. Reminding her of all the ugly things that had transpired.

The Council meeting was upon them and Eliza wondered what all the fuss was about. Gwen too had been dressed and made to look even more beautiful, but her wounds were still too slow to heal and she would be taken down to the meeting in a bed.

When the time had come, they'd found themselves in the grand hall of the Council, with its members, honorary representatives of the realm, and a few leaders of various communities. Eliza thought that the golden floor of the room seemed too delicate to walk on, and she limped as lightly as she could with Arden's assistance. Any moment now, she felt her heavy human footsteps would cause a permanent crack in the delicate faery dwelling in front of all these fae folk. Faeries that she knew were not only suspicious because she was human, but because she was a human walking in arms of a faery. Forget the minor detail of helping their realm.

"This way please," directed a fiery Salamander usher

pointing to their seat with the ends of her long scarlet plait.

They were sat in one of the front rows before a circular stage in the middle of the large, round hall. Eliza felt out of place in the regal hall among such ethereal beings. Faeries and beings of all kinds not only beautiful in themselves and how they appeared, but in how they sounded and in the very movements they made. Gwen lay beside her, and Arden stood to her other side. From the other side of the room Arden's mother eyed her brazenly. No doubt, Lady Drwyrwen's feelings hadn't softened. Arden took Eliza's hand in his. She could hear Gwen feigning a choke, definitely in reaction to Arden holding her hand, but before Eliza could say a thing to her silly friend, the meeting was called to order.

"Honourable beings of the realm, welcome," said Eolande in a neutral but full-bodied voice that filled the hall. "We have seen many dark days of recent, but even darkness has an end. As we clean up our realm, there is much work to do. We must ensure justice and peace are restored, and that evil is stamped out by good. We will not stop searching until the allies of the evil Sorcha are captured. The Key to the realm's doorways is secured and we have also relocated it to a secret location, with boosted security, but this is not why we have called you today. We owe not only thanks to these four beings before us—Arden, Arrae, Eliza and Gwen—but we also owe them an apology. They remained on the side of good while we hunted them without giving them a voice. Thank you for your kindness to this realm. It is a sacrifice that will not be forgotten. Eliza, we know this realm is not your home, but we will like you to consider it a second home from now on. We welcome you always. We are pleased to announce that from this day forth, humans are no longer outlawed. In your honour, we also wish to grant you and your friends each a gift of your choosing."

Gwen sputtered out loudly.

Eolande looked up at her briefly and then continued.

"Please, make your wishes known," she said.

"I don't want nothing from this realm," muttered Gwen, and all eyes widened in shock.

Eliza wanted to say something to her friend but how could she argue with her? She couldn't.

Without any further question, Eolande's eyes simply moved over to Eliza awaiting a response.

"You can't blame her. After what you did to her mum?" asked Eliza.

"Your wish, Eliza?" said Eolande in a flat firm voice.

Eliza's left brow went up. "Okay. You want my wish? Free Gwen's mum, and honour all those who have helped us. Stop ostracising those who are different or those who do not agree with you..."

Eolande butted in.

"I don't know who you've been speaking to Eliza, but—"

"Would you like a list?" Eliza sputtered, and Arden was rubbing her knee in a calming motion.

Eolande looked behind her to her fellow council members.

Arden shot up from his chair. "I want the same as her," he said nodding over to Eliza.

"And me too" said Arrae standing up.

In the hall, the sound of the odd shuffling chair sounded magnified among the hushed whisperings of the council members.

Eventually, Hiatar spoke from behind Eolande.

"You have our word we will consider and work on your request," he said.

Eliza and Gwen smiled at each other, each friend not wanting to expect much but nonetheless excited of the possibility of freeing Niada. Gwen had dreamed of this day for many a year.

Much of the remainder of the meeting consisted of talks

on how the human realm would be cleansed of any mess left by Sorcha and the wild phookas, and how, despite the change of law on humans, the human victims would be administered potions to remove any memory of Annwn and their abduction.

"What?!" Arden and Gwen shouted in response.

"Humans are no longer outlawed, and they are allowed to live here again but given the circumstances of how the little human girl and the man came to be here, it is too much a risk for us. And they wish to return to their homes."

"You owe them! What about the families of the two fishermen who were killed? It's not their fault you couldn't handle a rogue faery," argued Gwen.

"Agreed, and we are working on finding suitable, anonymous means of compensating them, but it is law that humans generally should not be allowed to return to their realm unless their memories cleared."

It was a while before Eliza realised the obvious.

"Wait," she interjected. "Does that include me? Will my memory be erased too?"

"Yes, all humans," said Eolande.

"You can't!"

"Eliza," Eolande tried to reason.

"Don't 'Eliza' me!" and she, Gwen, Arden and Arrae all began to shout at once.

"Your human life will never be the same if you retain knowledge of this realm and given your newly acquired gift, it is just too big a risk. Besides you've had many a traumatic encounter...." Eolande calmly spoke over them.

Eliza considered it. Could she really forget all the horrific things she had met on her journeys through the realm? Could the purple scar on her forehead just appear a curious mark of which she could have no memory? The thought bore much appeal to her. She would like to forget the many dark days she had seen in that place, but no the painful reality beset itself on her. To remove the trauma would also be to remove the good. The kindness she had met, the friends she had made. Loridel, who nursed her wounds and carried her heavy heart for many days with care, Niada, who had rescued her in the dark mountainous tunnels, Aquila who had caught them while falling into the depths... so many friends she owed her life to.

"No," she stood up and Arden stood up beside her.

"You will not do it. You will not take my memories. You can't take the bad without taking the good. So I'll keep them both, thank you, if it means I get to remember my friends," she said with determination fixed on her face.

The groaning beside her was the sound of Gwen struggling out of bed to stand beside her in agreement and she did, propping herself against Eliza who wrapped a firm arm around her friend.

Surely, the Council could not deny her this and after careful deliberation, they didn't, given the sacrifices she'd made. To turn down a now honorary member of the realm would be a mockery. Eolande hated this but couldn't argue, as most of her fellow council members seemed to agree with Eliza.

"Okay. You may keep your memories. You could also stay," said Hiatar, "and learn to develop your new gift."

What an appealing thought. Not.

Eliza feigned the best smile she could muster up. "Thank you for allowing me to keep my memories, but I have to return to my family. They need me," she said and it was settled.

At the end of the meeting, it finally hit Eliza that she'd soon be going home, and she was overcome with excitement.

"Can we go home now?" she asked Urhouri as the great hall emptied.

"Most certainly," she gleamed.

"Oh, Gwen! Eliza leaned over and hugged her friend

tightly. "Your dad's going to be so happy to see you!" she babbled on and on about their return, but then she realised the silent reaction and loosened her grip on Gwen, who sat back down.

Gwen's face was sombre and she tried avoiding eye contact.

"Gwen?" she said, but her friend was unusually quiet. So were Arden, Arrae and Urhouri.

"Eli," Gwen said in a most gentle voice uncharacteristic of herself. "My wounds are still pretty bad. You see how poorly I am, and...."

"And what?"

Urhouri interjected to help Gwen out. "Eliza, if Gwen went home now, she would...well she would die, definitely. She needs the medicines of our realm for her healing."

"No, no, no, can't you bottle them up and we'll take them home with us?" Eliza said.

"I'm afraid it's not that simple. Many of the medicines Gwen needs must be brewed soon after the plants are picked. And they must be blended by the skilled hands of one of our physicians."

"No, no..." Eliza said shaking her head profusely. "I am not leaving her here with you, not in this place, never, never," she said repeatedly almost as if trying to convince herself. Then without thinking, she threw Gwen's arm over her and started helping her up.

"Come on, we're going home."

"Eli," Gwen cried, and Eliza dropped her arm and fell to her knees before her friend, burying her head in Gwen's skirt.

"I promise I'll be home as soon as I'm better. You know I'll never leave you, right?" Gwen said in tears.

Eliza stared into her friend's bright eyes. It was an unusual thing to see Gwen cry.

"Promise?" Eliza said in a childlike way, her voice muffled in Gwen's skirt.

"Promise."

Later that evening, Eliza and her two human counterparts were taken to the nearest doorway to the human realm. Eliza couldn't wait to see her Ma and her Grampie and Aunt Rosie. Of course, she couldn't. She'd dreamt of the day for so long, but she also couldn't bear to leave Gwen behind and Arden. She hadn't been able to even think of not seeing him, not being next to him, but now the reality weighed heavily on her heart.

"I will see you again," he said gently pressing his lips against hers, and she rested her hand on his chest.

"Soon," he added. "Until then, I will think of you every time I see the blooming flowers. For you are the most delicate and beautiful of them all. Forget me not?" he asked.

"How could I?"

"Then don't."

"I won't, I promise," she said.

She gave Gwen one final embrace and was forced to let go. Taking little Emily Wetherspoon's hand in her own, they started through the nearest doorway, temporarily opened for their departure. It was flanked by Eolande and two guards. By the time they reached the other side, the little girl and the surviving fisherman would have no recollection of where they had been all this time away from home, thanks to potions that had been administered to their food. Before stepping through the door, Eliza looked back one more time. One more time at Gwen's face. One more time. She looked to Eolande whose hand was outstretched. For a moment, Eliza wanted to leave her hanging but decided it would be bad manners and accepted Eolande's hand. In the firm embrace, Eliza felt a sharp sting in her palm.

"Ouch!" she said looking down to the spot of blood appearing on her hand. Her head suddenly went light.

"Apologies, human. I wanted to wish you well," nodded Eolande.

Eliza nodded nonchalantly, and looked over Eolande's shoulder to Gwen, Arrae, Arden, and Aquila one final time, before stepping through the doorway carved through the trunk of a giant tree.

When they reached through the other side of the doorway, they walked a while before they entered the familiar setting of the quaint little village backdropped by a picturesque orange lit evening sky.

"Where's my mummy? I want my mum," moaned an irritable Emily.

"What are we doing here? Who are you?" asked the fisherman.

Eliza lifted Emily and showed them to her Aunt Rosie's house where she thought her grandparents could fix everything.

She pressed the doorbell and her heart pounded like an eager dog lost, awaiting its owner to find it.

When the door swung open, Indira was standing before her all agasp, hands covering her mouth. She threw her arms around Eliza and the child and kissed Eliza's face all about.

"Oh child," cried Indira.

"Ma," Eliza whispered in tears of happiness, and before she knew it or could control it, she was croaking a steady flow of tears. Jose and Rosie rushed into the room to the commotion. On seeing them, Eliza burst into a fresh set of tears. She was being kissed, hugged, tugged, and stroked when Indira asked, "Wait, child, where is Gwen? What happened to you? Who took you?"

"Oh, Gwen!" exclaimed Eliza remembering suddenly, and staring back at her grandmother.

She looked over to the fisherman and little Emily and eventually muttered, "Where's Gwen? Where've I been all this time?"

Acknowledgements

To my editors for their hard work. This feat would be impossible without them. Thank you Samantha.

The process of self publishing my first story has been very daunting, and I could not have done it without the guidance and support of author A.D. Starrling and Streetlight Graphics.

Dad always said I would do it. Thanks Dad.

To Elena, Jackie, and Lynda for their patience, and never ending support.

To Mama Claire and Aunty Mello for always showing a keen interest in my stories.

To all my loved ones who supported me – with special thanks to Neidi, Sue, Jhaye-Q, Denesia, Gayshiel, Jaqs and Nikki.

Last but not least, thanks to my Lord for His grace and favour.

Website: www.authoralishanurse.com

Made in the USA
Charleston, SC
26 December 2014